D0531041

Dear Reader,

I'm so thrilled to bring you *Lord of the Vampires*, the first tale in the dark and sizzling ROYAL HOUSE OF SHADOW series.

Writing this book was such a blast! A world with vampires, werewolves, witches and monsters? Hell, yes! A prince known for his wicked ways and fearsome temper? Even better! A human woman who will either save or destroy him—bringing him to his knees in the process? Yes, yes, a thousand times yes.

Throw in upcoming stories by Jill Monroe (*Lord of Rage*), Jessica Andersen (*Lord of the Wolfyn*) and Nalini Singh (*Lord of the Abyss*) and I'm practically drooling about this series. E-mailing these ladies about the different books was truly inspiring.

I hope you enjoy our modern takes on beloved fairy tales. We certainly had fun writing them.

All the best,

Gena Showalter

GENA
SHOWALTER

LORD OF THE VAMPIRES

MILLS
BOON®

First published in Great Britain 2011
by Mills & Boon, an imprint of Harlequin (UK) Limited,
Eton House, 18-24 Paradise Road, Richmond, Surrey TW9 1SR

© Gena Showalter 2011

ISBN: 978 0 263 88330 5

089-1011

Harlequin (UK) policy is to use papers that are natural, renewable and recyclable products and made from wood grown in sustainable forests. The logging and manufacturing processes conform to the legal environmental regulations of the country of origin.

Printed in the UK
by CPI Mackays, Chatham, ME5 8TD

New York Times and *USA Today* bestselling author **Gena Showalter** has been praised for her "sizzling page-turners" and "utterly spellbinding stories." She is the author of more than seventeen novels and anthologies, including breathtaking paranormal and contemporary romances, cutting-edge young adult novels, and stunning urban fantasy. Readers can't get enough of her trademark wit and singular imagination.

To learn more about Gena and her books, please visit www.genashowalter.com and www.genashowalterblogspot.com.

This one is for Jill Monroe, Jessica Andersen and
Nalini Singh. Amazing ladies and talented authors.
I'd plot with you guys anyday!

And to Tara Gavin, for her amazing support and
enthusiasm for the ROYAL HOUSE OF SHADOWS

Prologue

Once upon a time, in a land of vampires, shape-shifters and witches, the Blood Sorcerer coveted the only power denied him: the right to rule. He and his monstrous army attacked the royal palace, slaughtered the beloved king and queen of Elden and sought to do the same to Nicolai, the crown prince, as well as his three siblings, Breena, Dayn and Micah.

The sorcerer succeeded in all but the latter. He had not counted on a king's hunger for retribution and a mother's love for her children.

Just before expelling his final breath, the king used his power to fill his offspring with an unbreakable need for vengeance, ensuring they would fight for eternity to claim their due. At the same time, the queen used her power to send them away, saving them. For the time being.

Only, the king and queen were weak, their minds fogged from pain, and their magic conflicting.

And so, the royals were now bound to destroy the man who had slain their parents, yet they were also cast out of the palace, each flung to different kingdoms within the realm with only one link to the Royal House of Elden: a timepiece, given to them by their parents.

Nicolai, the Dark Seducer as his people called him, had been in bed, but not alone. He was never alone. He was a man known for the violence of his temper as well as the deliciousness of his touch; and after his youngest brother's birthday celebration, he'd adjourned to his private chamber to sate himself on his newest conquest.

That's when the dual natures of the enchantments struck him.

When he next opened his eyes, he'd found himself in *another* bed—and not with his chosen partner. He was naked still, only now he was chained, a slave to the very desires he'd evoked in his lover. Desires that had mingled with the magic and sent him straight to the Sex Market, where he was quickly sold to a princess of Delfina, his will no longer his own, his pleasure no longer his own, his timepiece stolen and his memories wiped from his mind.

But two things could not be taken from him, no matter how fervently the princess tried. The cold rage in his chest and the blistering need for vengeance in his veins.

The first, he would unleash. The second, he would savor. First with the princess, and then with a sorcerer

he could not quite remember, but a sorcerer he knew
he despised all the same.

Soon.

He had only to escape....

Chapter 1

"I need you, Jane."

Frowning, Jane Parker placed the note on her kitchen countertop. She studied the scarred, leather-bound book resting inside an unadorned box, surrounded by a sea of black velvet. A few minutes ago, she'd returned from her five-mile jog. This package had been waiting on her porch.

There'd been no return address. No explanation as to why the thing had been left for her, and no hint as to who "I" was. Or why Jane was needed. Why would anyone need *her*? She was twenty-seven years old and had only recently regained the use of her legs. She had no family, no friends, no job. Not anymore. Her little cabin in Smallest Town Ever, Oklahoma, was secluded, barely a blip in the neighboring expanse of lush green trees and wide open, blue sky.

She should have tossed the thing. Of course, curiosity far outweighed caution. As always.

She carefully lifted the book. At the moment of contact, she saw her hands covered in blood and gasped, dropping the heavy tome on the counter. But when she lifted her hands to the light, they were scrubbed clean, her nails neat and painted a pretty morning rose.

You have an overactive imagination, and too much oxygen pumping through your veins from the run. That's all.

Cold hard logic—her best and only friend.

The book's binding creaked as she opened to the middle, where a tattered pink ribbon rested. The scent of dust and musk wafted up, layered with something else. Something…mouthwatering and slightly familiar. Her frowned deepened.

She shifted in her seat, a twinge of pain shooting through her legs, and sniffed. Oh, yes. Her mouth definitely watered as she caught the slightest trace of sandalwood. Goose bumps broke out over her skin, her senses tingling, her blood heating. How embarrassing. And, okay, how interesting. Since the car accident that ruined her life eleven months ago, she had experienced arousal only at night, in her dreams. To react like this in daylight, because of a book…odd.

She didn't allow herself to ponder why. There wasn't an answer that would satisfy her. Instead, she concentrated on the pages in front of her. They were yellowed and brittle, delicate. And beaded with blood? Small dots of dried crimson marred the edges.

Gently she brushed her fingertips along the handwritten text, her gaze catching on several words.

Chains. Vampire. Belonged. Soul. More goose bumps, more tingling.

Some blushing.

Her eyes narrowed. At last the sandalwood cologne made sense. For the past few months, she'd dreamed of a vampire male in chains and woken to the fragrance clinging to her skin. And yes, he's the one who had aroused her. She'd told no one. So, how had anyone known to give her this…journal?

She'd worked in quantum physics for years, as well as what was considered fringe science, sometimes studying creatures of "myth" and "legend." She'd conducted controlled interviews with actual blood drinkers and even dissected the corpses brought to her lab.

She knew that vampires, shape-shifters and other creatures of the night existed, even though her coworkers on the quantum physics side of the equation had not been privy to the truth. So, maybe someone had found out and this was a simple joke. Maybe her dreams had no connection. Except, forever had seemed to pass since she'd had any contact with those coworkers. And besides, who would do such a thing? None of them had cared enough about her to do *anything*.

Let this go, Parker. Before it's too late.

The command from her self-preservation instincts made no sense. *Too late for what?*

Her instincts offered no reply. Well, the scientist in her *needed* to know what was going on.

Jane cleared her throat. "I'm reading a few passages, and that's that." She'd been alone since leaving the hospital several months ago, and sometimes the sound of her voice was better than silence. "'Chains circled the vampire's neck, wrists and ankles. Because his shirt and pants had been stripped away, and a loincloth was his only apparel, there was nothing to protect his already savaged skin. The links cut him deeply, to the bone, before healing—and slicing open again. He did not care. What was pain when your will, your very soul, no longer belonged to you?"'

She pressed her lips together as a wave of dizziness crashed through her. A moment passed, then another, her heartbeat speeding up and hammering wildly against her ribs.

Raw images tore through her. This man—this vampire—bound, helpless. Hungry. His lush lips were pulled taut, his teeth sharp, white. He was surprisingly tanned, temptingly muscled, with dark, mussed hair and a face so eerily beautiful he would haunt her nighttime fantasies for years to come.

What she'd just read, she'd already seen. Many times. How? She didn't know. What she did know was that in her dreams, she felt compassion for this man, even anger. And yet, there was always that low simmer of arousal in the background. Now, the arousal took center stage.

The more she breathed, the more the sandalwood scent clung to her, and the more her reality altered, as if this, her home, was nothing more than a mirage. As if the vampire's cage was real. As if she needed to stand up and walk—no, *run*—until she reached him. Anything to be with him, now and forever.

Okay. Enough of that. She slapped the book closed, even though so many questions were left dangling, and strode away.

Such a strong reaction coupled with her dreams utterly nixed the idea of a joke. Not that she'd placed much hope in that direction. However, the remaining possibilities upset her, and she refused to contemplate them.

She showered, dressed in a T-shirt and jeans and ate a nutritious breakfast. Unbidden, she found her gaze returning to the leather binding, over and over again. She wondered if the enslaved vampire were real—and okay. If she could help him. A few times, she even opened to the middle of the book before she realized she'd moved. Always she darted off before the story could snare her.

And perhaps *that's* why the stupid thing had been given to her. To hook her, to send her racing back to work. Well, she didn't need to work. Money was not a problem for her. More than that, she no longer loved the sciences. Why would she? There was never a solution, only more problems.

Because when one puzzle piece slid into place, there were always twenty more needed. And in the end, nothing you did, nothing that had been solved or unraveled, would save the ones you loved. There would always be some dumb guy throwing back a few cold ones at the local bar, getting into his car and hitting yours. Or something equally tragic.

Life was random.

Jane craved monotony.

But when midnight rolled around, her mind still hadn't settled in regards to the vampire. Giving up, she returned to the kitchen, grabbed the book and stalked to bed. Just a few more passages, damn it, *then* she'd start craving monotony again.

Jane's oversize T-shirt bunched at her waist as she propped the book on her upraised legs, opened to the middle of the story, where the bookmark was still set, and returned her attention to the pages. For several seconds, the words appeared to be written in a language she did not understand. Then, a blink later, they were written in English again.

O-kay. Very weird, and surely—hopefully—an I-just-need-sleep mistake on her part.

She found her place. "'They called him Nicolai.'" Nicolai. A strong, luscious name. The syllables rolled through her mind, a caress. Her nipples beaded, aching for a hot, wet kiss, and every inch of her skin flushed. She thought back. She'd never interviewed a vampire named Nicolai, and the one in her dream had never spoken to her. He had never acknowledged her in any way. "'He did not know his past or if he had a future. He knew only his present. His hated, torturous present. He was a slave, locked away like an animal.'"

Just like before, a wave of dizziness slammed through her. This time, Jane pressed on, even as her chest constricted. "'He was kept clean and oiled. Always. Just in case Princess Laila had need of him in her bed. And the princess did have need of him. Often. Her cruel, twisted desires left him beaten and bruised. Not that he ever accepted defeat. The man was wild, nearly uncontrollable, and so filled with hate anyone who looked at him saw their death in his eyes.'"

The dizziness intensified. Hell, so did the desire. To tame a man like that, to have all of his vigor focused on you, pounding into you…his participation willing… Jane shivered.

Lose the ADD, Parker. She cleared her throat. "'He was hard, merciless. A warrior at heart. A man used to absolute control. At least, he thought he was. Even with his lack of memory, he was patently aware that every order directed his way scraped his nerves raw.'"

Another shiver rocked her. She grit her teeth. He needed her compassion, not her desire. *He's that real to you?* Yeah, he was. "'At least he would have a few days' reprieve,'" she read on, "'forgotten by one and all. The entire palace was frothing over Princess Odette's return from the grave and—'"

The rest of the page was blank. "And what?" Jane flipped to the next, but quickly realized the story had ended on an unfinished cliff-hanger. Great.

Thankfully—or not—she discovered more writing toward the end and blinked, shook her head. The words didn't change. "'You, Jane Parker,'" she recited hollowly. "'You are Odette. Come to me, I command you. Save me, I beg you. Please, Jane. I need you.'"

Her name was in the book. How was her name in the book? And written by the same hand as the rest? On the same aged, stained pages, with the same smudged ink?

I need you.

Her attention returned to the part directed to her. She reread "You are Odette" until the urge to scream was at last overshadowed by curiosity. Her mind swirled. There were so many paths to take with this. Forged, genuine, dream, reality.

Come to me.

Save me.

Please.

I command you.

Something inside her responded to that command more than anything else in the book. The urge to run— here, there, anywhere—beat through her. As long as she found him, saved him, nothing else mattered. And she could save him, just as soon as she reached him.

I. Command. You.

Yes. She wanted to obey. So damn badly. She felt as if an invisible cord had been wound around her neck, and was now tugging at her.

Trembling, Jane closed the book. She wasn't searching for anyone. Not tonight. She needed to regroup. In the morning, after a few coffee IVs, her head would be clear and she could reason this out. She hoped.

After placing the tome on her nightstand, she flopped into her bed and closed her eyes, trying to force her brain to quiet. An unsuccessful endeavor. If Nicolai's story was true, he was as trapped by those chains as surely as she had once been trapped by her body's infirmities.

The compassion grew...spread....

While he was kept in a cage, she had been bound to a hospital bed, her bones broken, her muscles torn, her mind hazed by medication, all because a drunk driver had slammed into her car. And while she had been— was—tormented by the loss of her family, since her mother, father and sister had been in the car with her, Nicolai was tormented by a sadistic woman's unwanted touch. She felt a wave of regret, a crackle of fury.

I need you.

Jane inhaled deeply, exhaled slowly and shifted to her side, clutching her pillow close. As close as she suddenly wanted to clutch Nicolai, to comfort him. To be with him. *Uh, not going there.* She didn't know the man. Therefore, she wasn't going to imagine sleeping with him.

But that's exactly what she did. His plight was

forgotten as she imagined him climbing on top of her, his silver eyes bright with desire, his pupils blown. His lips were plump and red from kissing her entire body, still moist with her flavor. She licked at him, tasting him, tasting herself, eager for anything and everything he would give her.

He growled his approval, flashing his fangs.

His big, muscled body surrounded her, his skin hot, little beads of sweat forming, causing them to rub and glide together, straining toward release. God, he felt good. So damn good. Long and thick. A perfect fit, stretching her just right. Rocking, rocking, faster and faster, taking her to the edge of sensation before slowing…slowing…tormenting.

She clawed at him, her nails scouring his back. He groaned. She raised her knees, squeezing his hips. *Yes. Yes, more.* Faster, faster still. Never enough, almost enough. *More, please more.*

Nicolai's tongue thrust into her mouth, rolling with hers before he bit down, drawing blood, sucking. A sharp sting, and then, finally, oh, God, finally, she tumbled over.

Ripples of satisfaction swept through her entire body, little stars winking behind her eyes. Her inner muscles clenched and unclenched, liquid heat pooling between her legs. She rode the tide for endless seconds, minutes, before sagging against the mattress, boneless, unable to catch her breath.

An orgasm, she mused dazedly. A freaking orgasm from a fantasy man, and she hadn't even needed to touch herself.

"Nicolai…mine…" she whispered, and she was smiling as she at last drifted off to sleep.

Chapter 2

"Princess. Princess, you must wake up."

Jane blinked open her eyes. Muted sunlight pushed into the bedroom—an unfamiliar bedroom, she realized with confusion. Her room was plain, with white walls and brown carpet, the only furniture an unadorned bed. Now, a lacy pink canopy was draped overhead. To her right was an intricately carved nightstand, a bejeweled goblet perched on top. Beyond that, a plush, glittery carpet led to arched double doors framing a spacious closet bursting with a rainbow of velvets, satins and silks.

This wasn't right.

She jolted upright. Dizziness hit her—familiar, but not comforting—and she moaned.

"Are you all right, princess?"

She forced herself to focus and take stock. A girl stood beside her bed. A girl she had never encountered before. Short, plump, with a freckled nose and frizzy red hair, wearing a coarse brown dress that appeared uncomfortably snug.

Jane scrambled backward, hitting the headboard. "Who are you? What are you doing here?" Even as she spoke, her eyes widened. She knew five different languages, but she wasn't speaking any of them. And yet, she understood every word that left her mouth.

No emotion crossed the girl's features, as if she were used to strange people yelling at her. "I am Rhoslyn, once personal servant to your mother but now personal servant to you. If you agree to keep me," she added, unsure now. She, too, spoke in that weird, lyrical language of flowing syllables. "The queen has bid me to rouse you and escort you to her study."

Servant? Mother? Jane's mother was dead, along with her father and her sister. The latter two had been killed on impact, the drunk driver having slammed his car into their side of the vehicle. Her mom, though…she had died right before Jane's eyes, her life dripping out of her and onto Jane, their car propped against a tree, their seat belts holding them in place, the metal doors and roof smashed so completely they'd had to be pried out. But, by then, it had been too late. She'd already taken her last, pained breath.

She'd died the very day she was told her cancer was gone.

"Don't you dare tease me about my mother," Jane growled, and Rhoslyn flinched.

"I'm sorry, princess, but I do not understand. I tease you not about your mother's summons." How frightened she sounded now. Tears even beaded in her dark eyes. "And I swear to you, I meant no offense. Please do not punish me."

Punish her? Was this some sort of joke?

The word *joke* was as familiar as the dizziness. But, really, *joke* still didn't fit. Nervous breakdown, perhaps? No, couldn't be. Breakdowns were a form of hysteria, and she was not hysterical. Plus, there was the language thing. *Come on. You're a scientist. You can reason this out.*

"Where am I? How did I get here?" Her last memory was of reading the book and—the book! Where was the book? Her heart thundered uncontrollably, a storm inside her chest, as she panned her surroundings once more. There! Her book rested on the vanity, so close, yet so far away.

Mine, every cell in her body screamed, surprising her. Equally surprising, the absolute rightness of the claim. But then, she'd practically made love to the thing. And, oh, damn. Her blood heated and her skin tingled, her body readying for absolute, utter possession.

I need you, Jane. The text. She remembered the text. *Come to me. Save me.*

Consider this logically. She'd fallen asleep, dreamed of a vampire's decadent touch and, like *Alice in Wonderland,* had woken up in a strange, new world. And she *was* awake. This was not a dream. So, where was she? How had she gotten here?

What if…?

She cut off the thought before it could veer into a direction she didn't like. There had to be a rational explanation. "Where am I?" she asked again.

As Jane scooted from the soft confines of the feather-lined mattress, the "servant" said, "You are in…

Delfina." She spoke with a question in her tone, as if she couldn't quite grasp the fact that Jane didn't already know the answer. "A kingdom without time or age."

Delfina? She'd…heard of it, she realized with a start. Not the name, but the "kingdom without time." A few of the beings she'd interviewed had mentioned another realm, a magical realm, with differing kingdoms outside the notice of humans. At the time, she hadn't known whether to believe them or not. They'd been prisoners, locked away for the good of mankind. They would have said anything to gain their freedom. Even offer to escort her into their world.

What if…?

What if she'd crossed the threshold from her world and into the other? Jane finally allowed the thought to reach its conclusion, and her stomach churned with sickness.

Before the car accident changed her life so radically, she'd studied more than the creatures of myth. She'd studied the manipulation of macroscopic energy, attempting the "impossible" on a daily basis. Like the molecular transfer of an object from one location—one world—to another, and she had succeeded. Not with life-forms, of course, not yet, but with plastic and other materials. That's why she'd been deemed an acceptable risk for interacting with the captured beings, both dead and alive.

What if she'd somehow transferred *herself?* But how would she have done so, she wondered next, when the necessary tools were not in her cabin? Latent effects of her contact with the previously transferred materials, perhaps?

No. There were too many variables. Namely, her new, royal identity.

"Rhoslyn," she said, keeping her narrowed gaze on the girl as she settled her weight on her legs. Her knees knocked together, and her muscles knotted, but thankfully the dizziness did not return.

"Yes, princess?"

She gave herself a quick once-over, blinked with another dose of surprise and had to look again. She wore a lovely pink gown she hadn't purchased herself and had never before seen. The material bagged around her reed thin body, dancing at her ankles.

Who the hell had dressed her?

Doesn't matter. She focused on the here and now. "What do I look like?"

Rhoslyn reached out, and Jane pursed her lips as she darted away. "Please, princess, you have been unwell. Allow me to assist you."

"Stay where you are," Jane told her. Until she figured out what was going on, she would trust no one. And without trust, there would be no touching.

The girl froze in place. "Wh-whatever you command, princess. Did you wish me to fetch something for you?"

"No, uh, I just want to grab something from over there." Jane lumbered forward. The carpet fibers were as soft as they appeared and caressed her bare feet, tickling the sensitive areas between her toes. She moved slowly, allowing the tension to drain from her abused legs. By the time she swiped up the book and turned, she felt normal. Still the girl had not moved, her arm extended toward the bed, shaking now. "At ease," she found herself saying.

With a sigh of relief, Rhoslyn dropped her arm to her side. "You asked what you look like. Beautiful, princess. As always." Said automatically, with no real feeling.

Half of Jane's attention remained on her while the other half focused on the book. She frowned. The dark leather was unmarred. She flipped to the middle. There was no bookmark, and the pages were new, fresh. Blank. "This isn't my book," she said. "Where's my book?"

"Princess Odette," Rhoslyn replied smoothly. "To my knowledge, you did not arrive with a book. Now, would you like—?"

"Wait. What did you call me?"

"Pr—princess Odette? That is your title and name. Yes? Did you wish me to call you something else? Or, perhaps I can summon the healer, and have her—"

"No. No, that's okay." Princess Odette, returned from the grave. Jane had read those very words. She'd also read, "You, Jane Parker. You are Odette."

She twisted and leaned into the vanity, watching her reflection in the mirror. The moment she came into view, she stiffened. Light brown hair flowed over one shoulder. *Her* hair. Familiar. Her dark eyes were glassy, crescent-moon bruises underneath. Also familiar.

She reached out. Her fingertips pressed into the glass. Cool, solid. Real. If she lifted her gown, she would see the scars that marred her stomach and legs. She knew it.

She hadn't morphed into Princess Odette overnight, then. Or, hell, maybe she and the princess looked alike.

"How did I get here?" she croaked, swinging back around to face the girl.

I need you, Jane.

Nicolai. She sucked in a breath as his name suddenly filled her mind. Nicolai the enslaved vampire, chained, abused. Nicolai the lover, sliding into her body, her legs parting to welcome him, then squeezing to hold him captive.

Come to me.

Come to him, as if he knew her. As if she knew him. But she'd never met him. At least, not to her knowledge.

Such a thing *was* possible, she supposed. Paradox theory suggested—damn it. No. She wasn't going to hypothesize about paradox theory until she had more information. Otherwise, she'd be lost in her head for days.

Rhoslyn paled. "Yesterday evening a palace guard found you lying on the steps outside. He carried you here, to your bedchamber. You'll be happy to note it is in the same condition you left it."

Falling asleep at home, waking up…here. Princess Odette, returned from the grave, she thought again. Alice in her Wonderland.

"I hope you do not mind, but I bathed and changed you," Rhoslyn added.

White-hot heat in her cheeks. Plenty of strangers had bathed and changed her over the past eleven months, and she was relieved Rhoslyn had done so, rather than some sweating, panting guy. Still. *Mortifying.* "Where's my shirt?"

"It's being washed. I must admit, I have never seen its like. There was strange writing on it."

She closed the book and clutched it to her chest. "I want it back." Just then, it was her only link to home.

"Of course. After I escort you to your mother, I—oh,

I'm sorry. I did not mean to mention her again. I will take you to…the study below and fetch the garment for you." Before Jane could comment, Rhoslyn added through gnashed teeth, "I am so happy—as are all your people—that you have come back to us. We missed you greatly."

A lie, no question. "Wh-where was I?"

"Your sister, Princess Laila, witnessed your fall from the cliffs what seems an eternity ago. After you were stabbed and drained by your new slave. Though your body was never found, it was assumed you were dead, as no one has ever survived such a drop before. We should have known that you, the darling of Delfina, would find a way." She flashed a stiff smile that lasted a single second, no more.

Princess Laila. That name, too, reverberated in Jane's head, followed on the heels of "cruel, twisted desires."

"Nicolai," she said. Was he here? Real?

The servant chewed on her bottom lip, suddenly nervous. "You wish me to bring the slave, Nicolai, to you?"

Jane's blood quickened and warmed, her skin tingling just as before. The girl knew who he was. That meant he *was* here, that he was as real as she was.

Her mind fizzed and crackled like her favorite candy. The book. The characters. The story, coming to life before her eyes…Jane now a part of it, deeply integrated, though she was someone other than herself. Finally. A puzzle piece slid into place.

The book could have been the catalyst. Maybe, when she'd read aloud, she'd somehow opened a doorway from her world into this one. Maybe Nicolai had somehow sent the book to her, and she was his only hope for freedom.

"Nicolai," she repeated. "I want you to take me to him." She had to see him, and was too impatient to wait. Would he know her? Was she right about the events that had unfolded?

Rhoslyn gulped. "But he's the one who stabbed you, and your moth—I mean, er, the queen does not like to be kept waiting. She visited you once already, but you were sound asleep and could not be roused. Her impatience grows, and as you know, her temper..." Her cheeks flushed as she realized what she was saying. "I'm sorry. I meant no disrespect to the queen."

Nicolai had stabbed Odette, the woman Jane was supposed to be? Talk about a plot twist Jane hadn't seen coming. Damn. What if he tried to do the same to Jane?

He won't, some deep, secret part of her said. *He needs you. He said so.*

"A few minutes more won't hurt the queen." Whoever the queen was, whatever she was supposed to mean to her, Jane didn't care. Although, the fact that the woman was in charge, her word law and she apparently had a temper, unsettled her.

"Your sister—"

"Doesn't matter." She, too, was dead. Although, according to the book, *Odette* might just have a sister. That other princess. But again, Jane didn't care. "Take me to Nicolai. Now." Time to find another puzzle piece.

A breath shuddered through the girl, the seconds ticking by in tension-filled silence. Then, "Whatever you wish, princess. This way."

Chapter 3

They called him Nicolai. He didn't know if that was his real name. He didn't know anything about himself, really. Whenever he attempted to remember, his head throbbed with unbearable pain and his mind shut down. All he knew was that he was a vampire, and the females here were witches. That, and he despised this kingdom and its people—and he would destroy them. One day. Soon. Just as he'd destroyed one of their precious princesses.

Anticipation rushed through him. His captors thought him weak, ineffective. They kept him on the razor edge of hunger, giving him a drop of blood in the morning and a drop of blood at night. That was all. He was teased and tormented constantly. Especially by the Princess Laila. *So highborn, but look at you now. At my feet, mine to do with as I wish.*

Highborn? He would find out.

They assumed, just because he was chained and starved, he could not harm them. They had no idea of the power that swirled inside him. Power that was caged, like him, but still there, ready to burst free at any moment.

Soon, he thought again, grinning darkly.

They'd had their healer bind his powers, as well as wipe his memory, and they made no secret of those facts. Why they'd done the latter, however, they'd never said. What did they not want him to remember? Again, he would find out.

What *they* didn't know was that the witch had lacked Nicolai's inner strength, and already a few of his abilities had seeped through that mental cage, allowing him to summon a woman who could set him free.

A woman who had at last arrived. Urgency and relief rushed through him, driving him to pace, back and forth, back and forth, his bare feet pounding into the cold concrete, his chains rattling. Even his guards were shocked by the miracle of Princess Odette's appearance. Or rather, the girl they assumed was Princess Odette.

The real Odette was dead. He'd made sure of it. He had drained her, stabbed her, then shoved her over the cliffs outside this palace. Excessively violent, perhaps, but an enemy was an enemy, and his temper had been roused. And, as he'd known, not even the most powerful of witches could recover from that.

Hurry, female. I need you.

Nicolai had spent countless days, weeks, years—he wasn't sure—with Odette before he'd killed her. She was the one who had purchased him at the Sex Market, after all. She'd been a cruel girl, with a taste for delivering pain, unable to reach her climax until her unwilling partner screamed.

She had never climaxed with Nicolai.

Remaining silent had been a source of pride for him. No matter the instruments used on him, no matter how many males and females the bitch had allowed to touch and use him, he had only ever smiled.

When Odette took him outside the palace, threatening to throw *him* over the cliffs if he continued to defy her, he was finally given an opportunity to strike. She'd made the mistake of leaving his muzzle behind. She'd also made the mistake of stepping within his reach, chained though he'd been. He'd fallen on her, pinned her and sunk his fangs into her neck. Starved as he'd been, he'd drained her in minutes. And after that last, life-ending gulp, he'd stabbed her with her own dagger, just to be sure, and shoved her over the precipice.

Too late had the guard realized what had happened, and Nicolai had turned on him, ready for another snack. They'd fought like animals. More beastlike than most, Nicolai had won. The guard had never stood a chance, really. When provoked or hungry, vampires became frenzied and ravenous—unpredictable, uncontrollable predators who scented prey.

As he'd drained his second victim, Princess Laila had swooped in. Having coveted her older sister's right to the throne, as well as her possessions, including Nicolai himself, she had watched Odette, waiting for the perfect time to act.

Nicolai had inadvertently given it to her. She and her guards had moved faster than his gaze could track, unfettered magic giving them strength and speed, and though his first meal in weeks had rallied him, the chains had slowed him down. He'd been overpowered with embarrassing ease.

Footsteps suddenly sounded, followed by the waft of something sweet in the air, both catching his attention. Nicolai stiffened and stilled, his ears twitching, his mouth watering. Absolute hunger bathed him, his stomach twisting. *Must...taste...female...*

The desire did not spring from his mind, but from deep inside him. An instinct, a need.

Usually those footsteps heralded the arrival of Laila's servants, sent to drag him up the stairs and into her bedroom. This time, a plump redhead rounded the corner. He inhaled deeply, growled. Not her. She was not the source of that sweetness.

Nicolai stopped breathing, hoping his head would clear, if only for a moment. He was so damn hungry for the one responsible...had to see her. He rooted his feet in the center of his cage, his pallet behind him, thick bars in front of him, waiting. Who would next enter the dungeon?

And then, he saw her. The summoned female. His "Odette."

He sucked in another breath. Her. She was responsible. A second growl rose, this one straight from his soul. *Must taste female.*

She did not smell like the real Odette. To everyone else, she would. She would smell of too-strong floral perfume mixed with the raw ooze of a putrid wound— evidence of her rotting heart. But to him...oh, to him... He inhaled again, unable to stop himself. Mistake. The sweetness, thicker now, almost tangible, fogged his mind. *Must. Taste.* His fangs and gums actually ached with the need to sample her. *Must taste.*

He studied her, his blood practically on fire. Anyone who looked at her would see the mask his shifted glammor had created. The mystical illusion of being someone else. Hair as dark as the Abyss, eyes of vivid emerald, skin as pale as cream. But that was where the gift of her father's famed beauty ended, and the cruelty of her mother's ugliness revealed itself. Odette was tall yet thickly built, her cheeks puffed from excess, her jaw squared with jowls. Her dark brows were substantial, and nearly connected in the center. Her nose was long with a definite hook.

What Nicolai saw, however, was the woman his summoning had chosen. The one from his dreams. Dreams in which she stood off to the side, watching him, never speaking. Dreams he had not understood. Until now. All along, his magic had known what he needed.

She was just as tall as Odette, but reed slender, with hair the color of a honeycomb. Her eyes were seductively uptilted, a shade darker than her hair, and filled with haunting secrets. Her skin was slightly bronzed and radiant, as if the sun was hidden underneath. Her cheeks were perfectly sculpted, her chin stubborn and yet delicate.

Delicate, yes. That's what she was. Amorously delicate, utterly fragile and delightfully feminine. Almost... breakable. Would he kill her when he drank from her? And he *would* drink from her. He would not be able to resist that scent for long.

The protector in him rose up—a part of him he had not known existed, not for some stranger—demanding that he sweep her away from this and save her from the horror to come. Horror he would be responsible for. Not only from his dark embrace, but also from the evil of those around her. The people of Delfina wouldn't savor her blood if they learned the truth of her identity. They would spill it and kill her. Painfully.

Do you want your freedom or the girl out of harm's way? You can't have both.

He hardened his heart. He wanted his freedom.

Their gazes locked a second later, a shock of awareness blasting him. Perhaps she felt it, too, for she gasped, stumbled. She righted herself and stopped at the bars, her amber eyes wide, her lush, pink mouth open, revealing straight white teeth. She held a book.

Taste her...

He wished he could see her tongue. Wished he could capture that tongue with his own. His desire surprised him. How long since he'd experienced true, willing arousal?

"You're real," she whispered, gripping the metal with her free hand. She squeezed so tightly her knuckles bleached of color. "You're really here. And you look exactly as I dreamed."

He nodded stiffly—and that wasn't the only stiff thing about him. His cock filled, lengthening, thickening. "I am real, yes." She'd dreamed of him, as he'd dreamed of her? He liked the idea.

He motioned to the servant with a tilt of his chin. *Get rid of her.*

Her attention whipped to the girl, and she uttered another gasp, as though startled to find they weren't alone. "You may go, Rhoslyn. And thank you for bringing me here."

"Anything for you, princess." Expression softening with her relief, Rhoslyn curtsied. She raced around the corner and pounded up the stairs.

"You are confused," Nicolai said. How harsh his voice was, pushing through his teeth and slicing up his tone.

A shiver slid down her slight frame as she faced him. "Yes. One minute I was at home, reading a book—about you! The next I was here. How am I here? Where *is* here? At first, I thought I was hallucinating or that this was a joke, but that isn't right. I know that isn't right. I'm calm. I see, I feel."

"No hallucination, and no joke." His frown deepened, his fangs cutting into his bottom lip. Just a taste, one little taste. "You were reading a book about me? Is that it?"

Her gaze fell to his teeth, and she gulped. "Yes. Written by you, I think." Her voice was as soft and delicate as her features. "Or at least, part of it was. But no, this isn't it. This one is blank. Or maybe this *is* it, but the writing just hasn't happened yet."

To his knowledge, he had not written a book, and had not sent a book to anyone. That did not mean anything, however. The memory of doing so could be buried with all the rest of his past.

He closed his eyes for a moment, enjoying the scent of her—and felt the ache in his gums intensify. He was walking toward her, determined to grab her, bite her.

When he realized what he was doing, he forced himself to stop. He would scare her, and she would scream. Guards would rush inside to save her.

He could cover her mouth with one hand, of course, and tilt her back with the other, giving himself a wide playing field. He could lick…finally, blessedly taste…

Concentrate. "Do you know who I am?" Again, his

tone was harsh, demanding. "Have you met me before? Besides in your dreams?"

"No."

Disappointing. "I will explain everything. Later," he lied. The less she knew, now and in the future, the better it would be for her. "Right now, we must hurry." Ever since he'd woken up in the slave market—weeks, months, *years* ago?—he'd been driven by more than a need to feed and escape. He'd been driven by an urge to reach the kingdom of Elden.

He must get there. And soon. More than that, he must slay the new king. He didn't know why, he just knew that even thinking of the man filled him with rage. And every day that this man lived, a piece of Nicolai died. The knowledge was separate from his memories, springing from the same place as his need to taste this woman.

Taste. How many times would he think the word?

Countless. Until he got what he wanted, he was sure.

"Give me your arm." He licked his lips at the thought of touching her, of knowing the texture of her skin. "I will mark you." A little nip of her wrist, and he would stop. He would make himself stop. For now.

She shook her head, honeycomb hair dancing over her shoulders. "No. Explain now. Afterward, we'll *talk* about the marking thing, whatever that is."

Surely the female was not as stubborn as she seemed. "We might be separated." Before she freed him. "I want to know where you are at all times."

"Uh, I'm not sure how I feel about someone knowing where I am at all times. But again, we'll discuss it. After."

All right, she was *more* stubborn than she seemed.

"As you can see, I have been enslaved. Tortured." Uttering the words enraged him further. He should never have allowed himself to be placed in this situation. He should have been stronger. He *was* stronger. But he had no idea how he'd ended up in the Sex Market. "I don't even—"

"Know if your name is really Nicolai. Blah, blah, blah. *I know.* I told you, I read a few passages of the book. I just don't understand this." She motioned to the prison, to him, to her gown. "'Jane, I need you,' you said. How did you know to write to me when we've never met?" Desperation wafted from her. "Unless I came here before, but returned home to a time before we'd met, and my dreams were echoes of what was to be. That would mean history is now looping, but of course, that creates a paradox, and—"

"Enough." Jane. Her name was Jane. Somehow familiar, causing his arousal to ramp up...up. Maybe because the syllable was as soft and lyrical as her strange—though slight—accent. *Focus.* If she had asked anyone else these questions... "What have you mentioned to the others?"

"Nothing." She laughed without humor. "I don't know them."

"Good. That's good." But she knew him, even though they had only seen each other in their dreams? As he had claimed to know her in that book? Something more *was* going on here. "Where are you from, Jane?"

"Oklahoma."

Oklahoma was not part of this magical realm. "You are human, then? Not a witch?"

A sweep of dark lashes, momentarily hiding undiluted shock. And pride. "I was right. I crossed over, didn't I?"

"Jane. I asked you a question." And he was used to getting answers immediately. He felt it in his bones.

"Yes, I'm human, and no, I'm not a witch. But you, you're a vampire."

He nodded. He knew this realm coexisted alongside the mortal world—a world mostly ignorant of what surrounded them.

Crossing over, as she had mentioned, happened more often than it should. How and why, though, no one knew. One moment you would be talking to a shifter or fighting an ogre, and the next moment a human would be in his place. And if not a human, a useless, bendable object.

Disappointment nearly felled Nicolai. Why had his magic chosen this woman? What good was a human here? Even so luscious a human? If Jane were asked to perform a ritual, as Odette had often been asked, she would be unable. She would fail. Everyone would know she was not who she claimed to be, *before* he could get what he wanted.

He had to act faster than planned.

"Listen. I summoned you here, and I am the one who protects you." A small truth meant to pacify her. "Trust no one else. Only me." A lie meant to save him. For once she set him free, he truly planned to leave. This palace—and her. As unstable as his abilities were, he could not remove the mask that made her Odette while they were together without the possibility of sending her home. Plus, he needed her able to travel freely through this palace as only a princess could. What a princess *couldn't* do was travel unfettered outside these walls.

The moment she let him go, Jane would have nothing but her wits to shield her.

Guilt filled him. Before the emotion had time to settle, develop roots and grow, he ground it into powder and scattered every speck. He could not soften. No matter how desperately he craved this woman's blood.

"So, you wield some type of magic?" she said. "All right. I can roll with the idea of a magical vampire. But really, a lot of people assume science is magic, so are we talking about planar, natural, runic, divine or metaphysical, because I can—"

"Jane." She was a babbler. He found the trait… charming. He frowned. Charming? Truly? The need to taste her must be clouding his judgment.

Abashed, she smiled. "I'm sorry. Curiosity and puzzles are my downfall. At least, they used to be. I thought I'd come to hate them, but, well, as you can see, that's no longer the case."

That smile…had he ever seen so open and innocent a sight? Another spark of guilt ignited in his chest, but again, he quickly ground and scattered it. Easier done this time, as the force of his arousal intensified, becoming his sole focus.

No. Only escape mattered, he told himself.

"Why me?" she asked. "I mean, how did you know to summon *me?*"

He'd wanted a female susceptible to the lure of a vampire, one untainted by the evil of the Queen of Hearts, one who was not afraid of blood, who would understand his plight. He told her none of that. He knew women—or, at least, thought he did—and knew it would not please her. "Order my release. Now. Hurry."

Frustration suddenly radiated from her. "How?" she demanded.

"Summon the guard," he said. "Tell them to unchain me, that you wish to take me to your bedchamber. Then, tell them to bring the healer to us."

"The healer?" Her concerned gaze swept over him. "Are you hurt?"

No. But the healer had bound his memories and powers, and so the healer could easily free them. And, he mused darkly, he wanted to kill the bitch. "I do not hear you calling for the guard, Jane."

"Then your ears are working perfectly, Nicolai. So, the guards will do what I tell them?" She snapped her fingers. "Just like that?"

"In their minds, you are the princess Odette. Oldest daughter of their queen, and soon to be their ruler." Nicolai finally allowed himself to stride the rest of the way to the bars, his chains rattling. Closing in… "They will do anything you tell them to do."

She released the metal and backed away before he could touch her. As if he were dirty, unworthy. He probably was. "Yes, but why do they believe I'm Odette?"

A muscle ticked below his eye. Her continued questioning irritated him, yes, but her distance irritated him *more*. When close to her, the scent of her was nearly overpowering and so delectable he was probably drooling. "Because."

"Because why?"

Stubborn baggage. "Because my…vampire magic made them," he said flatly. To tell her more was to, perhaps, send her running. Humans were so easily frightened by what they did not understand.

For the moment, he needed this woman on his side,

and calm. Although, to be honest, she'd handled things very well so far.

"How?" she insisted.

He shook the bars. "Do as I told you, Jane. We must hurry."

She arched a brow. "You're cute when you're ordering me around, you know that?" The color in her cheeks brightened, and her breath became shallow. "And you... you smell like sandalwood."

She liked his scent as much as he liked hers, he realized. It aroused her. Her nipples were pearling beneath her robe, begging for a touch, a kiss. Did her belly quiver? Was she already moist between her legs?

His hands fisted at his sides. "I don't know why I'm here or how they captured me, but I do know that I don't belong here. I know that if I stay, I will be tortured again and again. Tell me you are not like them, Jane. Tell me you do not like to watch a man be tortured."

Her dark gaze fell to the metal linked around his neck, then dipped lower, perhaps following the beads of dried blood that rode the ropes of his stomach before stopping at his tented loincloth.

Another shiver from her. "I don't," she said on a broken wisp of air. "But what happens if they realize I'm not truly Odette?"

"They won't find out." This lie did not leave him smoothly. "All right? All you need to know to aid the illusion is that you bought me at the Sex Market. You own me. Demand my release, and escort me to your—"

The sound of footsteps echoed, and Nicolai pressed his lips together. Jane tensed. An audience, exactly what they did not need right now. Then Laila rounded the corner, a scowl marring her already ugly face. She was as short and squat as her mother, her cheeks just as padded as Odette's, and her jowls just as noticeable.

Without the hooked nose, however, she was the "beauty" of the family. The length of her dark hair was coiled on top of her head, ringlets hanging at her temples. She wore an opulent gown of bright green velvet to match her eyes, though there was nothing in this kingdom or any other that could make her attractive. The evil of her soul was simply too dark.

A silver timepiece hung from a chain around her neck. She was never without it, and the sight of it never failed to twist Nicolai's stomach with rage. Why?

She ground to a halt when she spotted Jane, hurriedly smoothing her features into a doting expression. "What are you doing here, sister dear? And in your nightgown, no less." An anxious laugh. "You should be resting. We don't want you getting sick, do we? You've already suffered so much."

Her voice never failed to disgust him, either. He'd heard it over him, under him, behind him, her warm breath trekking over his skin. Now, so close to escape, he had to bite his tongue to hold his curses inside.

Soon, he would destroy her.

Jane gulped, looked at him.

Do what I told you, Jane, he projected at her, a part of him resenting the need to do so. He'd never had to beg for anything in his life. He'd always—a sharp ache erupted in his temples, cutting off his thoughts. A memory, dead and gone before it had a chance to live.

"You are Princess Laila. My sister. Yes." Jane breathed deeply, squared her shoulders, and faced her "sister." "He's—he's mine. I own him." What she lacked in conviction she made up for with determination.

Good girl.

Laila gritted her too-white teeth, and shifted from one sandaled foot to the other. "Yes, but you were gone, darling. I took over his care. He's mine now." She stroked the timepiece. "In situations such as this, Mother always sides with the one in possession."

"I don't care. He's mine."

"Odette, be reasonable." How patient Laila appeared. A falsehood. "He attempted to slay you once, and nearly succeeded. He is too much for you to handle and I have grown used to—"

"I said he's mine."

Good girl, he thought again. So badly Nicolai wished he could unleash the torrent of power inside him, now rather than later. He would crush Laila, smile when she screamed, laugh when she died, then raze this palace brick by brick and dance atop the rubble.

Soon. The word was a constant inside him.

He didn't know what powers he could wield, or if they'd be strong enough to do everything he wanted to this kingdom. Absolute, total destruction. But he wasn't worried. Were his powers not too weak, he would raise his army and they would march—

Another ache tore through his head, another memory destroyed. He hissed from the pain, clearing his mind before he shut down completely.

Both women flicked him a glance before refocusing on each other. But Laila's attention quickly returned to him, to his erection—still pulsing with need of Jane— and her mouth hung open with shock. "You're aroused."

Silent, he reached under his loincloth and stroked his

length up and down, taunting her with what he'd never willingly offered her.

Laila gave a strangled choke, her eyes widening as she faced her sister. "How did you arouse him?"

"I—I—" Jane blushed as becomingly as she smiled. So innocent and sweet, sunlight and moonlight twined together. *Taste…*

"Never mind," Laila snapped, all pretense of love and patience vanishing. "It doesn't matter. Mother's on a rampage and demands a word with you. She mourned your death for days, and was ecstatic by your return. But that happiness will not save you from a whipping if you continue to defy her."

A mother, mourning her child *for days*. How sweet, Nicolai mentally sneered. But then, the Queen of Hearts was known as a brutal tyrant, an unforgiving bitch and a power hungry murderer. Nicolai's own mother had—

He clenched his jaw against the pain.

"I heard you were on your way down here," Laila went on, "and came to get you. You don't want to keep your queen waiting, do you?"

"I—I—"

"No. You don't."

Damn this. Jane was letting Laila direct her, proving she had not the strength of will to lead. His one and only chance for escape was withering with every second that passed.

"Laila, no. I—"

"Your poor, addled mind hasn't yet recovered from your fall, has it, darling? But you like having skin on your back, I know you do. Guards," Laila called.

Jane twisted her fingers together, clearly agitated.

"I—I— there's no need. I don't want to be whipped, but I really need to—"

Two armed guards swung around the corner and stopped behind Princess Laila. They kept their gazes straight ahead as they awaited orders.

If they touched Jane, Nicolai would execute them. He would cut their throats, and spit on their remains. The ferocity of the thought should have surprised him. Jane was here for one purpose, and one purpose only, whether she acted like it or not, and remaining untouched by the citizens of Delfina was not it. Surprised, Nicolai wasn't. Nothing would stop him from attacking these men in cold blood. Jane was his. His savior, his to handle. Only his. No one else was allowed.

Until he left her.

He bit his tongue so hard he tasted his own blood.

"Muzzle the prisoner and cart him to my chamber," Laila commanded, and he relaxed somewhat. The men weren't here for Jane, then. "My sister and I will visit with the queen."

"No," Nicolai growled before he could stop himself.

"No?" Astonished, Laila leveled her attention on him. She wrapped her fat little fingers around the time-piece hanging from her neck and squeezed. "You dare issue commands, slave? To *me?*"

"Odette stays." Jane might have fooled the servants and her sister, but she would not find the Queen of Hearts so gullible. She had groomed Odette in her image, and no one knew her better. Jane and her odd speech would be found out. Killed before Nicolai could use her.

Heart...hardening.

Softening...

Laila floundered. "You'll try and kill her again. That's why you want her here. I know it. That's why you're pretending to desire her."

He flicked his tongue over his fangs. "I need inside her. *That's* why I want her here."

Once again, Jane blushed.

"You...you're lying," Laila stammered. "You hate her. You wouldn't want to bed her."

"I crave her."

A pause, heavy with tension. Motions clipped, Laila closed the distance between her and her sister and wrapped an arm around Jane's waist. "Don't listen to him. He'll say anything to gain a second chance to harm you. Come now. I'll protect you."

"No!" Jane jumped from Laila's embrace and glared up at the guards. "Take Nicolai to *my* chamber, but don't muzzle him. And tell M-Mother that I'm in need of rest. I'll speak to her later."

Laila paled as the men leaped into action. Seconds later, hinges were squeaking as the door to Nicolai's cage swung open. There were more footsteps, then a key was inserted into the metal base that pinned him to the wall.

His relief was palpable.

"But...but, Odette. You are placing yourself in danger," Laila said, desperate.

"He. Is. Mine. Nothing more needs to be said."

Wrong words. The claim—*he is mine*—affected him, giving birth to a savage animal inside him. Hers, he was hers, and he would have her before he left her, no matter the consequences. Over and over again. In every way imaginable. He would drink her, and possess her body.

There would be no stopping him, no reasoning with him. Not now.

Chapter 4

The guards forced Nicolai onto the bed, the feathered mattress dipping and puffing under his weight. They anchored the metal links curling around his neck to a steel hook in the wall, just above the headboard, then removed the chains from his ankle and wrists—only to cuff him to the bedposts.

Odette had brought slaves here before, Jane realized. The posts were scarred, the deep grooves evidence of their resistance. A *lot* of resistance. How many times had Nicolai suffered this kind of indignity with the princess?

At least he didn't try and bite the guards, and they didn't try to hurt him, and Jane didn't have to side with a "slave," fueling suspicion. Already she felt as if she had a neon sign blinking over her head: Imposter.

Thank God Laila hadn't realized the truth. And wasn't the other princess a shocker? Short, squat and

foaming-at-the-mouth-rabies mean. Seriously. If the
Wicked Witch of the West had slept with Hannibal
Lecter, and the two of them had a baby, that child's
name would be Laila.

*Pay attention to what's happening around you,
Parker!*

Right. Jane focused. She watched, flabbergasted, as
one of the guards cleaned Nicolai from head to toe and
the other oiled him.

She placed the book on the nightstand, considered
protesting what was being done to him, but wasn't sure
"Odette" would do such a thing. Therefore, she held
her tongue. Through it all, Nicolai remained silent, his
expression blank, but his gaze, oh, his gaze was glued
to her. His pupils were huge, his irises still sparkling
with…desire.

For her, or for her blood? His fangs were sharp and
long, revealing the depths of his hunger.

Just then, he was the poster child for bondage, blood
and a badass fetish. He was chained, yes, but he would
be in control. He was strong, in body and in mind, and
he exuded something, pheromones, perhaps, that drew
slavelike desires from *her*. Every cell in her body ached,
frantic to know his touch. He was the most physically
perfect being she'd ever encountered.

Seeing such a proud, strong man bound like that,
lying atop a bed of pink lace and ruffles, being readied
for her use, should have caused her stomach to churn
with sickness. But she only wanted him more.

Her mind had pictured him before she'd ever met
him, yes, but her mind had not done him justice. He
was tall, at least six foot four, with wide muscled shoulders, a stomach roped and corded, and skin as smooth

as cream mixed with coffee. He had shoulder-length hair as dark as midnight, and eyes the color of moonlight glinting off snow, silvery yet threaded with gold.

She didn't see her death in those eyes, as the book had promised. She saw her seduction. How many times had she had to stop herself from reaching out, letting him "mark" her, whatever that meant, just to feel his skin against hers? Too many. That's why she'd jumped away from him when he'd reached for her. She'd feared her reaction, afraid of an increase in the desire she felt. Already being near him was becoming a need as necessary as breathing.

The same force that had brought her here had to be responsible for what she was feeling.

Though he was cut and bruised, with dried blood caked along his arms and legs, he had not a single scar. In fact, he did not have a flaw, period. The closest thing to an imperfection he had was the thin trail of dark hair traveling from his navel to the waist of his loincloth—and that wasn't an imperfection so much as a roadway to heaven.

Speaking of the final destination of that naughty roadway…down in the cell, he'd been aroused by her, and he hadn't tried to hide it. He'd *boasted* about it, drawing attention to his groin. With very good reason. Besides her dreams and single fantasy about him, she had been with only one man. And that man could not compare. She doubted any man could. "Big" was an understatement in Nicolai's case.

When he'd touched himself, running his fingers up and down his length, her body had ached. She'd forgotten her circumstances and imagined dropping to her knees. Tonguing him, drinking him in.

Mind, stop dipping your toes in the gutter pool!

Finally the guards finished and strode toward the door. Her shouted command, "Leave the key," stopped both men.

The shorter of the two faced her and bowed. "You have the key to these restraints, princess."

Oh. Odette would have known that. "Well," she said, swallowing, "the fall…from the cliffs—you heard about the cliffs, right?—must have caused me to forget. You can, uh, leave us." She waved toward the door, as princessy as possible. God, acting like someone other than who she was—like someone she'd never met—was not fun.

The door shut with a soft *clink*.

She rounded on her "prisoner," closing the distance between them, stopping only when the edge of the bed forced her. Again, she wanted to touch him, but she couldn't allow herself the luxury. Those teeth… He could take her jugular as a souvenir.

"The key is in the drawer of the nightstand," Nicolai said, breaking the silence first. "Use it."

Even his voice was a delight. A sensual feast of tones and nuances. Raspy, husky, a wisp of smoke. She shivered, licked her lips. "You might have summoned me or whatever, but you are not in charge. So listen up. I'll get the key—*after* you tell me more about what's going on."

"You and your 'afters.'" He glared at her, the long length of his lashes fused together and shielding the uniqueness of his dual-colored irises. "This is blackmail." As irritated as he appeared, he also seemed… proud.

Why proud? In and out she breathed, luxuriating in

the scent of sandalwood. Far stronger now than when she'd dreamed or read the book. "Yes, it's blackmail, and I won't back down."

Cruel of her, but she suspected the moment she released him, he'd feed first, then race out the door, leaving her behind without giving her a single answer. He had the look of a cornered panther, ready to bite and bolt. Plus, he hadn't wanted to talk to her in the dungeon and wouldn't have, if she hadn't pressed him. Therefore, she would continue to press him.

"Apparently, I'm risking a whipping by being here with you," she added. "You kind of owe me."

"You wouldn't understand," he gritted.

She'd graduated high school at the age of fifteen. Acquired her master's at eighteen. Then, while working toward her doctorate, she'd joined a highly classified branch of the government to research unexplainable abilities and phenomenon, as well as find ways to *accomplish* the unexplainable. The only reason she'd quit and changed the focus of her studies to health sciences was to move back home and help her mother, who had just been diagnosed with breast cancer.

"I think I can keep up," she said dryly. She anchored her hands on her hips, the material pulling tight over her chest.

His gaze lowered to her breasts, and his lips stretched taut over his teeth. "Very well. We'll talk. *After* you straddle me."

She blinked at the sensual request, even as her body responded to him, readying for penetration. "What… why?"

"You get what you want, I get what I want."

"Blackmail?" she parroted, not nearly as controlled

as she sounded. Blood rushed through her veins at an alarming rate.

"Yes."

Tempting. So tempting. And probably meant to cow her. "Well, I'm not caving." One of them had to keep things on a business level.

"Are you wet?"

Breath caught in her throat. Clearly that someone was not Nicolai. Really, what kind of question was that? "I—I don't even know you, of course I'm not...I can't be...what you asked."

"Jane. I saw the way you looked at my cock. You can be. So. Are you wet?"

"Yes," she whispered, blushing. She'd done that a lot today. And just as clearly, she wasn't that someone, either.

"I'm hard for you."

I know. I sooo know. "That doesn't matter." Oh, God, that mattered. She wanted to introduce herself to that hardness properly. Meaning, a nice, firm handshake. "I mean, uh, are you planning to hurt me like you hurt the real Odette?"

A beat of silence. "Odette, I hated. Jane, I crave."

Such sweet, intoxicating words, all the more potent because she couldn't accuse him of only lusting for what was available. Laila, too, had wanted him in a bad, bad way, but he hadn't wanted the princess at all. So, logically, Jane had to believe he was as attracted to her as she was to him. Yeah, logically. And not just because she was trembling and desperately wanted it to be true.

He could simply be trying to soften her up.

Oh, great. The upsetting thought poked its way from

an ugly place inside her. A place that never wanted her to be happy. A place that felt she didn't *deserve* to be happy. They'd been butting heads for months; more and more, she won the battles. Today, she might not.

"If I hurt you, you would not help me," he said in a silky tone. "I want you to help me, and I am not a foolish man."

No, he was a sexy one. "You're a violent man. I know you are."

"Yes."

His honesty deflated her upcoming argument before she could start.

"Do you fear me, little Jane?"

"Maybe. What if you bite me? Or do that marking thing?"

"You'll like it, the bite and the marking, but I won't do either until you beg. You have my word. Now. Straddle me," he repeated. "I'm also capable of giving pleasure. Giving and taking. That's what we'll do here and now. Give and take pleasure while we talk."

Beg… Sweet heaven, she just might. Because deep inside, at the core of her femininity, she wanted to be with him. As if she'd been born for him, and him alone. Or bespelled. But even the thought of magic couldn't dull her desire for this man. The desire was somehow as familiar as his scent.

"I'm not taking off my robe. Or my panties. We just met. That would be, uh, tacky." *Idiot.* "I'm trusting you to keep your word. And I'm only doing this for answers," she lied.

"Don't care why. Just want to feel you."

Slowly, unsure, she climbed on top of him, placing a knee on each side of his waist. Her robe hiked up, revealing the length of her thighs. Just as slowly, she lowered her body until her female core brushed his erection. She gasped at the contact. He moaned.

This was better than her fantasy. He was hot, so hot. Hard, so hard.

"Talk," she said, flattening her palms on his chest. Before she did what she'd said she wouldn't and stripped out of her panties.

He arched up, pressing more firmly against her. They moaned in unison, his heart drumming as erratically as hers. She liked that.

A moment passed. "You said you enjoy puzzles," he mentioned huskily. His gaze settled on her neck.

Her pulse fluttered, as though happy to have gained his notice. "Yes."

"We fit together very nicely, don't you think?"

"Yes." God. How moronic she sounded. Yes this, and yes that. It was just, he'd fried her circuits. She was on top of him, poised over his cock. And she ached. Ached like a drug addict in need of a fix. Why else would she have practically thrown herself at a vampire?

He waited. When she said no more, he arched his hips again. "What did you want to know, Jane?"

She rubbed against him. An accident, she told herself, and just once, but enough to leave her sweating. "I want…to know…about you. About why you summoned *me* to free you?" There. She'd found her voice, without panting like she was climbing a mountain. Or a well-endowed man.

"You never said," she continued. "Do I look like Princess Odette or something?" If so, Odette and Laila must have been an odd sight. The blond giant and the brunette toddler. *Jealous?* "I mean, you told me that, in everyone else's mind, I'm their princess." She rubbed again, harder, but slow, so slow, and impossible to label as accidental. Need drove her. "But when I looked at myself in the mirror, I saw, well, myself."

Little beads of perspiration formed on his brow as he met her, moving with her. "You look nothing like her. Yes, keep doing that."

"Then how does your magic work?" The tip of his erection brushed her most sensitive spot, and she moaned. "Why does everyone assume I'm her?"

"When I summoned you, I also shifted my ability to cast illusions to you, projecting Odette's image." His chains rattled as he attempted to lower his arms. When he realized he couldn't, he scowled. "To everyone around you, with the exception of me, you look and sound like her. But gods, you smell divine."

"So do you." He'd spoken of intrinsic power. So very, very good...uh, *interesting.* Getting answers had never been this wonderfully agonizing in class. "Can you remove the illusion?"

The leather of his loincloth was soft between her legs, a startling contrast to his erection, creating a dizzying friction. Her heart hammered against her ribs with so much force, she feared the bones would crack.

She needed to slow down, or she would explode before the conversation ended.

"No, I cannot. Not while we're together. My power... they did something to me. Bound my abilities in some way, as surely as they bound my body." He licked his lips, revealing and hiding his fangs. So sharp, so deadly. "Do you like this, Jane? Do I please you?"

So much it scared her. "Yes."

"Lean down. Kiss me."

Another urge to obey… She stilled instead. Yes. She wanted to kiss him. Yet she knew that if she leaned down, if she kissed the breath out of his lungs as she wanted him to do to her, they would have sex. They wouldn't be able to help themselves. Look how close she was to begging for it already!

She couldn't have sex with him. They were strangers. Worse, he was a vampire, a drinker of blood, and she'd studied his kind for research. Oh, God. Talk about a mood killer. If he ever found out, the mood wasn't the only thing that would be killed.

He wouldn't find out, she assured herself before she could panic. Wasn't like she'd tell him, and who else knew? No one. Although he might wonder why she knew more about his physiology than she should. Like the fact that he was alive, and not dead, with the same basic organ alignment as a human.

Besides, she would return home at some point. She hoped. More than that, they were in danger and under a time crunch. She needed answers from him, not pleasure. Not kisses.

Reluctantly she crawled off him and stood beside the bed. Her knees almost buckled. Amazing that she was able to maintain her balance, since her muscles had the consistency of Jell-O.

"Jane?"

She couldn't look at him. She would cave. He was just so damn beautiful, those eyes so hungry. For her. Plain Jane, as the kids at school had once called her. Already she was tempted to fling herself back on top of him, rubbing her way to ecstasy. The scent of him clung to her. Sandalwood. Delicious. Every time she inhaled, she smelled him, weakening her resolve.

"Can someone else remove the illusion?" she asked, keeping her profile to him. "While we're together?"

"Why did you leave me?"

"I wasn't concentrating. I was only..."

"Thinking of me. And sex."

Her cheeks heated as she nodded.

He uttered a low growl. "If you will not take pleasure from me, at least sit beside me. I would rather have part of you than none of you."

Said the spider to the fly. A born seducer, this one. Nicolai knew just how to lure, how to tempt. Against her better judgment, she sat. Her fingers brushed his ribs, and the heat of him had her shivering all over again.

"The answer to your question is yes," he said, gruffer still. "If someone's power is greater than mine, my illusion can be broken. But do not go around asking for such a thing. You do not want the witches here knowing what was done to you."

She waited, tense and silent, for him to go on. He didn't. Finally she gasped out, "You can't leave it at that. What happens if they discover the truth?"

Another round of silence.

Her heartbeat increased in speed. "What if your magic fails while I'm here?" Again, she waited. He didn't rush to assure her all would be well. *Still no need to panic. Not yet.*

"Feed me," he said, his fangs extending over his bottom lip, "and I'll strengthen. *No one* will be stronger than me." There, at the end, his words were slurred.

One half of her trembled in pleasure, the other half shuddered in fear. The vampires in the lab had fed from bags of plasma. She'd never been bitten. Had never wanted to be bitten. Until now. If anyone could make her enjoy something like that, it was this man.

"I'll think about it. Now let's backtrack a little. If you can make anyone look like the princess, why did you summon me specifically?" Why place *her* in such danger? Not that he'd truly wanted her, and her alone. She recalled his disdain when he'd learned she was merely a human, recalled his surprise. "I asked before, but you never answered."

He leaned toward her, forcing her fingers to press into his skin. A silent command—and an unrelinquishing demand—for contact. "I did not summon you specifically."

She'd realized that as she'd spoken, but hearing him confirm it depressed her. She had to remain on equal footing with him, and even though he was chained, he kept leaping to the next level without her.

"Who did you mean to summon, then?" she asked, tracing an *X* next to his navel. She blinked. His navel? Damn it! Her willpower sucked. She'd told herself not to touch him so, of course, the first thing she did was claim his belly button as her personal property.

"Jane?"

His deep voice startled her, and she jerked her spine ramrod straight. An instant later, her gaze met Nicolai's. A mistake. Liquid silver eyes, smoldering with passion. Languid expression masking a sea of desires.

"Yes?" *Danger, Jane Parker, danger.*

"I lost you, even though I'm having this conversation only because you wished it. We could be doing—"

"Sorry," she said before he could finish. No reason to discover if what he thought they could be doing meshed with her own desires, and every reason not to.

She stuffed her hands under her butt, her weight pinning them in place. Hopefully. "I'll pay attention from now on."

He flicked his tongue over one of his fangs, and she couldn't help but imagine that tongue flicking between her legs. "I summoned whoever would save me."

Oh, dear God. Her bones melted. Climbing on top of him a second time might actually be a good idea, she mused. She'd be able to hear him better. Yeah, yeah, because she was having trouble hearing him and... *Damn it,* she thought again. *You knew better than to look at him!*

She cleared her throat. "So I release you, and then what happens?" Good. Back on track.

"I am...not sure."

The truth or a lie? That hesitation... "Will I go home?"

"I told you. I do not know. Do you have a man waiting for you?" he asked, the words grated, as if pushed through a grinder.

"No. Otherwise, I wouldn't have straddled you. Fidelity is important." She had nothing and no one except the routine she'd developed. Wake up at six-thirty in the morning and jog five miles. Take a shower, dress, fix breakfast. Read for a few hours, usually something on macroparticles, sometimes a romance, fix lunch. Read for a few hours more, shop online for anything she needed, walk the treadmill to release the knots in her muscles. Bathe, fix dinner. Watch TV, sleep. *Exciting.*

She didn't need to work because one, she'd made so much money through her research, she could never spend it all; and two, she'd made so much money in the car accident settlement, she could never spend it all. Only problem was, she wanted something money couldn't buy. Her family. A second chance.

"But I'm not in danger there," she added softly. "So tell me. What will *you* do when you're free?"

Absolute determination cloaked her features. "Kill my tormentors." Flat, cold. A vow. "After that, I will journey to Elden."

The "kill my tormentors" part shouldn't have cranked her engine, but it did. A lot. All that ferocity… He would protect what was his, and fight for what he wanted. Always. Anyone who tormented him or those he loved would suffer. And with him, a woman would never have to worry about anything. Well, except her panties. Those might be ripped a few times.

"If I summon the healer and she does her thing, and then I let you go, but I don't instantly go home, will you take me with you?"

She was not staying here; she knew that much. Nicolai might plan to kill everyone, but he was only one man. Or vampire, whatever. There would be survivors. Survivors looking to punish the person who had unleashed the big bad vamp.

And the longer she resided in this palace, the more danger she would be in, he'd said. Yet, she couldn't strike out on her own. She knew nothing about this land. This *magical* land, where spells could be cast, memories erased and powerful vampires enslaved.

He opened his mouth, closed it. Then he relaxed, his body sagging against the mattress. His expression softened, heated. "What would you do to stay with me?" he asked, his voice once more like smoke, curling around her, trying to lure her back in.

Her hand itched to reach out, the urge to touch him springing to new life. She wanted to learn the texture of his skin—she hadn't paid enough attention before. She wanted to rediscover the warmth of his body. Was already reaching toward him…

She jumped back to her feet and backed away from him. Sitting next to him had been a mistake. She couldn't concentrate, and she couldn't keep her dumb hands to herself.

"Jane," he said, exasperated.

"What?"

His eyes narrowed, the gold flecks brightening, bursting through the silver. "Forget it. Have I answered your questions?"

"Yes. Wait, no, I—"

"Too late. You said yes. There's no changing your mind. Now summon the healer." He lifted the arm closest to her as best he could, the cuff rubbing against the iron poster. "And remove the chains."

Damn him. He'd never promised to take her with him. "All right. Chains first. Healer second. But you'll owe me. Big time. And don't feed from me. I didn't beg you."

"Noted."

"I'm trusting you. If you go back on your word, I never will again. Once out of my trust circle, always out of my trust circle." She turned and bent over the nightstand, pulling out the top drawer. Sure enough, a long, thin key rested atop a bed of crimson velvet. "Lookie there. So simple."

"Odette!" Hinges squeaked a second before her bedroom door slammed against the wall.

Gasping, Jane spun. A short, obese woman with

ruddy cheeks huffed and puffed in the now open entryway. She wore a navy blue and gold robe, the material far too tight for her rotund frame. She had jet-black hair peppered with silver, the strands slicked back and greased.

The city without time had managed to take its toll.

"You dare defy me, girl?"

The queen, she thought with dread and just a little panic. Her "mother." The gal with the whip. *Don't forget you're supposed to be Odette.*

Fear pumped through Jane's veins at an alarming rate, joining the dread and panic. *Danger, danger, danger,* her mind shouted, and it was not the succulent kind Nicolai offered. If this world was anything like her own had once been, this woman, this queen, had absolute power over every one and thing in her kingdom. Including Jane.

"I—I'm sorry." Jane's gaze fell to Nicolai. His expression was now blank, his features smoothed out. Yet, he couldn't hide the coiled tension in his biceps and stomach. He practically vibrated. As stealthily as possible, she tossed the key at him. "I didn't mean to disrespect you, M-Mother. Queen."

"And yet you did. You, my successor, the one my people look to as an example, have made me appear the fool." At least she hadn't noticed the key. "Rather than seek out your doting mother, you sought out a slave." As the queen spoke, two guards filed in beside her.

Jane didn't recognize them; they were taller and meaner looking than the others.

"Now, you'll be punished."

The men continued to advance.

"But…I… You can't do this! Stop. Don't you dare touch me. Let go!"

A snarl left Nicolai. One that promised pain. Lots and lots of pain. No one but Jane seemed to notice. The guards snagged her by the arms and began dragging her out of the bedroom.

"Mine," Nicolai snapped. "No touching."

Again, he was ignored.

"Stop! Let go!" She struggled, kicking and screaming, but they never loosened their hold.

Behind her, she heard Nicolai jerking against his chains. "Mine!"

"I can do anything I wish," the queen said, so superior Jane wanted to slap her. "Perhaps your little bump on the head made you forget. But no worries, my pet. I will remind you—and ensure you never forget again."

Chapter 5

She never cried, never even gasped as the whip flayed her delicate skin.

Nicolai was chained to Odette's bed. He hadn't marked Jane as he'd wanted, but he was somehow attuned to her in a way he doubted he had ever been attuned to another. He should not have been able to focus on her, especially since he'd been fighting sizzling desire for her—her body, her blood—and all other thoughts had become fogged and insignificant in comparison.

Now, he felt fury. So much fury, and every bit of it was leveled on the guards.

They had dragged Jane along the opulent corridor filled with portraits of the queen and her daughters, down the winding stairs with dark velvet carpeting, and to the extravagant banqueting hall. Though she was no longer in the bedroom, Nicolai saw her still.

As if their minds were somehow connected. She struggled the entire way. Only when they bent her over the dining table, her face pressed into the polished wood, only when they stripped away the back of her gown, had she settled.

Panting, she twisted her head to gaze over at the queen. The Queen of Hearts, a woman known to dine on the still beating organ during the spells and incantations used in her never ending quest for youth.

"Don't do this," Jane pleaded. "I meant no offense."

The queen raised one of her many chins, the ones beneath it jiggling. "And yet it was offense that you gave."

"I'm sorry."

"You will be more so."

"Please," Jane said, her skin both pallid with fear and bright with exertion. "Give me another chance."

Perhaps the queen replied. Nicolai would never know. He was too focused on Jane's back. Already she bore scars. More than he could possibly count. They twined from her spine to her rib cage, red and angry, badges of pain. They stretched past the robe's gaping material, perhaps even riding the length of her legs.

What the hell had been done to her?

His guilt sprang back to instant, shattering life, and he was unable to destroy it this time. *He* had placed her in this situation. This delicate, haunted woman with the tantalizing scent, who had offered him the only glimpse of sunlight in a darkened void. She had come to save him, had trusted him enough to straddle him while talking to him. To rub against him, ratcheting his desire to unequaled heights, even without climax. And her resistance…gods, he'd wanted to quash it. Still did. Wanted her to know his bite, his kiss.

His possession.

Perhaps she was merely a challenge he had to triumph above. He didn't care. Quite simply, she was his. That was not in question. *Mine,* his cells continued to scream. *All mine.*

He could not allow her to be whipped.

Nicolai looked at the key resting at his side. Jane had tossed it at him, and it had landed on the mattress. A brave gesture on her part, but useless. He could not bend enough to reach it with his mouth. He could not angle his hands to grab it. He could not do anything with it. Yet the fact that she'd tried, that she'd thought of him in the face of her own peril…affected him.

He *would* escape. However necessary. He would save her.

Never before had he been left on his own outside of his cell, with no guards within sight or hearing distance. He jerked at his cuffs. The metal links scraped his already cut skin, digging deeper, deeper. He'd pulled at them while straining toward Jane, but at the time he hadn't cared, hadn't felt any sting but that of passion. Now, he felt the pain. That didn't stop him, however.

Just as before, the latches held, both to him and to the bed. He gritted his teeth. His hate for Laila, her mother and even Delfina grew exponentially. *Destroy…*

He closed his eyes, concentrating on the power still swirling inside him. There it was, dark, so dark, churning, an untapped storm just waiting, desperate to be unleashed; and all he had to do was break through the glass cage that had been erected within him.

A glass cage with thin, riverlike cracks running through the center.

Exploit. He banged against the mental glass, over and over again. Nothing. He clawed at it. Still nothing. Damn it!

"Now," he heard the queen say, pulling Nicolai back to the present. To Jane and their connection. Somehow, enough of his magic had escaped to allow him to continue watching her despite the distance between them.

Leather whistled through air. The first blow landed. Jane squeezed her eyes shut and pressed her lips together. She grimaced, but not a sound did she make.

They had done it. They had whipped her.

Just like that, something inside of Nicolai broke. Not the glass cage, but something far more dangerous, roaring like a wild animal pushed beyond its limits.

From the first moment Nicolai had spotted Jane, his body had reacted to her. He had experienced lust, guilt and possessiveness in varying degrees. Now, the possessiveness simply took over.

Mine, he thought again.

This time, the word sprung from deep inside him, as unstoppable as an avalanche. He did not understand the fierceness accompanying the thought, and refused to ponder it now. Later. He would ponder later. Right now, more than before, he knew only that she was his—his savior, his woman—and nothing else mattered.

The guards had touched her, hurt her. They would die. Painfully. By the time he finished with them they would probably thank him for killing them.

All he had to do was free himself. And he would. Nothing would stop him. Not now, not anymore.

"Soon" had at last arrived.

Being a magical vampire, as Jane had called him, was not going to aid him; he admitted that now. Still his determination intensified, blending with the hate, the burn of that possessiveness. He would reach her by grit alone; he would save her. No matter what he had to do. His gaze strayed to the wrist cuffs and narrowed. Without his thumbs, his hands would slide right through.

He didn't have to think about it. Goodbye, thumbs.

Biting his tongue against the pain he knew was to come, he slammed his hands, thumbs out, into the headboard. *Crunch*. The bones broke with that very first punch. He sucked in a breath, but, like Jane, he did not utter a sound. Punch, punch, punch. Each new blow caused even more damage, ripping tendon, tearing muscle, flattening bone.

By the time he finished, he was sweating, bleeding, his hands limp. But his top half was free. With a growl, he jolted upright. Heard the whistle of leather through air, a soft inhalation of breath. Another lash against Jane's delicate skin.

Skin he wanted to caress.

His hands were too mutilated to grab the key. In fact, his efforts sent the little piece of metal sliding to the floor with a clink. He would need it later, to remove the neck cuff, and so he would pick it up with his mouth—after he'd freed himself.

Through narrowed eyes, he peered down at his feet. At a different angle, those feet would glide straight through the metal rings. And all he had to do to achieve that different angle was break every bone that ran from his ankle to his toes.

Nicolai started kicking the footboard.

* * *

Jane closed her eyes to hide the tears trying so determinedly to form and spill. It wasn't like she'd never experienced pain before. For God's sake, her spine had been broken, her legs unusable for months. Then there'd been the surgeries. Surgery after surgery to pin her bones in their proper places. Then, of course, the rehabilitation.

So, this whipping? Not even a blip on her agony radar. And yet, the humiliation of being bent over a table, her clothing ripped away, her scars revealed to those who sought to harm her, her body bound with ties she couldn't see—magic?—nearly undid her. And for what? For failing to speak with a fat, ugly woman when summoned?

Poor Odette. Was this how she'd lived? Always fearing the next punishment? And poor Nicolai. Jane could not blame him for doing everything within his power to save himself. She would have done the same.

In fact, she could blame only herself for this. Had she listened to Nicolai, had she freed him when he'd wanted, they would have been far, far away from this dreadful place. Well, *he* would have been. He would have left her behind. And he still might, she thought. During their talk, she had not garnered a promise from him. Not to keep her with him, not to protect her. And now, it was too late. There was no way she'd leave him bound after this. Not for any reason. She would free him the moment she was physically able, then take off on her own.

Dumb on her part, maybe. Probably. Okay, definitely. Allowing herself to be separated from the one person who knew who and what she was, the one person who could get her home…so damn foolish. But that still wasn't going to stop her.

And, wow. Jane Parker, considered a dummy. That was a first. She laughed without humor. A novelty in the face of pain. *Nice.*

"This amuses you?" the queen demanded.

Jane refused to acknowledge her.

There was a squeak of outrage. "Clearly you are not hitting her hard enough. You." The queen snapped her fingers. "Take over the whip. Your arms are stronger, as I can well attest."

Oh, gross.

A pause, then the whip continued to descend. Harder, so much harder. Over and over again, minutes ticking by. Still Jane did not utter a sound. She wanted to go home. Back to her boring life, where she was in control.

The whip stopped falling. Finally, a reprieve.

"Have you at last learned your lesson, Odette?" the queen asked, expectant. "Or shall I have him remove the skin on your legs, as well?"

She opened her mouth to tell the bitch to go to hell—no ignoring her this time—but she stopped herself before a single word escaped. Did these people believe in hell, or even know what it was? Would she announce her humanity and lose the protection—what little there was—in being thought of as Princess Odette?

"Silence will not—"

A roar echoed from the walls, harsh, guttural and a promise of pain.

Everyone in the room stilled. Jane forgot to breathe. That sound…she'd never heard its like. There was an animal on the loose, a lion probably, there just had to be. And people were clearly on the menu.

Another roar, followed by the crash of furniture and the shattering of knickknacks. Screams of agony. Gasps, racing footsteps. Had her guards left?

"Don't leave me here," she shouted.

"What's going on?" the queen snapped. Okay. Good. She was still here. Bitch that she was. "You, find out. You, shield me."

"Free me," Jane demanded. "Now."

They paid her no heed.

One of the guards headed toward the entryway, where other guards were pouring inside to *escape* the beast, but he didn't make it outside the room. Not alive. There was a blur of movement, then blood was squirting, a headless body falling.

From the corner of her eye, she spotted Nicolai. He was a mess, covered in blood, limping, his arms hanging at his sides. His fangs were bared in a fearsome, crimson scowl, and she knew.

He was the animal.

Thank God. Some of the tension drained from her. Somehow, some way, he'd managed to escape. His plan to destroy the people who lived inside this palace was well under way.

Before, she'd thought there would be survivors. Now, not so much.

He barreled into another guard, his shoulder slamming into the man's middle and knocking him backward. The guard propelled into another, the one with the whip. The two fell to the floor. Nicolai slashed into the whipper's neck and shook, a wolf with his first meal in months. Screams…silence…death…

Just like that, Jane was freed from whatever had bound her. She straightened. Sharp lances of pain shot from her back, spiraling though the rest of her. She hardly noticed. Her gown sagged from her shoulders, momentarily exposing her breasts. Hurriedly she righted the material, holding it up.

Nicolai's silver-gold eyes landed on the queen, who was no longer shielded by a man. Blood—and other things—dripped from his mouth. His expression was so dark, so murderous, even Jane backed away from him. He was a terrifying sight. A warrior lost to bloodlust, his only goal the destruction of every one and every thing around him.

He advanced on the queen. "Die. You die."

"How dare you threaten me and my people this way?" the bitch snapped. "I allowed you to live after you tormented my eldest daughter, and now you think to spit on my mercy? Guards!"

No guards came. Perhaps they were too busy being dead.

"She...mine," Nicolai snarled, moving in front of Jane while still advancing on the queen. There was something wrong with his feet, his ankles twisted at an odd angle, yet his steps were measured, clipped with determination.

The queen lifted her mountain of chins. "You think to protect my daughter from me? The daughter you tried to slay?"

"Mine!"

"Come on, then, slave. Come get me."

Jane's heart pounded with renewed force. Her legs shook. This was a showdown the queen couldn't hope to win. Right? *Please be right.*

Nicolai leaped.

Grinning, the queen stretched out one arm and ripples of power pulsated from her. The air around her shimmered, thickened. Nicolai slammed into a wall Jane couldn't see, ricocheting backward.

Another roar ripped from his throat as he jumped to his feet. He pounded his injured fists into that invisible shield, his fangs flashing.

The queen laughed, smug. "Do you see now? Even were you at your strongest, you could not touch me. I am beyond your reach."

Booted footsteps reverberated, and Jane watched, wide-eyed, as the second line of defense marched into the room. So. There were more guards, after all. This new contingent held swords and spears, and when they spotted the bloody Nicolai, they bolted into action.

"No!" Jane threw herself in front of him, the action born of instinct rather than thought. As she well knew, even vampires could be killed, and she didn't want Nicolai to—couldn't watch him—experience that.

Strong arms banded around her waist and jerked her into a hard body. Instinct still drove her and, for a moment, she fought, kicking and elbowing.

"Mine. Be...still."

Nicolai. She relaxed, despite his raging animal nature. He was warm against her. Solid, sturdy despite his wounds. Even decadent. Her inhalations were coming so quickly, she scented the sandalwood she was already coming to love.

Okay, then. They would die together, she thought distantly. She'd survived so much the past year. The car accident, injuries that would have killed most people. Injuries that *should* have killed her. Especially since she'd yearned for death, and hadn't done anything to aid her own cause.

She'd been so lost, wondering. Why her? What was so different, so special, about her that she could endure what others had not? Nothing, that's what.

And now that she wanted to live, she would finally die. Irony at its finest. She would not be allowed to know Nicolai better. She would not get to spend time with him, laugh with him or make love with him.

She should have kissed him earlier.

"Mine," Nicolai repeated against her ear. "Safe." He had stretched out an arm, mimicking the queen, and the air around them had shimmered, forming a...shield? For *them?*

Her jaw dropped as the guards slammed into it and flew backward, just as Nicolai had done.

A gasp escaped her. "How did you—?"

"Walk," Nicolai said in that gravelly voice. His one-word sentences were as frustrating as they were welcome. He nudged her forward.

One step, two, she lumbered over the fallen, savaged bodies sprawled around her. Those who remained standing were pushed out of the way by the shield. Outside the dining room was a foyer. Spacious, with doorways in every direction. Exactly where was she supposed to go?

Laila raced down the staircase, dark hair flying behind her, the silver timepiece banging against her chest. When she spotted Jane and Nicolai, she ground to a halt.

Nicolai snarled at her. He released Jane as if he intended to pound up those steps and attack, but quickly changed his mind. His free arm banded around Jane once more, the other ensuring the shield never wavered. "Mine."

She was really starting to like that nickname.

The younger woman was breathing heavily, her green eyes glittering with jealousy and hate. "Yours? She isn't yours. Odette, he means to kill you. Fight him! Use your magic."

Jane flipped her off.

Shock replaced the anger, but only for a moment. When the princess regained her wits, she shouted, "Someone stop them. Now!" but still the guards could not penetrate the shield. "He's bespelled Odette."

"We need magic, princess," one of them said. "Cast a spell for us. Anything!"

"No magic," Laila gritted without hesitation and with the briefest flare of panic. Then to Nicolai, she said, "You think I'd bind your vampire strength and abilities, and not bespell you to remain here forever? You might be able to leave the palace, but you'll be back. That, I promise you."

Another growl erupted from Nicolai's throat, so fervent even Jane's body vibrated.

"You can kill her if you want," Jane said. "I'll wait."

He tightened his hold. "Mine."

Apparently protecting her was more important than avenging himself. What had changed his mind, she didn't know, but his decision was a gift, better than a diamond and not something she'd ever regift.

Yes, she really should have kissed him when she'd had the chance. Once they were safe, she'd remedy her mistake.

Laila raised her chin(s), reminding Jane of the queen. Smiling, she drew circles around the center of the timepiece with the tip of her index finger. "Go ahead. Try. Fail."

"Walk," Nicolai repeated.

"Where?" Jane asked, tightening her hold on her robe.

He didn't speak again, but guided her toward one of the doorways. He used his big, strong shoulders to nudge it open, careful not to jar her. Endorphins were swimming so potently through her veins, he could have poured salt into her slashed-up back and she wouldn't have felt it. Yet.

Silvery moonlight came into view. As did a large expanse of flatland, with robed men and women moving unhurriedly, happily, children dancing around them. Beyond that, Jane saw trees. Mile after mile of white trees, their leaves swaying, dancing together like drunken ghosts. The landscape was somehow familiar to her, as if she'd been here before. How…why…?

Jane could only gape, struggling to understand— until Nicolai released her, and her thoughts took a nosedive. He was leaving her already? Disappointment rocked her. She'd liked his touch, had wanted more. Perhaps forever, which made her as dumb now as she'd been earlier. Thankfully, he didn't allow the separation for long. He moved beside her, clasped her hand as strongly as he was able, which wasn't much considering the damage he'd sustained, and jerked her into the throng.

"This way."

A child spotted her, and dropped into a bow. Murmurs arose, and everyone else quickly followed suit. Jane's steps faltered.

"Uh, hi," she said, not knowing what else to say.

"Princess," they muttered. Not happily, but with fear.
"Escape…faster…" Nicolai said with a nudge.
"My pleasure," she muttered, leaping into a sprint.

Chapter 6

They traveled for hours—or so it seemed—though they never managed to exit the forest. Nicolai suspected they were going in circles, his doom in the center. Just when he would think they'd made progress, he would spy the glittering palace rooftop. A rooftop Delfina was famous for, the shingles comprised only of elf tears. No matter what he tried, he could not alter his path.

Fail. The word Laila had used. *Go ahead. Try. Fail.* She had used her magic on him as promised, he realized. But what spell had she used? Unless he figured it out, he could not fight its power. Even as the question and answer formed in his mind, a sharp lance of pain jetted through him. He gnashed his teeth.

At least the guards never caught his trail. Even when the magical shield around him evaporated in a puff of smoke. Magic he wasn't sure how he'd wielded. He knew only that the queen had constructed a shield of her own, and he had instantly known how to do the same.

Now, though, he could not reconstruct it; the ability was gone as if it had never been. And its absence infuriated him. At all costs, he must protect Jane.

Mine. The possessive claim was now so much a part of him, he wasn't sure how he'd survived without her. So, yes, he would protect her. Even from himself. His hunger was completely sated, he'd drained so many guards to reach her, and yet, he could still scent her. His female. So sweet. He still wanted to taste her. So damn badly.

She was injured, though, and needed to rest. Not that she had complained. She had not spoken a word since they'd left the palace courtyard. She had remained behind him the entire time, accepting his every dictate, following his directives. Limping, he thought, and sometimes using his arm as a crutch.

He hadn't allowed himself to look at her, knowing he would have stopped long before now if she appeared fatigued in any way. He wanted her as far from the palace as possible. As far away from Laila and the queen—who should be dead right now, already rotting in a grave.

That they lived...

Worth it. Jane lived, too.

His ankles throbbed as he led her to a cave he'd noticed each time he'd unintentionally backtracked. "Here," he said, voice gruffer than he'd intended. "We'll be safe here." He was sure of it.

"Oh, good. You're back to your normal self."

Normal self? What did that mean? "Rest." Once they were strengthened, he could return to the palace, sneak inside, kill Laila and her mother and find the healer, as planned. Before he left, he would erect defenses so that Jane could stay here, safe.

Once his memories had been returned, his powers restored, he would come back for her. They would travel to Elden together.

His hands tightened into fists. Elden. What awaited him in Elden, besides his desire to kill a king he had never met? At least, not to his knowledge. All he knew was that the man had slaughtered the former sovereigns, claiming the crown by brute force.

Nicolai had heard palace servants gossiping about the royal change. Yesterday, or a hundred years ago, he wasn't sure. Whatever time spell the witches had cast over the palace caused minutes to eke by for everyone inside, the days blending together, a blur you could never count.

Nicolai wondered if he'd ever met the former sovereigns. Perhaps even guarded them. While he could not picture them, he could visualize their palace without problem. A towering monstrosity built more for withstanding attack than aesthetics. A lush green forest surrounded a lake, and that lake surrounded the structure. There was no discernable entryway other than the guard walkway—a walkway he knew better than he knew the angles of his own face.

He *longed* for that palace, that lake, that forest. Knew the land would smell of sea salt and pine. Thought he could hear the echo of his booted footsteps as he ran to…do something, hug someone, perhaps. Thought he could hear a woman's deep throated chuckle and a man's gruff grunt of approval. A pang of love and homesickness, followed by a wave of hate, swept through him.

Love? Homesickness? Hate? Why? He must learn the answers. He must kill the new king.

A dull ache bloomed in his temples, and he ceased that line of thought. For now.

Jane hobbled in front of him, and placed her hands on his shoulders. At the moment of contact, his fangs lengthened and his gums ached. Just a little taste…

No! Not yet. He soaked in her presence instead, distracting his unnecessary hunger with her electrifying beauty. Electrifying, because she had somehow brought him back to life.

That fall of honey-colored hair, framing a face as pure and unique as a snowflake, begged for a man's fingers. Her ocher eyes were no longer haunted, but determined. Her cheeks were rosy—with desire, despite her weakened, abused condition—a sheen of perspiration from the sultry night air making her glow. She'd tied the fabric of her robe together and the knots on her shoulders teased him. With only a tug, they would unwind and he could—

No, he thought again. He would not entertain such lustful thoughts until she was healed. Then… Oh, yes, then.

Seeing her whipped for his actions had not only broken something inside him, it had awoken something inside him. Not to mention that smile of hers… She shouldn't have smiled at him.

"The key," he said. "Free my neck." He used his tongue to move that key from the side of his mouth to between his teeth.

"My pleasure." She unlocked the ring. The heavy binding tumbled to the ground with a thump. "We should probably get going. The sun will come out soon."

Though she'd hobbled, her voice was firm, strong. "If you guys have a sun? And if time has kicked back into gear for us? Someone mentioned Delfina is ageless."

"Not ageless. Those who reside in the palace age much slower. And yes, out here there is a sun, a day and a night."

"We have to hide you, then. We don't want you bursting into flames."

His brow furrowed. "I am not a nightwalker." How had she known about nightwalkers and the way they burst into flames?

"Oh, well…" She paled, swallowed. "Well, in my world, vampires are considered a myth. In books and movies, you guys always burst into flames—or glitter—when you step into sunlight."

Glitter? "I am, perhaps, more sensitive to the sun's rays than others in this realm, but I am nothing like the nightwalkers. At worst, I will burn and blister."

"Oh. Good." Her relief was palpable.

Such a strong reaction, when she'd had no cause to worry. And yet, that worry pleased him. He liked her concern. Liked what it meant. Already she cared.

"I've been thinking," she said, nibbling on her bottom lip.

His stomach clenched at the sight of her teeth, doing what he wanted to do. "Something you enjoy." He placed his throbbing hands over hers, preventing her from drawing away.

"Yes, well." Her tongue emerged, swiping where she'd bitten. "We've been going in circles, which means Laila the harpy told the truth. You are cursed to remain in Delfina."

The sight of her tongue did far more damage to his

control than the sight of her teeth. How easy it would be to lean down, lick, sample, savor. *Not until she heals.* Another reminder. *Also, not until she begs. You promised.* "I know," he said more harshly than he'd intended.

"Oh." Her nose scrunched adorably, easing the sting of his self-directed anger. "Well, you could have told me. I've worried, expecting you to argue and trying to formulate my own argument for whichever direction you could have taken. Anyway, you might have been bespelled to think the most dangerous places are the safest, and the safest places the most dangerous. Actually, cancel that 'you might.' You were. You bypassed the water six times!"

River? "You saw a river?" The kingdom of Elden was surrounded by the lake, a lake that connected its northern shore to Delfina. That had always been a point of contention for him while rotting inside his cell. So close to his goal, yet so far away. Now, he was glad.

"No," Jane said. "I didn't see. I *heard* the water."

He hadn't. The only landmark that had stood out to him was a dark, too dark, part of the forest that had made his skin crawl. Had he been alone, he would have braved that forest without hesitation. His mind had been centered upon Jane's protection, however, and he'd opted to brave nothing. A mistake.

His swollen fingers intertwined with hers, squeezing. "Why didn't you say something?"

"You were all scary alpha and in charge, and I didn't want to, you know, poke at the bear. Plus, I was kind of distracted by the scenery and maybe lost in my thoughts. So, here's what we're going to do," she went on. Now who was all alpha and in charge? "You're going to lead us to the most dangerous place in this forest. And when you think you should turn left, you're going to turn right. You're going to do the opposite of everything you feel is correct."

Smart, his Jane. And so damned arousing he doubted he would ever get enough of her.

He wanted to keep her. In his bed, his arms, his fangs buried in her neck, his cock buried between her legs. Even though he was destined to wed the… Another sharp lance tore through his mind, and he grunted.

"What?" Jane asked, concerned all over again. "Are you okay?"

Her back was a mess of welts, and she asked if *he* was okay. He pressed his tongue to the roof of his mouth and nodded. "You are well enough to travel?"

"Of course," she said, as if there was no doubt in her mind.

"All right, then."

Though his body protested, he trudged forward once again, leaving the cave behind. He followed Jane's advice—orders—and did the opposite of what his "instincts" demanded, even plunging into a patch of thorny clinging vines guarding the darker part of the forest. He expected to be scratched, but the leaves merely caressed him, tickling.

There were no thorns, he realized. Even though he saw them, they were not there. Laila—or her healer—was more powerful than he'd ever suspected.

Male laughter cut through the night, springing from just ahead. Nicolai stopped, stiffened, and Jane bumped into him. Her breasts mashed into his back, and he had to press his lips together to halt his moan.

"Did you hear that?" he whispered.

"Hear what?"

That answered that. Still he did not move forward, but stood there, waiting, listening. Jane's nipples hardened, rasping over his flesh as she breathed. Her scent enveloped him. *Must taste female...soon.*

This physical desire was new to him. Oh, he'd had sex. And recently, too. Many times, but with Laila, or someone of her choosing as the princess watched and directed. Always chained to her bed, muzzled, her mouth and hands forcing him to respond to her, even though he hated her.

Sometimes, when even that failed to arouse him, she had used her witch magic to elicit an erection from him. Unlike her sister, she hadn't needed someone else's pain to spur her into orgasm. She had ridden him with abandon, while he had stared up at the face he despised, scowling, trying with every ounce of his strength to prevent her—and himself—from climaxing.

Sometimes she had, sometimes she hadn't. Sometimes he had, sometimes he hadn't. But each time, no matter the outcome, his hatred for them both had grown.

He did not remember ever being with another woman—besides Odette—though he was sure he'd had many lovers throughout the years. Because, as Laila had writhed atop him, he'd instinctively known what would bring her pleasure. Gliding his thumb along the bundle of nerves between her legs. Laving his tongue there. Kneading her breasts, plucking at her nipples. All the things he had refused to do, and now wanted to do to Jane.

He wanted to watch her expressive face as she reached her peak. Wanted to feel her inner walls clutch

at him. Wanted to hear her cry out his name. Sweet
heavens, even the thought delighted him.

"Seriously. What are we listening for?" Jane asked.
The warmth of her breath trekked down his spine. "I
don't hear anything."

Taste…

Distracted again*, Nicki?* The stray thought jolted
him back to full awareness. Someone had once said
that to him; he knew it. A woman. He wanted to know
who, but now was not the time to try and access his
memories. He had to remain alert.

"Come," he said, leading Jane deeper into that dark
part of the forest. More laughter echoed. Evil, promis-
ing retribution. Once again, he stilled. "Did you hear
that?"

"What?"

More laughter, blending with yet another man's.
"That."

"No. I hear the rush of water now, but that's all."

Damn it. The laughter must be another trick of Laila's, meant to send him fleeing. Nicolai kicked back into
gear. Five minutes passed, an eternity. He remained on
guard, without a weapon—he should have grabbed a
damned weapon—but willing to shield Jane with his
body.

Another five minutes eked by. Then another. He
wasn't sure how much longer he could go on, but he felt
like he should stop, so he did the opposite. He pushed
onward. Another five minutes. Another.

"Wait. Nicolai. You have—"

Jane's words cut off when Nicolai felt the cool rush
of water against his feet, droplets splashing up his calf.
Brows knitting in confusion, he paused and looked

down. He hadn't noticed the water, even though it had been directly in front of him.

The rocks were slippery as he backtracked to the edge. *Dangerous,* he thought. *This place is dangerous. He should—*

Stay. Finally.

"You did it," Jane said. "You found the source." She laughed, soft and carefree.

Without thought, Nicolai found himself whipping around to catch a glimpse of her. Her expression was lit up, brighter than the sun on its best morning. Her plump pink lips were curved at the corners, inviting him to lick, to finally taste. To devour. The hem of her robe was wet and plastered to her ankles.

She was safe. He could have her. Yes?

His chest constricted, and his stomach quivered. He reached out. A touch, until she healed, he'd allow himself only a touch. Except, his knees gave out just before contact and he fell into the water. His chin resting on his sternum, he breathed quickly and shallowly, trying to fill his lungs but failing.

His energy was draining, absolute fatigue taking its place.

"Oh, no, you don't. Not there. You'll drown." Jane latched on to his arm and managed to drag him to the shore.

Once there, he just kind of fell the rest of the way, crashing into a mossy embankment. He tried to rise, but couldn't find the strength. He needed to forage for food. Jane must be starving. He needed to build a shelter. The bugs would eat his woman alive. He needed to stand guard. She must not be hurt.

"Relax," she said.

"Protect," he murmured.

"Yes, I'll protect you." Gentle hands smoothed over his brow,

"No, I…" Oblivion claimed him before he could utter another word.

Nicolai…

The deep male voice that called to him was familiar. Always in his dreams, when his defenses were weakened, but it was stronger now than ever before. And… beloved?

Nicolai…time…save…

In the back of his mind, he heard the *tick, tick, tick* of a clock.

"Who are you?" he demanded.

An image flashed in his mind. Not of the speaker, but of huge, grotesque monsters crawling toward him. Each had eight legs, with sharp, deadly points. They were black and hairy, their eyes big and beady, their tails pointed and curling toward him. They were staring him down, as if he were a tasty snack. Bile rose in his throat, but he pressed on, ignoring them.

"Where are you? What can I do?"

Nicolai…brother…heal yourself, and come. Time… save…

Brother? Nicolai tried to picture a brother. Nothing. He could not picture his mother, either. Nor his father. Even in his dreams, pain exploded through his head, shutting down his memories.

Tick, tick, tick.

Kill! an equally familiar male voice suddenly boomed. Deeper, harder.

Damn it. He had to find out who was speaking to

him. Had to know. Had to, had to, had to. Life—and death—rested on his shoulders.

As he considered their identities, he thrashed, his hand connecting with something solid and warm.

He heard a gasp. For some reason, the female's pain only increased his agitation. Must protect…

"Everything's fine. You don't have to worry," she said, soothing him. "I'm here. You're safe now."

Jane, he thought, stilling. His Jane. Such a sweet voice, such a pretty face. Such a commanding personality, worthy of a queen. She was nearby.

Heal yourself…time…save…

Yes, he thought. With Jane nearby, he could do anything. Heal himself, and even replenish the store of power he'd burned through. He relaxed, willingly sinking back into oblivion. This time, he had a purpose.

Chapter 7

Jane spent two days gathering supplies and making weapons. She never strayed far from the unconscious Nicolai, just in case he needed her or they had unexpected visitors, so those supplies were limited. However, she managed to find fruits and nuts to eat, as well as small, thin twigs and mint leaves. Those, she'd turned into surprisingly efficient toothbrushes, which she used liberally on both of them.

Because they were near a stream, bathing her patient was easy. In fact, there'd probably never been two cleaner people trapped in the wilderness. Nicolai was no longer oiled, his skin was scrubbed to a healthy pink shine, and yet, the scent of sandalwood was stronger than ever. Every time she breathed him in, she tingled, her blood heating, her mouth watering.

It hadn't helped that in bathing him, she'd had to run her hands all over him. As dirty as he'd been—cough,

cough—she'd had to bathe him *a lot*. Those muscles… so hard, thickly roped and laced with sinew. That trail of hair from his navel to his penis…always tempting her to wickedness.

And God, she was shame spiraling.

Nicolai might desire her, but he didn't need another woman lusting after him while he was helpless. What's more, he didn't need another grabby woman touching him without permission, and already Jane had pushed the boundaries of his trust by bathing him (so many times).

Hands off from now on, she decided. And one day, she'd apologize for her behavior. Maybe. She wasn't sure she would sound sincere. Despite his past, she'd *liked* touching him. *Bad Jane*. But, well, he'd seemed to like being touched by her. He tossed and turned intermittently, only calming when she was within reach.

Sometimes he questioned a man who needed his help, sometimes he cursed Laila for the vile things she'd done to him, and sometimes he fought ugly monsters, his arms and legs flailing. After the latter two, he always vowed retribution. Painful, slow retribution.

Something he was fully capable of delivering now. The swelling in his wrists and ankles was gone, his thumbs having snapped back into place, his feet having realigned right before her eyes. Even the abrasions on his skin were gone. It was quite an amazing process to witness.

The vampires she had studied had healed quickly, as well, but not *that* quickly. Nor had they slept this long in a single stretch. She worried about him.

Did he need blood? He'd had so much at the palace, and overfeeding could cause as much damage as starvation. Perhaps more so, because overfeeding caused an insatiable need for more, more, more. Nothing else mattered ever again, and dead body after dead body was left in the wake.

She shouldn't know that. She'd almost given herself and her knowledge away with the whole "bursting into flames" thing. And while she hated herself for having experimented on his brethren, she wished she'd done more, knew more. Anything to help Nicolai right now.

Jane sighed. She'd give him another day. And then what? she wondered.

She would have to construct some kind of hamper and drag him through the forest and into a town, find a healer and get him checked out. *If* there was a town other than Delfina nearby.

The problem—besides her lack of strength and direction—was her face. Her magical face. As Odette, she simply couldn't lose herself in a crowd, as proven by the reaction of the people outside the palace. Word of her arrival might travel to Laila. Someone might attempt to capture Nicolai.

That someone would have to die by Jane's hand, and she wasn't quite ready to become a killer.

Another sigh slipped from her, this one weary. As a golden moon settled into a black velvet sky, she placed her handmade weapons—twigs sharpened on rocks until becoming daggers and spears—beside Nicolai. Then she lay next to him.

She'd washed her robe about an hour ago, the still-wet material now draped over a nearby tree limb. Except for her panties, she was naked. By necessity. Of course. So she wasn't going to castigate herself over needing

Nicolai's warmth. Well, not too badly. The baths had been frivolous; spooning wasn't.

Lying next to him provided a wealth of wondrous experiences. Peace, after so many months of fear and regret. Soul-deep contentment. Hope for a future she had once dreaded. He shouldn't affect her this quickly and this strongly, even with magic.

After some thought, she'd realized magic could not change a person's feelings. He had never welcomed his captors; and had they possessed the ability to force the issue, they would have.

Though she was exhausted, falling asleep proved difficult. Her back had scabbed, and those scabs pulled and reopened with her every movement. And her legs… Without her morning jogs and physical therapy, her legs were stiffening up more and more frequently, aching and throbbing. She could practically feel atrophy setting up camp in her muscles.

What she wouldn't give for a handful of painkillers.

At least she didn't have to dread the approach of the sun. Their very first night here, she'd constructed a big, leafy canopy above the small site. Nicolai had claimed he wouldn't burst into flame with ultraviolet contact, but she wasn't willing to risk it. Granted, the sun here was muted, always shaded by clouds, and not nearly as hot as she'd experienced back home. But in her world, she *had* witnessed other vamps burning to ash. Maybe even one of his friends.

Stomach cramp. She wouldn't let herself go there.

Also, the canopy offered them camouflage from the enemy, hiding them from prying eyes. As proud as she was of her efforts, they'd so far been unnecessary. Laila and her men had never even marched past.

Most likely they weren't even looking for the escapee, the princess expecting Nicolai to walk himself straight back to her bed.

Bed. Exactly where *Jane* wanted Nicolai. A soft mattress underneath him, Jane on top of him, her nails digging into his chest as she balanced. A tantalizing rush of desire poured through her, and she moaned.

Nicolai was right beside her. He could wake up at any moment and realize what she yearned for. But… maybe another sex fantasy was in order. For his sake. After all, she had to be disturbing him, rolling around like this. And last time, she'd fallen asleep the moment she'd climaxed.

Yes, for Nicolai's sake, she thought dazedly, inhibitions crumbling as she imagined the hard thrust of him inside her.…

A low moan caused Nicolai to jolt upright.

Out of habit, he cataloged his surroundings in an instant. The moon was high, golden, the stars bright, winking from their scattered perches. Ghost trees swayed against a cool, sultry breeze. A river rushed along a pebbled bank.

His brows drew together with confusion. He was enveloped by the sweetest scent of passion…fading…and the ripe scent of pain…intensifying. Who was in—?

Another low, female moan sounded, broken and harsh. His attention whipped to the left, down. Jane. Jane lay beside him. And gods above, she was practically naked. Her only covering was a tiny scrap of white material between the apex of her thighs.

He should remove it. With his teeth.

Instantly his fangs ached. A familiar sensation in

her presence. For a moment, he could only drink in the sight of her, his gaze greedy. Her breasts were small, her nipples pink as berries and beaded deliciously. Her stomach hollowed, showcasing every single one of her ribs.

Clearly she had been hungry for a long time. He would feed her, he thought, delighted by the very idea. She would never lack for food again. Would eat from his hand. Only the very best morsels, too. She would close her eyes at the succulent taste, savor every nibble, groan in joy when he sampled the meal with her, and then directly from her.

While blood was the source of his life, he needed food, as well. Perhaps because he was not fully vampire. He had a witch for a mother, and—

A witch for a mother?

Pain sliced through him, and he nearly pounded his fist into the ground. Not again. Frustration ate at him.

Then he spied the scars on Jane's abdomen, and thoughts of offering her the choicest of meats fled, right along with thoughts of his family. Hunger of a different nature asserted itself. He ached to commit murder. Those scars…Dark Abyss… He'd known she had them, but not how many or how deeply they cut her.

From her navel down, she looked as if she'd been sliced up and sewn back together by a blind weaver. Thick, red scars crisscrossed in every direction, badges of pain most in the world would probably never experience.

How had she survived whatever had been done to her?

Whoever had hurt her would die, just as the guards who touched her had.

She deserved pampering. Not just the food from his table, but gowns of rich velvet and a bed of the finest goose feathers. Never would she work. She would relax, enjoy, perhaps spend her days naked, lounging in his bedroom, and her nights sweat soaked from passion.

He would feast from her body, her veins. Sample every part of her, dining between her legs at his leisure. Riding her hard and fast, letting her ride him slow and sweet. Taking her in every position imaginable, then perhaps inventing a few. His cock hardened, already aching.

She needs her rest. Needs to heal. Deep breath in, deep breath out. But gods, much more of her incredible scent and he would fall on her, perhaps drink too much of her blood. She was like the morning dew on the petals of a rose, fragile, and he must always be careful with her.

Trembling, he reached out to smooth that honey hair from her brow…. When he saw his hand, he stilled. Turned his palm up to the moonlight. Wiggled his thumb. Healed. He was completely healed; there was no pain.

How much time had passed?

How long had he left Jane unguarded?

He looked around with fresh eyes, astonished by what he found. Enough time had passed for her to construct a hut, weapons, wash her clothing and his body. He was the man, the warrior, yet *she* had taken care of *him*.

Mine. Worthy of being queen.

She'd told him she did not have a man waiting for her, and he was glad. Had she, he would have killed the man. Not painfully, not unless the man had once hurt her, but he would have died all the same. After Nicolai found a way into her world. And he would have done so. No one but him would lay claim to this woman, not in any time or in any place.

And if you have someone waiting for you? Someone you've forgotten? He frowned, not liking the thought. Fidelity was important. Jane had said as much. He didn't know a lot about himself, but that he, too, believed.

But…he wanted Jane. And right then, he could not even conceive the idea of wanting anyone else, of being with anyone else. Ever. Truly, every cell in his body burned for Jane, only Jane. Somehow, she was already a part of him. Somehow, her essence was rooted so deeply inside him, he suspected they had always been destined to meet, to be together. But…

If someone *was* waiting for him, what would he do? Despite his fearsome temper, he revered the law and never went back on his word. Right?

Perhaps. But… There was that awful, awful word again. The law, his honor, fidelity, none of those applied to this situation. If he didn't want another female, he wouldn't accept another female. He wouldn't cheat *Jane*. It was as simple as that.

While he thought himself somewhat decent in this matter, he did not think he fought honorably. He thought he won his battles through fair means or foul, and punished his enemies without a shred of mercy or remorse. Look at what he'd done to the guards of the Queen of Hearts.

And many years ago, he had led his army through the Wolfyn realm, the moon hidden behind clouds, the citizens of one of the kingdoms sleeping peacefully in

their beds. He and his men had razed the entire structure. He'd hated to do it, but that hadn't stopped him.
Anything to save his brother….

A sharp pain, his mind shutting down. The memory,
lost. For the most part. Once, he'd led an army. He'd
thought such a thing before, but now he knew. He had.
He'd led them. But…an army of what? Other vampires?
Mercenaries? Or had he been royally sanctioned?

The answers were not forthcoming, and he gritted
his teeth in renewed frustration.

He focused on the here and now. On Jane. He was
willing to fight for her. He wanted her in his life, and
she might very well protest. If so, they would verbally
brawl and he would do *anything* to keep her.

At last he smoothed the hair from her cheek and…

She had a black eye.

Nicolai stiffened, rage blooming through him, stronger than ever before. Someone had hit her. Who had
dared hit her?

The animal instinct roared to the surface, snarling,
desperate for blood.

Calm, he had to remain calm. For now. Was she injured further? As tenderly as he was able, he rolled her
to her back. There were no other bruises on her face.
The long length of her lashes cast spiky shadows over
her cheeks, and he traced them just to be sure. They
were smooth, soft and warm. Her lips were puffy and
red, as if she'd chewed them from worry.

Didn't matter. She was beautiful…a priceless work
of art.

There were several cuts on her hands, but those came
from the making of the blades. He had borne those same
cuts on multiple occasions. Another memory, and it

came without pain. He did not pursue it. Jane was more important.

Bruises wrapped around her rib cage, stretching from her back, where she'd been whipped. Thankfully, though, she possessed no other battle marks. So. How had she gotten the black eye?

She shifted in her sleep, and another pained groan left her.

Her back must agonize her in this position. He should have left her on her side. Could he never do the right thing where this woman was concerned? He eased back down and gently worked an arm under her shoulder. Then he lifted her until she was plastered to his side, her injuries free of all contact. She burrowed her head in the hollow of his neck and raised her top leg, fitting herself against him like the puzzle piece she'd once praised.

She flattened her hand over his heart, as if measuring the erratic beat against her own. So trusting she was, so trust*worthy*. She hadn't left him when she'd had the chance. So forgiving, too. He'd allowed her to be whipped, yet still she'd taken care of him. Had even, he mused, cleaned his teeth. His mouth tasted fresh, like mint.

She groaned again, but this time, oh, this time, there was no pain in her voice. Only pleasure. Such a decadent sound. Instantly his cock stood at attention, filling, hardening, readying. He bit his tongue, his fangs sinking deep into the tissue.

"Nicolai?" Jane breathed sleepily.

"All is well, Jane. Go back to sleep."

"No, I—"

"You're right. You may sleep after you tell me

who hit you," he interrupted before she could make a demand of her own.

"You did." Warm breath trekked over his chest, tickling his skin.

"What?" he shouted. "Me?"

"Accident. No worries. And I didn't mean to cuddle up to you. I'm sorry."

She was sorry? "Jane. *I* am sorry." Shame beat at him more stubbornly than any opponent ever had. "Name a punishment and I will render it against myself immediately."

"No punishment necessary, you silly man. I told you, it was an accident."

Even in this, she forgave him so easily. Her worth far surpassed his. "I will never hurt you again, you have my word."

"You were out of it. You couldn't help yourself. I'm just glad you're finally awake. I've been so worried."

She was going to roll away from him, he thought, feeling her muscles bunch, preparing for movement. He tightened his hold on her. "No. I put you here." *And here you will stay.*

"Oh," she said, and he couldn't decide if she was pleased or upset. "Are you, uh, thirsty? For blood, I mean."

Yes. "No." She was in no condition to feed him. But even the idea of tasting her had his fangs extending, moisture filling his mouth.

"Okay. Well, you might be wondering about the number of times I bathed you, but I promise you I never touched you more than necessary. Okay, maybe I did, but not by much. And I cut up the hem of my gown to use as rags, so that you wouldn't have to endure skin-to-skin contact while you were out."

Endure? The thought of her delicate little hands on his body caused his testicles to draw up tight and his erection to throb, close to exploding. "Thank you for taking care of me."

"My pleas—I mean, you're welcome. So how are you feeling?"

"Better." Now that she was relaxing against him. "You?"

"My legs hurt."

Her legs, not her back. It was the first complaint she had ever uttered, yet she'd cast no blame his way. Determination consumed him, suddenly and completely, blending with a sense of urgency. "Hurt, from the walk?"

"From an old injury."

"Tell me."

"Car accident." She paused. "A car is a vehicle used for traveling along roads at high speeds. Anyway, two of them smashed together. I was inside one. My family, too. I survived. They didn't."

He could not imagine what she described, but could identify with her pain. "I will make you better." He eased her to the ground and sat up.

"You can't. Only time can. I only just started walking again a few months ago."

"You could not walk?" When he turned and moved between her legs, a hot blush flooded her cheeks and she quickly covered her breasts and stomach. She also kept her gaze on the large emerald-and-white leaves forming a barrier between them and the sky.

"Not for almost a year. So, hey, did I tell you that I

washed my gown and that's why I'm practically naked like this? The material wasn't dry, and I didn't want to wake you up if I accidentally rubbed against you and the gown was cold and wet. But I probably should have risked it," she babbled. "My scars, I know how ugly they are and as perfect as you are, you're probably used to perfect women, too. I mean, not that you had a choice with Laila, and not that she's perfect. But before her you probably—"

"Jane."

She licked her lips. "Yes?"

"Let's tackle this one issue at a time. You think I'm upset by your nakedness?"

"Well, yes. After what Laila did, I—"

"You are not Laila." And every part of him knew it.

"I know that, but you are a victim of sexual abuse and I…I just don't want to push the boundaries and upset you."

Upset him? *Him?* "I've told you how much I crave you, Jane."

"Well, you needed me to save you. You might have been buttering my toast, so to speak." When he looked at her blankly, she added, "You know, softening me up so I'd do what you wanted."

Indeed, that had been the plan. From the first moment he'd spied her, however, everything had changed. He'd operated only on instinct. "You are also too smart for your own good and convince yourself of the silliest notions."

Her eyes narrowed, just not enough to hide the fire inside them. "Anything else you want to complain about, you lazy vampire?"

His lips twitched. Even angry, the woman wasn't

concerned with his new position. Her knees were poised at his hips, his erection lifting his loincloth and nearly brushing what was definitely the sweetest spot in this world or the other. Despite her insecurities, she trusted him completely.

She was uncomfortable about her nudity for reasons that had nothing to do with him, and that he couldn't allow. "You know I've…climaxed recently," he said.

"Well, now I do," she replied cautiously.

"The last time was the morning of your arrival. Mere hours before, in fact. And not once, but twice. Yet, look at my cock, Jane."

A slight gurgle was her only response.

"Look at my cock," he repeated.

This time, she obeyed. Slowly, slowly, her gaze lowered. She gasped when she spotted the angle of his loincloth.

"If I did not want you, I would not be hard."

"I know." A heated sigh.

"Any time you doubt your appeal, just look here." He fisted his length and moved his hand up and down, up and down, hissing in a breath at the painful but very necessary pressure. "You'll remember how exquisite I find you. So much so you are in constant danger of being devoured."

"But my scars…"

"Your scars simply prove how strong and capable you are. They prove you survived a terrible accident. They are lovely."

"Really?" she squeaked, her cheeks brightening another degree.

"Really. And just so you know, there are no boundaries with us."

"There aren't?"

He stopped his assault on himself before he spilled. "No."

"But…but…there are always boundaries."

Oh, really. "Is there something you don't want me to do to you? Some place on your body you don't want me to touch?" He was tense as he awaited her response. He could have misjudged. He could be wrong about her feelings.

She gulped. "No."

He relaxed. "It is the same for me. Therefore, no boundaries."

"Okay, I believe you. But I—I don't think we've explored all the ramifications of this."

"This." A sexual relationship? "I think you think and reason too much. We will mate. One day. Not today, but soon."

Another sigh, her entire body sagging into the ground. "I know that, too. I'm too attracted to you not to give in."

He loved such an open, honest admission. "Good. Now. Have I covered everything that worried you?"

"Well." She chewed at her lip until a tiny bead of blood formed. "I've been thinking."

"I have already mentioned that you do that far too much." Before he realized what he was doing, he reached out, collected the blood with the tip of his finger and licked it away. Her flavor, as sweet as her scent, fizzed and crackled over his taste buds, and he moaned.

Dark Abyss, *nothing* had ever tasted that good. The need for more grew…grew…until he was sweating, panting, fighting for control.

He would not fall on her. He would *not*.

He had known she would delight him in this way, but he had not expected *this*.

"I could return home at any second," she said, unaware of the change in him. "I mean, you're free now and isn't that the reason you summoned me? So it stands to reason that the magic that brought me here will soon begin to fade, whether you want it to or not."

"No," he practically roared, his hunger forgotten in the face of his sudden terror of losing her.

Her eyes widened. "No?"

"I will not allow it." Not now, not ever.

Ever? Yes, he would keep her forever. Would never let her go.

"Just like that?" She snapped her fingers. "You won't allow it, so it won't happen?"

Sweat beaded on his brow as he sat back on his thighs. "I am not safe yet. Therefore, you have not fulfilled all of your duties." He would remain in perpetual danger, if need be. He'd lost so many loved ones already. He could not bear...the pain. The damned pain, wiping his thoughts. "That subject is now closed."

"Fine," she grumbled. "Are you always this grouchy in the semimorning?"

Only when you talk of leaving me. "Would a grouchy vampire tell you that you are the most beautiful female he's ever met?" he asked, determined to soothe them both.

A luscious softening of her eyes, her mouth. "No."

"Then I am not grouchy. Now close your eyes and relax." If that ocher gaze met his, he would forget his purpose, lean down, kiss the breath right out of her, then work his way to her vein. And if his teeth sank inside her, his cock would expect equal measure. "I'm going to ease your hurts."

Chapter 8

The most beautiful female he'd ever seen? He must be seeing Odette, then, Jane thought. Thin might be in, at least where she was from, but there was such a thing as too thin and Jane was it. After the accident, she'd been bed bound and tube fed. When she'd finally woken up, able to feed herself, she'd learned of her family's demise and hadn't had an appetite.

Now that her appetite had reasserted itself, she'd been forced to exist on only fruits and nuts.

Fruits…nuts…hmm… In that moment, she realized she was starving. For a juicy steak and a side of fries— on top of another steak. The food could wait, though. She was also starving for a man's touch. A touch Nicolai gave her. Liberally. His strong fingers massaged her calves, deep and hard, hitting her just right. Moaning, she sagged against the moss beneath her.

"Too much?" he asked in a gravelly voice.

"Perfect," she managed to gasp out. She kept her eyes closed, as he'd demanded. Not because of his order, but because his fangs were still out. There was a slight slur to his words.

Those fangs scared her as much as they aroused her. She'd seen the harm they could do, ripping through flesh and bone, but also wondered about the pleasure they could bring. Every time she wondered, she shivered.

Hell, even now she shivered. If he was hungry, she was going to feed him, she decided. After this massage, she would owe him a kidney, anyway. Because, oh, sweet mercy, nothing had ever felt this good. Not even grinding on top of him—in her fantasy and in reality—and that had felt like heaven.

Okay, so, maybe the grinding had felt just as good.

He worked on her calves for over an hour, and by the time he moved up to her thighs, she stopped trying to conceal her breasts and scars. Why should she? He'd already seen them and had claimed to find them exquisite. Her arms slid to the ground, useless. God, the man's hands were magic.

Magic. Yes. Somehow, he was using magic. Warmth flowed from his skin and into hers, an unnatural warmth, a drugging warmth, intoxicating her, stealing into her muscles, her bones, until every part of her was tingling—and his property. Oh, yes. Whatever he touched instantly became his, existing for him and only him.

When his knuckles brushed the edge of her panties, every nerve ending she possessed roared to sudden life, reaching for him. Soon she was panting, groaning, trying to anticipate his next move. At her knee, he rubbed, then stroked up, gliding along her thigh, sweeping over—*yes, there, please there, almost, almost*—only to pause, not quite stroking where she most needed, before reaching for her other thigh. She had to bite her lip to cut off her plaintive cries for more.

If he would prolong the contact, angle it just a little, she could climax. Oh, God. If she climaxed from this… it would be embarrassing.

The massage continued. And really, who cared about being embarrassed? She didn't. When would he brush across her panties again? She tensed, waiting, hoping, so damn eager. Her entire body vibrated. Even the air in her lungs began to heat. But time ticked by, and his motions became a little jerky as he kneaded the knots, never offering such wantonness again.

"Distract me," she said. Otherwise, she just might beg him for a happy ending. Something she couldn't allow herself to do. He said they would mate soon. Which meant, now was not the time.

Or *was* she supposed to beg? Before, in the bedroom, he'd said, *Not until you beg me.* Was that what he wanted now? What he expected? To work her into a frenzy and hear her plead? Well, she would—

"Distract you how?" he asked, surprising her.

Okay, so begging wasn't on the menu. Astonished with herself, she fought a wave of disappointment. "Tell me a story."

He stilled. "A story?"

"Yes." She cracked open her eyelids and added, "Whatever you do, don't stop massaging!"

His lips twitched despite the tension radiating from him, something she found endearing. Most likely amusement had not been a part of his life for a while, yet he seemed to enjoy her. As she enjoyed him.

"A story about what?" he asked. He remained between her splayed legs, with her knees bent and framing him.

"I don't know. Your family, maybe." The second she said the words, she wanted to snatch them back. She remembered the passage from the book. He did not recall his past. His memory—

"I have two brothers and a sister," he said, and stopped breathing.

A moment passed, then another. His fangs slid back inside his mouth, disappearing. Shock and pain replaced the desire and joviality in his expression.

"What's wrong?" she asked, even though she knew the answer. Or thought she did. He needed to speak, to release. Something she had learned—and maybe discarded—in her therapy sessions. But just because *she* hadn't tried it, didn't mean he should not.

"I didn't remember my siblings until just now. I suspected, but…I have two brothers and a sister. Right now I know, *know,* they are real." There was a challenging note in his voice, as if he expected her to argue.

"They're real," she agreed.

He grimaced, nodded. "At last I can see them in my mind. I just can't recall their names. When I try, my head nearly explodes with pain."

"Pain?"

"A *courtesy* of the healer."

"Oh, Nicolai. I am so sorry." To know you had a family and to be unable to recall the past you shared, well, that was a true torture, and far worse than not knowing they existed at all. For months, Jane had survived only on her memories. "Ease away from thinking about their names and describe what you see." Perhaps, when he relaxed, his mind focused on one portion of his past, other memories would follow more easily.

The glaze of pain faded from his eyes, and the corners of his lips quirked up once more. He dug into her muscles with more ferocity. "My youngest brother, just a boy, has green eyes and hair several shades lighter than yours. I see him chasing after me, and that makes me happy."

"I bet he looked up to you," she said to encourage him. "I had an older sister, and I was always chasing after her, desperate to play with her and her friends."

"Yes." Nicolai's eyes widened, but he was looking beyond her, to a place she couldn't fathom. "Yes, he did look up to me. To all of us. And we loved him. He was sweetness and innocence rolled into a mischievous package. I—I see us standing together, smiling, a unicorn prancing in front of us."

A *real* unicorn. Jane wanted details—like, had they saddled the creature and ridden it around?—but didn't want to interrupt the flow of Nicolai's recollection. "What about your other brother?"

"He is younger, as well, though very close to my age." He paused, as if searching his mind for validation. He nodded. "They are all younger than me. Even my darling sister."

"And what are these other siblings like?"

"My sister has her golden head bent over a spell book. I try to convince her to leave with me, as I must visit the market, but she refuses. She wants to stay, has too much to do. She works too hard, wants to please too many people. And he, the brother closest to my age, has black hair, like mine, and he's hunting in the forest, racing alongside the wolves."

The bookworm and the warrior, huh? "You are the dictator, I bet," she said with a smile. "And the youngest is the sweetheart."

"Micah is a sweetheart, yes." His eyes widened, a trace of pain returning. "Micah. Yes, that's his name. I wonder where he is, where they all are, what they're doing."

"You'll remember, just like you remembered Micah's name. And maybe you don't need a healer to do this. These memories came back without her."

"Maybe they came back because of you." Nicolai's gaze returned to her. He caught sight of her encouraging smile and licked his lips, his expression changing yet again. From wistful to heated, his cheeks flushing, his fangs peeking out. Little beads of sweat popped up on his brow.

"Me?" The rising sun cast muted, golden rays over their camp. Though he remained in the shadows, his bronzed skin seemed to glow. His eyes swirled, liquid silver, hypnotizing her.

"Yes. You are the only change in my life," he said. His attention moved to her breasts, and her nipples pearled for him, as if desperate to please him. "Mine," he added, reminding her of the beast he had become inside the palace.

This time, the beast delighted her.

The tingling reignited, more intense and spreading quickly. She might have moaned. Might have lifted her hips, seeking more of his heat. Hard to tell, because her thoughts were so consumed with what she wanted, *needed,* from him.

"You keep saying that." And she kept hoping it was true. But they'd made no promises to each other, had only stated their desire for each other.

And really, despite his earlier shout that she would stay with him, she had no idea how much longer they would be together. An hour? A week? A year? They were literally from two different worlds, and she could return as suddenly as she'd appeared.

"Mine," he said more forcefully, perhaps sensing her doubts.

"What do you mean by that? Explain."

"Want you. No secret of that. You want me, too."

God, those short, abrupt sentences were sexy as hell. As if his mind was locked on one thought—pleasure— and nothing could penetrate his determination to have it. With her and only her.

But…could she truly satisfy him? More than being from two different worlds, they were completely different people. One, there was his abuse. Would the things she wanted to do to him freak him out? Maybe, maybe not. Nothing had so far. Two, he clearly knew his way around a female body.

Odette and Laila had been willing to enslave him to experience the joy of his body. Jane knew her way around one man's. She knew what he had liked, but had no idea what another male might long for.

Her previous relationship had lasted three years, ending with her accident. Not because of him. Spencer had wanted to stick by her side. She had pushed him away, too grief stricken to deal with him or anyone. And the plain fact was, she had no longer desired him. Not in any way. She had tried, she really had, to make herself want him again. She had planned a date night, with every intention of seducing him. Yet, even the thought of kissing him had made her sick and she had sent him home directly after dinner.

So, the fact was, while she and Spencer had done everything lovers could do, she'd didn't have any other experience. None. In school, she'd been far younger than her classmates, so no one had wanted her. After that, she'd been too busy. Spencer was the first man to distract her enough to start something.

The lack hadn't bothered her before. There'd been no time to consider it, not even when she had been grinding on top of Nicolai. She'd been too busy trying to figure out what had happened to her, trying to survive her sudden appearance here.

Now, however, she wanted to be perfect. The best. She wanted to please Nicolai the way he had pleased her in her fantasy.

She had enjoyed sex. And she had missed it, despite her lack of desire, all these months. Actually, nearly a year now. Mostly, she had loved and missed the after-glow, lying in a man's arms, absorbing his heat, talking, laughing.

"I've lost you to your thoughts." Nicolai cursed under his breath, but there was humor in the undercurrent. "I'm trying to resist you, Jane, and I'm failing. The challenge of engaging your attention isn't helping."

"Why?" A breathy entreaty. "I mean, why are you trying to resist?"

"You need time to recover. And there's something I must tell you first. Something you will not like."

Stomach cramp. "What is it?"

One heartbeat, two. "Without my memories, I can't be sure…a woman could be waiting…"

Another cramp. "Oh, God. You're married?"

"No. No, that much I know. Just before my appearance in the Sex Market, I was with a woman…a servant. Yes. I remember that. I would not have been with a servant if I were married. But I might have *promised* myself to another."

Might have… No. Not possible. "You hadn't." This she said with a sudden surge of confidence. He was too possessive to sleep with a servant if a fiancée waited in the wings.

A glimmer of hope in his expression. "I mention this only as a possibility, not a reality. I could never want anyone as much as I want you right now." He was looming over her a second later, his mouth poised just above hers. He was breathing shallowly, his hands anchored next to her temples, his erection pressed between her legs.

Finally. The contact she'd yearned for. He was hers, hers, only hers. She could believe nothing less. "You may not know yourself, but *I* think I know you," she said. "Trust me, no one is waiting for you."

She wasn't being stubborn or blind about this. Discarding his possessive nature and the fact that any woman he committed to would have his full attention, he was vampire and vampires mated for life. Physically they couldn't stray. Research had proven that. So, memory or not, he would not react to Jane if his heart belonged to another.

"Perhaps I am a horrible person, because I don't care about a faceless stranger," he said. "I can't resist you. I won't resist you. Don't deny me, Jane. Must taste you, all of you. Please." He didn't wait for her reply but leaned the rest of the way down.

"Nicolai—" She meant to tell him that she couldn't resist him, either, and she would never deny him, that he wasn't a horrible person, but the words were lost in a scorching kiss as he meshed their lips together.

His tongue thrust past her teeth and rolled with hers. Hot, so hot.

He tasted of mint and…candy. Mmm. Yes, candy. Sugary sweet, the flavor all his own, consumed her.

Unable to stop herself, she glided her fingers into his hair.

"Yes. Please. Please," she said, finally begging.

Her nails bit into his scalp, holding him to her. She needed more, had to have more, everything else forgotten. Her knees squeezed at his waist, and she rocked herself against him. A gasp of hungry joy escaped her. God! The feel of his erection against her was mind-blowing, shattering, necessary, better than anything she'd ever known. Maybe because she was so damn wet and ready. So she did it again, rocking, rubbing, gasping.

With a growl of approval, he thrust his tongue deeper. Their teeth scraped together. Dizzying friction, welcome but torturous as her need ratcheted up another level. Then he angled his head for even deeper contact, and she felt the graze of his fangs.

No, *this* was need. True, undiluted need. She *wanted* to be bitten, again and again and again. To be everything to him. Lover, sustenance, breath.

Her blood was heating unbearably, her stomach quivering. On and on the kiss continued, until there was no more oxygen left in her lungs. Until Nicolai was her only lifeline.

"Please," she rasped. "Do it."

"Gods, Jane. You're…you're like fire. I want to be burned."

"Yes."

He licked his way to the pulse hammering at the base of her neck. Was he going to bite her at last? But no, he continued laving at her pulse, sucking on it as one of his hands cupped her breast and kneaded. He pinched the throbbing nipple, and a lance of delicious sensation shot through her entire body.

Heaven and hell, so sweetly offered…how close she was to falling over the edge. But when she did, if she did—*please, let her*—where would she land? The clouds, or the fiery pits?

Only one way to find out…

"Nicolai?"

"Yes, sweetheart."

Sweetheart. His sweetheart. "Bite me."

"Jane." A groan. "You tempt me. I shouldn't."

Shouldn't, because he still thought she needed to heal? Or because a part of him still believed another female was out there, waiting for him? If the impossible happened and he *was* committed… Why impossible? she wondered next. Jane was here, wasn't she? *Nothing* was impossible.

The knowledge caused the first tendrils of doubt to surface. Jane despised cheaters, but she also hated stories that forced two people to remain together because of a sense of duty, rather than love. Nicolai wasn't in love. And if he had a woman, why hadn't she searched for him? Saved him? Again, that made Jane think he couldn't possibly be committed. No girlfriend would have let this guy go. Therefore, Jane could still have him.

But, she didn't want him resenting her. Or feeling pressured. Or regretting what they did. "All right. We won't—"

"We will. Just don't want to hurt you."

Relief. So much relief, ecstasy shimmering, within reach. "You could never hurt me. Nicolai, please. Do it."

"Yes, yes, please. *I'll* beg if necessary. I must have more.…" His fangs returned to her neck and grazed her sizzling skin. "Must taste, will die if I do not."

"Do it." She hissed out a breath and stiffened as she mentally prepared herself for the onslaught. Of pleasure or pain, she wasn't sure. All she knew was that she needed this, too.

He dragged in a shaky breath. "You are sure? I don't have to. I can stop."

"Don't stop. Please, don't stop. I'm just wary of the unknown."

Liiick. "Do not fear, little Jane. I'll be careful with you. Will control myself." Then, with agonizing slowness, he sank his fangs into her neck, sucked on her, swallowed her blood.

Not once did she experience any pain, but the pleasure, oh, God, the pleasure…exactly as she'd imagined, beautiful in the most erotic way. The missing piece to the puzzle of her life.

The burn of his mouth, the suction of his tongue, both caused riotous reactions in her body. She clutched at his back, pulled at his hair, lost to a bliss that should have been impossible. Soon she was even writhing and thrashing against him, desperate for completion.

He purred against her, his breath warm. Then something hot, so wonderfully hot, entered her system.

And okay, she hadn't truly known pleasure before that moment. *This* was pleasure. Pleasure in its purest form. Strength, heat, power. She felt those, too.

Her thrashing became a single-minded pursuit for the elusive satisfaction that still hovered so close. She ground herself against his erection, over and over again, little shivers of sensation coursing through her every time he swallowed. God. She could climb him like a mountain. Could eat him up, one tasty bite at a time. Could remain in his arms forever.

He wrenched free of her vein. "Have to…stop. Can't take…too much."

There was no such thing as too much. "Take more."

"Promised to be careful." He licked the punctures, shooting more of that liquid heat into her system. He growled, "Now you are marked. Mine."

His, just as he was hers. Hers, and no one else's.

"So good. Never tasted anything…so sweet. Addicted…already…"

Yes. Addicted. He was a drug. Her drug, and she doubted there was a cure.

With her painkillers, she'd had to stop using cold and flat. The withdrawals had been nightmarish. Yet she knew with sudden, shocking clarity that those would not compare to what she'd experience without Nicolai.

He replaced the hand on her breast with his mouth, flicking his white-hot tongue over her nipple, shooting more of those gratifying lances through her. He didn't bite, though, not again.

She wanted him to bite her everywhere. "Please, Nicolai."

"Anything you want, I will give you."

She arched into him, locking her ankles at his lower

back. The long, thick length of his erection hit her just right, more liquid dampening her panties. "I want it all."

He still wore the loincloth, but the leather must have bunched up, freeing his cock, because she could feel the heat of his silky skin, soft yet, oh, so hard, pushing at the cotton in a bid to move it out of the way. Just a little more, and they'd be skin-to-skin. Strength-to-wet.

She ached for that. Wanted it with every fiber of her being. But Nicolai had other plans. He continued his downward journey, tracing her scars with his tongue, laving her navel. She would have been humbled by the decadent attention, but she was too aroused. Goose bumps broke out, sensitizing her skin to an almost unbearable degree.

"Mine," he growled.

Yes. *Yes!* His. Always. She frowned. No, not always. The repercussions of his druglike lovemaking hit her like a hammer to the head. She could go home at any moment. This wasn't permanent, and she couldn't forget that fact. Couldn't become attached to him. To this.

You already are.

Yes, she was.

How could she return to her old life now? She'd tasted the forbidden fruit, was addicted just as she'd suspected, and she needed more. More of his hands and his mouth and his teeth and his fingers. More of the heat and the sweetness and the ferocity. But if she didn't finish this, if she attempted to walk away now, she would always wonder about what could have happened.

So, she would worry about the consequences later. Right now, she would simply enjoy.

"Mine," he repeated.

"Yes," she found herself agreeing.

"You want me."

"You, and only you."

"You're so wet for me. I can feel you, feel how ready you are."

"Ready for you, and only you." She was repeating herself, but she didn't care. The words were true.

"You're so hot for me."

"Yes."

"You'll give me everything."

"Yes, I…" Jane's thoughts derailed completely. Finally he was there, between her legs, shoving her panties aside the rest of the way. She anchored her calves over his shoulders as his tongue stroked her.

At first contact, she screamed. So good, so damn good. He licked, sucked and nibbled at her, building her desire to a fever pitch. So close, closer than ever before.

"Like?"

"I like!"

His fingers joined the play. First one, sinking in and out, then another, in and out, in and out, stretching her, preparing her for his possession. "Could stay here forever," he rasped.

She was incapable of responding, what little breath she had left caught in her throat.

"Taste so sweet here, too."

A sound escaped the knot. A whimper.

"Come for me, sweetheart." A command from the animal he'd unleashed at the palace, frothed into a frenzy, desperate, a conqueror. "Let me see that beautiful

face light up." With that, he bit her, right there, between her legs.

He sucked the blood that beaded, and then, thank
God, then he shot whatever his fangs produced straight
inside her core.

Sparks of utter bliss ignited there, then spread,
quickly burning her up from top to bottom. Every
muscle she possessed clenched, spasmed, shooting her
to the stars. Another scream left her, this one tearing
through the encroaching daylight.

The climax was intense, soul shattering. Then Nicolai was looming over her, one of his hands ripping at her
panties, his cock probing for entrance. His eyes were
glitter-bright, his fangs bared in a determined scowl.
Not of anger but of agonizing need.

"More," he said with guttural harshness.

"Let me have you."

"Now," he growled.

Just before he thrust inside, the bushes to their
left rattled, the leaves dancing together. His attention
whipped there, a growl of pure menace leaving him.

Jane was still too lost in the throes of passion to care.
"Nicolai! Please. What are you waiting for?" *Make me
your woman in truth.*

"Protect." He jerked upright, severing all contact.
She reached for him, but he placed himself in front of
her, acting as her shield.

The time for pleasure had ended. The time for fighting had arrived.

Chapter 9

Nicolai's morph from tender lover to savage vampire warrior shocked Jane back to her senses. She was naked—ripped panties didn't count—and her camp had just been invaded. By giants. Four of them.

All four were eyeing her up and down like a barbecued slab of ribs—and they were starving vegetarians.

One by one, they confirmed her thoughts.

"Ugly," the tallest said, the *g* prolonged.

"Hideous."

"Fat."

"Woman," the shortest said. He was probably six-five.

The rest of them shrugged, the universal sign for *I guess she'll do.* Apparently Odette and Laila looked a lot alike, but sex was sex. They might find her repellant, but they'd still do her. Their gazes dipped and glued to her nipples, saliva dripping from the corners of their mouths.

Vegetarians now converted into carnivores.

Jane shuddered. The best thing about her robe, she decided then, was the ease of donning it. She grabbed the material still hanging from the limb where she'd draped it and jerked it over her head. Boom, done. She was dressed and ready to face the newest hazard in her life.

She'd expected to battle Laila's guards at some point, but as she snatched up two of her wooden daggers, she realized the giants weren't as humanoid as the guards had been. Their eyes were bright red, like twin crimson suns rising from the pits of hell. Sharp, fanglike teeth, bared now, still dripping, dripping, forked tongues flicking out and swiping over reptile-thin lips. Wide shoulders, with black wings arching above them. Rather than nails, they possessed claws.

Somehow, she recognized them as she'd recognized the forest. They were straight out of her darkest nightmares and deep down she knew these creatures were savage, mindless. And Nicolai was going to fight them? *He drank from you. He's strong enough.*

Please be strong enough.

He snarled a sound of pure menace, his scary animal nature racing back to the forefront. "Mine." He stopped just in front of them, daring them to act.

He was weaponless, his torso bare. His poor back was as scarred as her front. Not from a whip or an accident, she didn't think. There was a wide circular mass of scar tissue, raised and puckered, in the center of his back, as if someone had carved out the patch of skin.

He was a survivor. Like her. He *could* take these men—and win.

"We want woman," the tallest said. He was clearly

the leader. Also, he was as dumb as a box of rocks, because he added, "You give. Now," and expected Nicolai to rush to obey.

"No," she and Nicolai said in unison.

"You leave," another said with a frown, just as clearly not understanding why Jane wasn't being given to him.

"She please us. You live."

"No," Jane told them with a shake of her head. "*You* leave." Simple words they might understand. "And *you* will live."

They ignored her.

"Leave," one said to Nicolai. "Last chance."

Another said, "You look like someone. Who?" He shook his head, already losing interest in the question. "No matter. Give woman. We keep."

So. Her will meant nothing. Rape was on their menu du jour. "Rip them to shreds," she told Nicolai.

He didn't reply. He simply leaped forward and raked his claws—claws, longer and sharper than theirs!—along the face of the tallest, the biggest threat, sending the giant stumbling backward.

The grunt of pain that followed was like the starting bell to a UFC match. No rules, just pain.

The five males swarmed together in a tangle of limbs, fangs, blood and adrenaline. The blood, well, that sent Nicolai into an animalistic frenzy. He snarled like a panther, bit like a shark and held on to whatever he clamped his teeth into like a pit bull.

Jane knew better than to interfere. When she'd switched the focus of her work to the human body, hoping to find a cure for her mother, she'd learned quite a bit about physical reactions. A man worked into a rage was completely unaware of his surroundings. The chemicals shooting through his bloodstream would keep Nicolai on a short leash, the end of that leash bound to these giants, where only killing mattered.

So she stood there, and she watched, silently cheering for her man.

Not yours, she forced herself to add. *Not completely, and not yet.* She could share her body with him, her mind, but her heart and soul? No. Not when there was a chance the magic would fade and she would return home. Worse, if he fell in love with her, he would wither and die if she left him.

Oh…damn. She'd forgotten about that. Such a terrible fate had befallen several of the vampires brought to her lab. She couldn't let that happen to Nicolai.

She brushed the depressing, worrisome thoughts aside. No distractions, not now. The fight escalated quickly, the violence seemingly unparalleled. Someone's arm flew past her head—and it wasn't attached to a body.

Just then, Nicolai was walking death. His expression, what few times she glimpsed it, considering how quickly he was moving, was cold. He lacked mercy, never once pulling his punches. He went for the throat, vital organs and groin. Had the giants been human, they would have fallen to his superior power within seconds. But each time he dropped one to the ground, or tore off a limb, the bastard got up for more.

That only revved Nicolai's engine. The lethal grace of him…Jane was riveted, even shocked. Oh, she'd known he was capable of this. There, inside the palace, hatred and determination had radiated from him. And guts had spilled across the floor. Had he not rescued her, he would have stayed until every living being had died by his hand. Or teeth. That, she'd known.

But this man, this warrior, had also given her sizzling pleasure. He'd feasted between her legs, and he'd loved doing it. She thought he might have enjoyed it as much as she had. And, oh, he'd set her blood on fire, thrilled her to her very soul, ensuring both of them existed only for passion. That had happened minutes ago. Mere minutes ago. Now he was a being capable of rendering pain, only pain.

And all too soon the giants learned to anticipate his moves. They bit at him with their too sharp saber teeth. They swiped their claws at him, cutting him deep. They spun around him, above him, using their wings to slice at him. Nicolai was forced to jump between them and use his momentum to kick at them. They stumbled, but again, they always rose.

She would have to do something, after all. Nicolai would tire soon, surely. He was losing blood, crimson streaking down his chest where he'd been scratched. How should she—?

In less than a heartbeat of time, strong, trunklike arms banded around her, one just above her breasts, the other around her waist, and jerked her into a thick body. Fear bombarded her, nearly paralyzing her. Then fight or flight kicked in—as did a reminder that she held two daggers. Fight won.

She slammed her elbow backward, hitting her attacker in the stomach, meaning to turn and stab. He grunted, but held tight, and she wasn't able to twist around. She opened her mouth to scream. Before even the slightest sound left her, her mind shouted, *You can't distract Nicolai.*

The giant—and she knew a giant held her—dragged her backward, but she didn't allow herself to struggle.

Perhaps they weren't as dumb as she'd first thought. This one had known to hang back, to wait, to watch, and grab her while everyone else was preoccupied. Were any others waiting in the shadows?

How would she fight them all?

A cold rage of her own infused her. Thankfully no one else appeared, and when Nicolai and company were no longer in sight, leaves and branches shielding them, she erupted. *Fight*. She angled her arms, lifted both of her elbows this time, and then slammed them home. He gave another grunt, finally loosening his hold.

Another angle shift, and she thrust her arms down, using the makeshift daggers. The tips sliced deep into his thighs.

With a howl of pain, he shoved her away from his body. One of the daggers remained lodged, but the other glided free as she stumbled forward. Jane righted herself and whirled around, facing him. This giant was scowling, his fangs dripping with saliva. His red eyes glowed with menace.

"I punish you," he snarled as he ripped the other dagger free. A flick of his wrist. The sharpened wood clanked on the ground, now useless.

Fight. "Wrong. *I'll* punish *you*."

That confused him for a moment. He blinked, brows knitting together. Then he shook his head. "No. I punish you."

Okay. Back to her original assessment. Calling these things dumb as rocks was an insult to the rocks. "Bring it, big boy." Six months of self-defense lessons were about to pay off.

Or not. She'd never had to use her "skills" in a genuine life-and-death situation.

He stomped toward her, booted feet kicking up dirt with every step, the ground shaking. Blood poured down his pant-covered legs, yet he didn't limp or even seem to notice his injuries.

When he was within reach, he tried to grab her. She ducked, and when his claws encountered only air, she twisted and stabbed. This time, her dagger sank into his middle. Another howl rent the air. Before she could dart out of the way this time, his fingers were fisting her hair and pushing her face-first into the dirt.

Seriously? Over that quickly? Oh, hell, no! She rolled into a ball before he could pin her with his massive weight, maneuvered to her back and worked her legs between their bodies. She pushed. He didn't budge an inch. Damn it!

Think, Parker. She still had one of the daggers. She stabbed again, going for his neck. He reared back. Too late. Contact, just not where she'd hoped. His cheek split open, and blood poured.

He flashed his saber-fangs as he snarled.

"Punish." Then he was leaning down, those fangs sinking into her neck. This bite lacked the pleasure and heat of Nicolai's. This one provided only pain. So much pain.

He thought to drain and weaken her. A mistake on his part, she thought darkly, steeling herself against every ache and throb. He'd left himself wide open. Before her mind could fog from blood loss, she wilted into the ground. Either he assumed that she had been properly subdued or that she'd passed out. His fingers left her hair to move to her breasts and squeeze.

She struck, finally slamming the dagger into his jugular, all the way to other end. His entire body spasmed, his fangs locking down tight.

Okay, reassessment time. *This* was pain. She nearly screamed from the intensity of it.

There was no dislodging him, even when he sagged against her. His weight shoved the air from her lungs. She lay there, trying to catch her breath, his blood pouring over her.

For a moment, she was transported back to her car. Her mother dying, her blood dripping onto Jane. Both of them crying, because they knew the others were already gone. Unsavable.

I love you, Janie.

I love you, Mom.

Something sharp dug into her scalp, ripping strands of her hair. Her body was pulled out from under the giant. His teeth had still been buried deep, and the movement caused his fangs to tear through skin and vein, leaving teeth tracks down her neck, chest and stomach.

Another scream fought its way from her throat. *Still can't risk distracting Nicolai.* His battle royale hadn't ended. Otherwise, he would have been here. And she knew it wasn't Nicolai who had grabbed her, even before bright, crimson eyes were glowing down at her. Nicolai would have been gentle, would have tried to soothe her.

"Woman. Ugly. I will bed, anyway."

Peachy. Her eyesight fogged. Had this guy escaped Nicolai, or was he new? Even if she'd had twenty-twenty vision just then, she doubted she would have been able to tell. One hideous monster was the same as any other, she supposed.

"I'm a…princess," she said, trying anything to scare him. "Princess…Odette. Of Delfina. You have to…let me go."

Like the caveman he was, he continued to drag her through the dirt. Twigs and rocks scratched at her scabbed back, and she winced. Soon her robe was in tatters and tears burned her eyes.

She tried again, even as the fog migrated to her mind. "My mother…queen…will kill—"

"Witch queen not my queen. No queen. Only king." He rounded a corner and the new angle hurt worse. "He have you."

Extra peachy. "You're taking me…to your king?"

"After."

After. The same word she'd once thrown at Nicolai, while he'd been chained and helpless. Never again. *After* was now stricken from her vernacular. "You keep this up…and I'll be dead…before we get there."

A confused silence. Then a triumphant, "You not dead. You alive."

Box. Of. Rocks. "Pick me up…stupid shit. Carry me."

The simple order worked. He stopped, swooped down and hefted her up—over his shoulder, fireman style, squashing her stomach into her kidneys, but hey, anything was better than leaving a trail of scabs and blood on the ground. A trail Nicolai didn't need. Wherever this brute took her, Nicolai would find her. He'd marked her, he'd said. And thank God he had.

She and her abductor ran into another giant along the way, and stopped. An angry conversation ensued. She

caught words like *king* and *now,* and curses so dark her
ears were probably bleeding. Just like the rest of her.

Didn't take a genius to figure out the problem. Word
of a female's capture had already spread to the king.
Ugh-O here was not to sample her goods. He was to
bring her in and allow the king to decide her fate, as
well as become the first to rape her.

Come on, Nicolai. Where are you?

Ugh-O leaped back into motion, the messenger remaining close to his side, not trusting him to obey. Or
maybe not. Maybe she was the glue that held them together. A few times, the bastard reached out and patted
her ass. This always angered the hell out of Ugh-O, and
he would swat at the offending appendage, jarring her.

In fact, his footfalls were so heavy, she slammed up
and down, losing her breath over and over again. By
the time they reached a twisted maze of caverns, she
was convinced her lungs were flat as pancakes, and her
intestines were wrapped around her spine.

Even with her still-dimming eyesight, she watched
for Nicolai, hoping to catch a glimpse of him shadow-
ing the beast, ready to strike. While she did spy other
beings following her captor—little things with wings,
darting through the air, and wolflike creatures skulk-
ing around the trees—none of them were the vampire.

And when she heard a roar, pain filled and broken,
echoing in every direction, she wanted to vomit. That
had been Nicolai's voice. What the hell were the giants
doing to him?

Then the sound cut off abruptly, and she found the
silence was even more disturbing than the roar. Had the
giants just…killed—*No!* No, no, no. But what if…?

Oh, God. A sob caught in her throat. If he lived, he would have come for her.

She was his, he'd said so. Many times. And somehow, he was hers. She barely knew the man but she felt something deep and inexorable for him.

Only minutes before, she'd thought her heart and soul safe from his appeal, her mind too concerned with the danger to him. Now, as she was dragged to the unknown, death a possibility, when she thought *him* dead, the truth hit her.

Her heart and soul had never been safe.

Nicolai fascinated her. He was bossy and arrogant, yet protective when it mattered. He was a killer with a lover's hands. In his arms, she'd come alive, had been utterly undone. He was already a part of her. In her blood, her head, her everything. So, no. No, no, no. He couldn't be dead. He just couldn't be.

Whatever had been done to him, he would heal. He had to heal. His roar had probably cut off because he'd passed out or something. Yes, that was it. And since he healed when he slept, that was a good thing.

Right?

The beast had to duck to enter one of the caverns, and she forced herself to concentrate. The hallways were narrow, suffocating. Footsteps echoed as he marched, creating a symphony of terror in her mind. She attempted to memorize the path he took, but it was difficult. So many turns, so dizzying. Alice's rabbit hole, she thought with a humorless laugh.

Finally they reached a spacious chamber bursting with more of those winged giants. Murmurs of approval abounded the moment she was spotted, and those approvals swiftly mutated into lusty catcalls. Growling, stiff with anger, Ugh-O tossed her atop a pallet in the center.

Jane scrambled to her feet. More waves of dizziness accompanied the action, and she swayed. When her vision cleared, she spun in a circle, studying her new surroundings. A throne of glittering crystal grew directly from the wall. That throne would have made a majestic sight, if not for the bare chested maniac seated on top of it.

His nose was so far out of place, the left side rested against his cheek. One of his eyes was missing, and there was a hole in his bottom lip, as if one of his saber teeth had punched right through. His chest was a mass of scars, like slices of roast beef that had been glued together—but the glue hadn't held.

At least twenty others stood beside him, guarding him. All eyes were on her, bright red lasers she couldn't escape. Sweat dripped between her breasts, even as her blood chilled. Not one of these creatures would aid her. They all wanted, and expected, a turn.

In fact, only two people in the room were uninterested in her presence. The only other females. Both were naked, old and wrinkled, unwashed, with straggly hair and dead eyes. They'd been well used, multiple times, and were covered in bite marks and bruises. No wonder these guys were so hot for the repulsive "Odette."

Footsteps behind her caused her to spin. More dizziness, intent on lingering. Only when it passed did she realize these were the men who had attacked Nicolai. They were bloody, limping, missing a few body parts and barely breathing, but they were here.

"Where's my vampire?" she screeched.

Ignoring her, they fell before their king. "Vampire disappear."

He'd disappeared. That meant he was alive. Thank God. Oh, thank God.

"No fresh meat?" the king asked, speaking up for the first time.

"No fresh meat."

A rumble of angry muttering sprung from the sovereign, and he waved his fingers toward the men. Four other giants stepped forward, palming swords and swinging before Jane could compute what was going on. Heads rolled, stopping at her feet.

She hunched over and finally vomited. No, not vomited. She dry heaved. There was nothing in her stomach. Laughter and applause abounded as the bodies were gathered up.

"Fresh meat now. Cook," the king said with a nod of approval. "We dine."

They were going to eat their own kind. Oh, God, oh, God, oh, God. She straightened, preparing to run.

Ugh-O settled a hard hand on her shoulder, ending her escape attempt before she'd taken a single step. "I found. I get."

The king lost his good humor and frowned. "I give you my hag." He motioned toward one of the old women. The hag in question stepped forward automatically and bowed. "Now give me yours."

"No. I want the fat one."

Hisses abounded.

Telling the king no was a crime, she supposed. "Fight," she suggested, her voice trembling as much as her body. "Fight over me. Winner gets me." Fingers crossed they killed each other.

That dark frown leveled on her. "Fight, yes. After."
He crooked his finger at her, expecting her to close the
distance between them.

After. There was that word again. Gulping, she shook
her head. Ugh-O squeezed her shoulder harder, harder
still, and she winced.

"Come," the king demanded, speaking more sharply
now. He waved her over, and if she wasn't mistaken,
next waved to his crotch. As if he expected her to jump
on board right here, right now.

He probably did. She'd heard the unspoken *Or else,*
and rallied her wits. *Come on. I can do this.* "Take me
to your bedchamber." Never in her life had Jane attempted to seduce someone who repulsed her, and she
mentally cringed at the huskiness of her tone. Better
she fight this man alone than with all his people watching—and able to join in. "I'll do things you've only
dreamed about." *If your dreams involve strangling on
your own intestines.*

"Just want your mouth on cock."

I would rather die. "And I want to put my mouth on
your cock." *Lightning, strike me down. Please.* "So let's
go to your bedchamber. Because, and here's the kicker,
I do my best work in private."

He was on his feet in an instant, stalking toward her.

Chapter 10

Nicolai's head was a seething cauldron of thoughts, his body a tuning fork of emotion. One moment he'd been fighting the giants, protecting Jane, the next he was shouting in pain, unable to control the turmoil in his mind. Faces, so many faces. Voices, so many voices.

Clutching at his ears, he fell to his knees. The jarring helped. The faces faded and the voices quieted, allowing rational thought to form. Had to…protect…Jane…again… But when he pried his eyelids apart, he saw that the giants were gone.

So was Jane.

He was no longer near the river, no longer in the forest. A barren wasteland surrounded him. What trees he saw were gnarled, their leaves withered. Ash floated in an acidic wind, black snow scented with death and destruction. And he smelled something…rotting.

He recognized nothing.

He turned, saw a snakelike vine slither from one of the trees, then another, both headed in his direction. They dove for him, bit at him and, when they tasted his blood, seemed to cackle with glee. When they dove a second time, he jumped out of the way—and onto a pile of bones.

A need to slay the Blood Sorcerer, the new king of Elden, filled him, consumed him entirely. Was the bastard nearby? If so, this wasteland was Elden. Had to be.

Elden. *Elden.* The word reverberated in his head. And just like that, the faces returned to his mind, forcing their way to the surface of a man somehow unprepared for them. Faces, blurring together, becoming one. A scene built.

A blonde woman crouched in front of him, studying his skinned knee with soft concern in her green eyes. He was a boy, just a boy, and as she chanted a spell and blew warm breath on his wound, peace and love infused him. The torn flesh knitted back together, blood no longer dripping from it.

When the healing process completed, she grinned over at him. "See? All better, yes?" Such a sweet voice, tender and carefree. She brushed his frustrated, angry tears away with her knuckles. The tears had not formed because of any pain he felt, but because he'd wanted, *needed,* to inflict more damage on his opponents. "You have to stop fighting, darling. Especially boys who are twice your age, and far bigger."

"Why? I beat them." And he could have hurt them a lot worse!

"I know, but the more you damage their pride, the more they will hate you."

"They cannot hate if they do not survive."

"Besides that," his mother continued sternly, "you are in a position of power, and they are not. You must be a voice of reason, not a blast of violence."

He crossed his arms. "They deserved what I did to them."

"And what, exactly, did they do to deserve your claws in their necks?"

"They hurt a girl. Pushed her around in a circle and tried to look up her skirt. They scared her so badly she cried. And then they touched her. In one of her private places. Here." He flattened a palm on his chest. "And she screamed."

The woman sighed. "All right. They deserved your wrath. But, Nicolai, my love, there are other ways to punish those who do wrong. Permissible ways."

"Such as?" He could think of no way other than what he'd done. Like for like, hurt for hurt.

"Tell your father what they've done, and he'll lock them away or banish them from the kingdom."

"So that they can do more harm elsewhere? Or one day seek revenge?" he scoffed. "No."

"And what if you are hurt while you are hurting them?" she demanded.

"I'll come to you. You are the most powerful witch in all the world."

Another sigh, some of her upset fading. "You're incorrigible. And your faith in me is very sweet, if somewhat misguided. Yes, I am powerful, but not as powerful as you will be one day. That's why I want you to be careful. One day, your temper might cause you to accidentally destroy more than a few lives."

"All right, Mother. I will try and be careful, but I can't promise."

"Oh, your honesty…" She flashed a soft smile. "Off you go. After you pay my spell casting fee."

He scrunched up his face, leaned forward and kissed the softness of her cheek. "I'm a prince. I shouldn't have to pay."

"Well, I'm a queen, so you'll *always* have to pay. Go on, now. Find your brother and *study* with him, my darling. No more running away from your tutors to avenge the world."

With a wave, he was darting off, away from her—but not for the classroom. He had too much energy and needed to swim. Swimming always calmed him.

In the here and now, darkness swooped in, blanking Nicolai's mind. Another reprieve. He fell the rest of the way to the ground. One of the vines sliced his cheek, but he hardly noticed. He was remembering his past.

Why was he remembering? Why were the memories flooding him like this?

The healer who had bound his powers had not unbound them. Perhaps more of Nicolai's abilities had found their way free. That would also explain the split-second location switch. Perhaps those abilities had demolished the glass cage.

Except, a quick mental check proved the cage was still there, his abilities and memories still swirling inside it, faster and faster. However, now streaks of crimson were dripping from the top, eroding the glass.

Crimson…blood?

The guards from Delfina? No. Days had passed, and he'd had no reaction to what he'd consumed at the palace. And while he had bitten the ogres, he hadn't swallowed their blood, unconsciously knowing it was poison to him.

The last person he'd drunk from was Jane. He'd gulped from her neck, her taste so decadent he'd wanted to stay there forever. And maybe he would have. Maybe he would have drained her if the thought of losing her had not slammed through him. That, followed by the thought of sampling the heaven between her legs, had driven him to leave her neck and descend. And he'd never been so glad to end a meal. Between her legs, she was sweeter than the nectar of honeysuckle.

He wanted to taste her there again. Wanted to at last sink inside her, possess her fully, become a part of her. Wanted her passion cries in his ears, her limbs all around him, clinging to him. Wanted her nails in his flesh, leaving her own mark.

Where was she? Had she—?

Another memory grabbed hold of his attention, using so much force he could only grunt with the pain. Images, voices, blurring together, painting another scene.

"Tighten your hold, boy. You'll lose your sword in seconds with that puny of a grip."

He was still a boy, a little older now, standing in front of a tall, muscled man. Black-as-night hair, eyes of polished silver. He wore a fine silk shirt and leather trousers, his boots unscuffed and tied just under his knees. A man of wealth, no question. A man of authority and knowledge.

A warrior.

They stood in the center of a courtyard, lovely plants and flowers thriving all around them. The air was sweet, the ground beneath their feet a lush, springy emerald. Smooth marble walls enclosed the entire area, yet there was no ceiling, allowing morning sunlight to pour inside and reflect off the veins of gold. And just above them, balconies opened up from each of the royal bedrooms, welcoming spectators.

A young dark-haired boy was perched on the ledge of the balcony to Nicolai's right, watching while twirling a dagger. He wanted to puff up his chest and pound. He was about to be all kinds of impressive for his younger brother. He could toss with deadly accuracy, stab with lethal force and, when he concentrated, wield two swords at once.

"Nicolai," the man in front of him said, impatient. "Are you paying attention to me?"

"Of course not. Otherwise, I would have heard what you said, and you wouldn't be about to repeat yourself."

Dayn chuckled.

Father was not amused, and did not reward Nicolai for his honesty. "I have meetings to attend, son. Meetings in another kingdom, which means *you* will be in charge while I'm gone. I need to know you can defend yourself and those you love. Pay attention. Now."

"Yes, sir." He focused on the happenings before him, weighing the metal in his hands. "Why must we practice over and over again? I'm good."

"You're good, but you need to be great. Last time I managed to stab you in the back so badly you scarred!" There was hard admonishment in his father's voice. "You must learn to work with all weapons, at all times of the day and night. You must work with one hand, both hands, standing, sitting and injured. *Without* becoming distracted."

Nicolai raised his chin. "Why can't I just kill my opponents with my fangs and be done with it?" He'd done so before. Many times. Until his mother's prediction had come true, and he'd destroyed an entire village simply to punish a man for beating his wife.

He'd at last taken control of his emotions and hadn't lost his temper since. That didn't mean his fangs were useless, though.

"And if your fangs have been pried out of your mouth?" his father demanded.

"No one would ever be foolish enough to remove my fangs. Mother says I'm the most powerful vampire in the world. I can walk in the light, and I can steal power from anyone I choose."

"No, she says you *will be*." His father's expression hardened. "You are a prince, Nicolai. The *crown prince*. Many in this world and the other will covet your direct line to my throne. Many will try and hurt you simply to hurt me. You must know how to defend yourself, always, for every situation."

Nicolai gave the sword another once-over. Long, thin and polished to a vibrant shine. He was not used to its heaviness, or the thickness of the hilt. "Very well. I will train some more, but why are you not teaching Dayn?"

"So many questions." His father sighed.

"Why must he watch? He's a prince, too, you know." And so very eager to learn. Each day, after Nicolai's lessons, Dayn begged to be taught. Nicolai could never resist him.

He loved his brother, and would die for him. A boy most in the palace feared. Dayn had an affinity with the animals that roamed the grounds, preferring to run with them rather than to walk alongside his own people.

Nicolai understood his brother's need. Sometimes he, too, felt animalistic in nature, most especially when his temper used to overtake him, shattering his control and leaving only a need to destroy, to hurt others

"His time will come," the king said. "Soon."

"But not the new princess, right? She'll always be too delicate." He sneered the last.

"Breena is newly born, and she is not a blood drinker like you and Dayn. She is a witch like her mother. You and Dayn must always protect her. In turn, she will heal your people after battle as your mother used to do."

Shame had Nicolai looking down at his dirty boots. He was the reason his mother could no longer heal the wounds of others. He hadn't meant to, but he had stolen her ability. She hadn't blamed him, hadn't even yelled at him.

He would do anything to return the ability to her. Yet, he could not. Once taken, he could not give back. Ever. He'd tried, over and over again. The only thing he could do, his mother had said, was learn how to control his newly discovered talent for absorbing the magic of others. And he had, remaining in his bedroom for weeks, reading, studying and practicing.

"Do you think I'll be a great leader, like you?" he asked.

"I think you and your questions will be the death of me, boy." The king held out his own sword, touching the metal against Nicolai's. "Let us begin."

Darkness.

Nicolai was panting now, sweating uncontrollably. Trembling. His hands ached. He looked at them. He must have clawed at his temples, trying to stop the pain from exploding through him, because his nail beds were bloody, his claws mere stumps.

His father had warned him.

His father. The king.

His name truly was Nicolai. Odette had not lied about that. She'd known who and what he was. They all had. *So highborn,* Laila had liked to say, and now he knew why. He was a prince. A crown prince, and one day, a king.

A brother to Breena. His sister. His beautiful baby sister with her golden curls. She'd grown into a lovely woman with a heart of fire, despite the fact that she was always protected, always guarded. Nicolai had snuck her out a few times, wanting her to have a taste of the freedom he took for granted. Where was she now?

Dayn, the brother closest to him, as dark and dangerous as the night, and just as beloved. Where was he?

His father, proud and strong. Honorable, determined. Unwilling to back away from any challenge. Where was he?

His mother, soft and gentle, so nurturing, even in the face of his most violent tempers. Where was she?

Micah, the youngest son, so full of life. Where was he?

Nicolai pulled himself into a crouch. Somehow, he had moved out of the forest. He was now in front of a lake. Not the lake he'd shared with Jane. This water was thick and red. Every few seconds, a hissing, snapping, flesh-colored fish would fly from the surface, arch in the air, then dive back in.

The rocks around him were dagger sharp. A hundred yards away, in the center of all that crimson, was a castle. Dark mold clung to the walls, more of those slithering plants crawling in every direction. There was a walkway, a line of monsters patrolling it.

They hadn't noticed him, but they would. He was out

in the open and needed to find shelter. Perhaps feed to strengthen himself. Then he needed to find Jane. She was out there, somewhere. If she was hurt…

She had better not be hurt. He must protect her at all cost. Yet, even as determined as he was, he only managed to crawl a few feet before the next memory hit him, welding him in place.

In this newest scene, he was a grown man, his dark hair shagging around his shoulders. He was bare chested and seated on a bank of rocks, much like the one he'd just seen. Only, the rocks were smooth, the water clear. He'd removed his boots before sitting down, and those were dry, waiting for him on the beach, but his pants were soaked through and caked in salt.

The moon was high, golden, the sky bright with scattered stars. They winked down at him, mocking him with their tranquility. His mind offered more chaos than he thought he could bear.

His father, King Aelfric, was sick.

The healers did not know if he would recover. Nicolai's mother, Queen Alvina, was frantic with worry. She'd tried countless spells and incantations, yet nothing she'd done had worked. *Nicolai* had tried countless spells, using the healing magic he'd stolen from her. Not even that elicited favorable results. Alvina suspected foul play, but until she figured out what kind of magic had been used, her hands were as good as tied.

Nicolai loved his father, gruff though the king was. Besides that, he wasn't ready to take the throne. He wasn't sure if he would ever be ready. Becoming king would mean his father was dead, and he wanted his father to live forever.

And, to be honest, despite Nicolai's best efforts,

despite a few years without a single episode, his temper sometimes got the better of him. When that happened, entire villages suffered. He was simply too volatile to rule an entire kingdom.

His father might be gruff, but he was fair. Fair, except when it came to Nicolai's marriage. Though his father had demanded, ranted, raved, Nicolai had refused to settle down. He wasn't ready to take a queen.

Being saddled with the same woman forever? That could become a hell as dark as the Abyss. He spent every night with a new female. Sometimes two new females. And once, three.

And all right, fine. Perhaps that lifestyle had grown tiresome. Perhaps the prize was never worthy of the chase. But some of his friends had married, and though a few were happy, the rest were miserable—and there was nothing they could do to change their fate. Marriage was forever.

His father wanted him to wed a princess from a neighboring kingdom, but he had not found one that appealed to him. Giving such creatures his name, sharing his kingdom, would grate every hour of every day.

"Nicki," a young voice called. "Nicki!"

Nicolai was on his feet a second later, hopping along the rocks and racing toward his youngest brother. The youngest prince was on the beach, beside Nicolai's boots, and unharmed. Relief speared him.

"Micah, damn it. What are you doing out here? Until you're older, you're not supposed to be near the water on your own."

The little boy screwed up his lips, all determination and courage. "I'm not on my own! You're here." A mischievous glint in his eyes.

"Damn it." Just like that, Nicolai's anger deflated. As always he could not stay angry with the scamp. Micah looked up to him, wanted to spend time with him, and Nicolai loved that. Loved *him*. Even though the boy had butchered his name while learning to speak, and his family sometimes still teased him with the nickname. "O-lie."

At least he had later moved on to "Nicki."

The females who made their way to Nicolai's bed often called him by the shortened Nicki, as well, but that invited a familiarity he never seemed to feel toward them, and after a quick admonishment, they never did it again.

He was almost afraid something was wrong with him. He loved his family with his whole heart, but no one else could penetrate the barrier he'd unwittingly constructed.

"Did you come to swim?" Micah asked when Nicolai reached him.

"No, to think."

"Can I help?" the boy asked eagerly. Golden hair gleamed in the moonlight. He smiled, two of his teeth missing. He was not a vampire, like Nicolai and Dayn, but he was powerful all the same. Though he had a warrior's heart, he took after their mother and sister in so many ways.

"Of course you can." Nicolai sat and patted the sand.

Micah plopped down beside him. For several seconds, they breathed in the moist, salt laden air, silent. Of course, Micah did not do this calmly. He shifted and he kicked out his legs, trying to get comfortable but never quite succeeding.

"Thinking makes me tired," Micah finally said. "Not like playing."

Nicolai bit back a smile. "What do you want to play?"

The image changed in a heartbeat, not giving way to a single moment of darkness. Nicolai was suddenly lying in the bed beside his father. Somehow, he knew a few days had passed since his night on the beach.

The king was recovering. Healers had drained him and Nicolai had fed him blood straight from his own vein. Every drop that he could spare, Nicolai had given—and even some that he couldn't. Finally, success. The poison had been vanquished, and now, the two men were recovering together.

"Pick a female and marry her," his father said. "If not one of the princesses, someone. Anyone. Please, Nicolai. I nearly died. Might still, though I feel stronger every hour. Please. You need an anchor, like your mother is to me. Someone to pull you back from the madness. *Please.*"

His father had never begged for anything. That he was now, over this…Nicolai did not have the heart to fight him any longer. He'd been pushing himself to this conclusion, anyway.

"As you wish, Father. It will be done. A princess from a neighboring kingdom, as you've already approved."

Tides of relief permeated the room. "Thank you. Thank you, my son."

Darkness, there again. Indomitable.

Nicolai heard a female scream, jolting him.

This time, when he came back to himself, he was crouched on a flat rock in the middle of the crimson lake. Closer to the moss-covered castle. The monsters had scented him, and were peering over at him through beady eyes. Their tails swayed, ready to strike at him if he dared move any closer.

The moon was still high, the hooked edges bleeding into a sky covered in a thick film of ash, hiding all the stars.

Those fiendish fish darted around him, teeth chomping at him, closer, closer. He was soaked with sweat, his heart a sledgehammer against his ribs, his muscles trembling. His mind, still lost. Aelfric. Alvina. Names.

Every member of his family now had a name.

Damn it, where were they? Did they still live? How long had he been away from them?

Quite a while, if this landscape was any indication.

He needed to search for them, but that scream… female… His female, he realized. Jane was screaming. *Jane!*

His blood burned in his veins, singeing, leaving blisters. Those blisters caught fire, tiny infernos that swiftly spread. With a growl, he pushed to his feet. His boots slipped on the slimy rock, but he managed to maintain his balance.

The monsters tensed. He should challenge them. Wipe the castle stones with their entrails. Yes… His heartbeat slowed, becoming a sporadic fist in his chest. No, he decided next. He would have revenge, would find his family—after. Jane needed him now.

His gaze skated over the violated water, the crumbling cliffs farther ashore, the hideous castle straight from a nightmare. He'd traveled here through his memories. Therefore, it stood to reason he could reach Jane through his memories, as well.

He closed his eyes, pictured her as he'd last seen her. Underneath him. Her naked body splayed for his pleasure.

Her expression was soft and heated, her teeth nibbling on her lush bottom lip. Her eyes were at half-mast, the long length of her lashes casting shadows over her flushing cheeks. That long, glorious mane of honey-colored hair was spread around her, the ends curling.

Her breasts were small but firm, her nipples pink and beaded. He'd kissed them, sucked them. Her stomach was flat, her navel a work of art. He'd licked, down... down. Between her legs was the sweetest patch of honey-colored curls, shielding his new favorite place in this world or any other.

Her legs were long and lean, and they wrapped around him just right.

Nicolai, he thought he heard her whisper.

He would have liked *her* to call him Nicki. Anything that promoted familiarity between them. He wanted her tied to him, in every possible way, forever. A forever that Jane might refuse to give him. If he had proposed to a neighboring princess—and he did not delude himself into thinking that princess was Odette, making his life simple—someone *was* waiting for him.

They had not wed, though. Marriage was forever to his people, and his body would react to no one save his wife. But. Yes, but. He would have pledged his name, his life. Easy to dismiss when he'd had no memory of agreeing to do so. Not so easy now, but that wouldn't stop him.

Nicolai did not want to be without Jane. He *wouldn't* be without her. He would find her and return to Elden. *She* would be his queen.

Elden. This decimated land truly was Elden.

The bloody lake was as much a part of his kingdom as the wasteland he'd first appeared in. His kingdom. *Not* the Blood Sorcerer's. A man Nicolai had dreamed of destroying. Would destroy.

Sickness churned in his stomach, because he knew what that meant. The Blood Sorcerer had slain his parents. Aelfric and Alvina would never have allowed their lands to wither like this.

Nicolai ached with the need to return the favor.

Don't think about that now. Find Jane.

He opened his eyes, realized he had transported himself back to the wasteland. Those slithering vines were closing in… He squeezed his lids shut, imagined Jane, felt his body disintegrate, the ground disappearing from beneath his feet. When next he looked, the lush forest of Delfina surrounded him. However, he did not see the camp or Jane.

He breathed deeply, catching her scent. He kicked into motion, running faster and faster, cutting the distance between them as rapidly as possible. All the while, he continued to picture her, the trees around them, until he blinked and at last found himself in the camp she had constructed.

Unable to slow his momentum, he smacked into a thick trunk and stumbled backward, into the water.

Another scream reverberated in his head, this one louder and far more desperate. His fangs lengthened, slicing into his bottom lip. His hands curled into fists, but his claws, not yet healed, merely tickled his skin. The daggers Jane had made lay at his feet. He strapped as many as he could to his arms and legs.

He started forward, his stride determined. Her scent

was stronger now…tinged with fear… Every step closer to her heated his blood with fury. She was marked, his, the path she'd taken suddenly a beacon in the night.

Anyone who had touched her would suffer. It was time the entire kingdom of Delfina—and all the kingdoms in this realm—realized that truth. Even if that meant unleashing the deadliest force of his temper.

I'm coming, little Jane.

Chapter 11

Moving the festivities to the king's bedroom, Jane thought, had been smart. In theory. But she hadn't known all the variables, or "monkey wrenches" as she'd called them, while working in her lab, which very often proved to be fatal while experimenting. The biggest monkey wrench this time around? In the throne room, she would have performed on the king of the monsters, and the king alone, while everyone else watched and probably cheered. In the "privacy" of his bedroom, he expected her to service him and friends. At the same time.

This was explained to her on the march down the hallway.

So, even though they'd switched locations, and even though his personal guards had remained behind with the hags to keep them company, there were now four men waiting for Jane to kick things off.

Not that she planned to put on a performance. She would rather die. And she just might.

The moment the newest giants spotted her, their eyes began to glow that dark, eerie red. Their bodies tensed, getting ready for the pleasure they expected to receive. Like Nicolai, they wore loincloths. Those loincloths were now tented.

The king pushed her forward, and she spun to keep her eyes on him. Already he was stripping. Leather crisscrossed over his chest, creating *X*'s—*so* not a treasure map—but a second later off came the criss-crosses, then the cloth. Daggers were strapped to his waist. Those he kept on. Dread and horror blended, rushing through her.

Okay, think, Parker. Think.

He pointed to the spot at his feet. "On knees. Use mouth on me. Hands on men. Orloft fuck you."

The guards licked their lips, every one of them. Okay. Okay. Options appeared and disappeared in an instant—and all of them were disappointing. She could do as ordered, and bite the king so hard he wouldn't be using his penis on anyone for a long time. If ever. He'd hit her and dislodge her teeth. A blow that would break her jaw, surely. After that, he'd be able to shove whatever he wanted into her mouth and she wouldn't be able to stop him.

She could run. There was no door to stop her. In fact, the entryways and exits were open and airy. But as good as that was for her, that was also good for the men. Four here, plus twenty or so in the throne area. They would give chase. Nothing would block them, and she would be caught. They knew this cavern better than she did, after all. She'd probably be gang banged.

She could fight the king and his personal guards, here and now. They would win, no question, but she would have tried. And she might die *before* actual penetration, so that was a plus. If Nicolai was out there, this might give him time to find her.

He was out there.

All right, then. She had a plan of action. Next up, finding a weapon.

The cavern boasted no luxuries. There was a pallet in the far corner. In the other corner was a pile of bones. Bones. Okay. Not the greatest weapons of all time, but beggars couldn't be choosers. She could use one as a club.

"Woman. Knees. Mouth. Pleasure. Now."

Jane tried the easiest approach: walking to the pile. Midway, the king jumped in her path. Very well. Easy way, out. She pretended to lunge left. He followed. She quickly switched and ran to his right. The four giants who'd been watching and waiting moved directly in front of the pile and crossed their arms over their chests. Okay, so. Hard way, out, too.

There was only one thing left to do. She widened her stance and prepared for an attack. "My answer is no."

The king frowned, glanced at his men with splayed arms, all *Women, so stupid, but what can we do?* before again pointing at his feet. "You. Knees. Now."

"I understand what you're saying." Moron. Some people drank at the fountain of knowledge. He must have gargled and spit. Then again, he might not have done even that. "That's why I'm telling you no."

He flashed his saber teeth at her. "But you said—"

"I lied. You're ugly and mean and I wouldn't give

myself to you even if a flesh eating bacteria was ravaging this world, and your cock held the only immunization."

Confusion followed by relief bathed his monstrous features. "Cock. You. Yes."

Of course that's the only word he cared about. *"No."*

His eyes narrowed to tiny slits, and she would not have been surprised to find a red bull's-eye in the center of her forehead. "I make you."

"That what I thought you'd say." She lifted her chin and waved her fingers. "You're very predictable, after all. So, let's cut the chitchat and do this."

Growling low in his throat, he advanced. He stretched out a hand to grab her, and she ducked, swung around and elbowed him in the stomach. He grunted, hunching over to gasp for air. The others laughed and snickered. Their merriment surprised her. She'd expected fury.

The king straightened before she could render another blow, found her with his gaze and advanced. Again, she ducked and swung; again, she elbowed him. Again, he hunched over, breathless.

This time, the guards clapped. They must think this was foreplay.

She raced behind the king before he could gain his bearings and kicked. He stumbled forward. She jumped up and, as she came down, elbowed the top of his head. He went down, face-first. The success of her moves thrilled and strengthened her, pumping adrenaline through her system. One more blow to the king for good measure, and she'd turn her attention to the guards.

Except, as she thrust out her leg to kick him in the stomach, he rolled and latched on to her ankle. With only a tug, he sent her crashing to her ass. Oxygen exploded from her lungs. Black and white winked before her eyes, little spiderwebs and starbursts.

Before she had time to act, the king swung out his meaty fist. *Contact.* Her poor cheekbone cracked. Skin split. Her brain rattled against her skull, and the black in her vision completely overpowered the white.

Just like that, her advantage was lost. Not that she'd ever really had one.

Crawl away. Curl into a protective ball. Something!

Too late. Another punch landed, this one on her jaw. For an endless span, pain and dizziness and nausea became her only companions. Then the spiderweb of black expanded, closing in. *Don't you dare pass out!*

Another punch.

So. Much. Pain. *Okay, you can pass out now.*

Of course, that's when the darkness thinned against another blast of adrenaline, sharpening her wits. Jane wanted to scream for help, but knew no one here would do anything to help her. Only hurt her further. Plus, physically, she *couldn't* scream. As she'd feared, her jaw was broken.

Another punch.

More pain. No, *pain* wasn't an adequate word for what she experienced. Agony, perhaps, but even that seemed too tame a descriptor.

Hard fingers wrapped around her biceps and shook her, causing the agony to radiate through the rest of her. "Look at me."

She blinked opened her eyes. Or eye. One of them was already sealed shut, the upper and lower lid glued together, concealing what felt like a golf ball. She lay on her back, and the king loomed over her. The moment he realized she was awake, he began ripping at her robe.

He liked to fight his conquests, then. Well, she would give him one to remember. She gritted her teeth against a new onslaught of suffering and kicked him in the face. The action was unexpected, and he stumbled backward before at last hitting the floor. Somehow, she managed to pull herself into a sitting position. The starbursts returned, pushing a moan out of her.

"Hold her," the king said with an evil grin. He rubbed at his erection. His bare erection. He'd already removed his loincloth.

Eager to please—as well as get their hands on her, she was sure—the men jumped to obey. In a blink, she was flat on her back, her hands anchored over her head and her legs pinned and spread.

Just. Like. That.

In another blink, her breasts were being squeezed and her nipples pinched. And all four giants were staring between her thighs, waiting for her femininity to be revealed.

"No," she snapped, but the word was intelligible. "No!" Was this what Nicolai had endured?

They laughed. The king fisted the tattered hem of her robe. The rest of the fabric ripped.

Beyond the cavern, a scream echoed. Her attackers paused, frowned, looked at one another. Another scream echoed, followed by another. And another. Each was pain filled and panicked. Were the beasts fighting among themselves, perhaps over the hags, or had Nicolai arrived?

Hope bloomed within her.

The king shrugged, his attention returning to her

body. She wore only her panties now, and they already were ripped in the crotch and therefore useless as far as barriers went. He licked his lips as he stroked his cock once, twice, preparing to penetrate her.

"Big," he said, practically patting himself on the back. In this, he was right. His penis was thick, too thick, and as long as a battering ram. She would be torn apart.

Her hope withered, died. Tears blurred her good eye, and she whimpered, the sound as broken as her jaw. Any second now, and...

A snarl reverberated, deep and ominous. Closer now, so close.

Neither the guards nor the king looked away from her to check who had uttered the enraged warning. But suddenly Jane knew, sensed. Nicolai *was* here.

"You're gonna die real bad," she said flatly. Again, her injuries made the words incomprehensible, but she didn't care. Saying them offered a small measure of satisfaction.

"Never die." Still grinning, the king fell to his knees. The guards leaned closer, their hands inching up her arms and legs. Then, as the king guided his cock toward her, something swiped out faster than her eye could track. Blood sprayed. The king roared in pain and shock.

That same something—a real dagger Nicolai must have stolen from the ogres—swiped at the guards, hitting two at a time. More blood, more roars. The men fell away from her, and finally she was free. She lay there, panting, shaking. Then gentle arms were slipping under her and lifting her. She was carted to the pallet and laid down. Fingertips tenderly brushed her swollen cheek. Nicolai's face came into view. He was covered in blood, every part of him soaked with crimson.

Flames leaped and cracked within his eyes. "Rape?"

She gave a slight shake of her head.

Those flames died, leaving something far worse: cold, merciless rage. Then he was gone.

He attacked the guards first, those who had maneuvered back to their feet, ripping their tracheas out with his teeth and spitting them to the floor. But that wasn't enough for him, and he used the dagger to remove their heads from their bodies. Bodies he piled in the entry, effectively locking the king inside the room with him.

The two men circled each other.

"Suffer," Nicolai said, the length and sharpness of his fangs causing him to slur the words.

"Yes. You suffer."

"She's mine. Mine! You will die for touching what's mine."

The king blinked, his head tilting to the side. "You familiar. You vampire. You…prince?" A gasp of horror accompanied the realization. "Yes. You prince. Dark prince. Majesty, I beg sorry. I thought you dead. We all thought you dead."

Nicolai, the slave, was a prince?

The king dropped to one knee, a show of submission. "I give my sorries. So many sorries. Majesty. No offense. Take woman. She is yours."

Nothing Jane had done had humbled the king. Nothing had evoked fear in him. Now, at the thought of battling royalty, he was on his knees, pleading.

"You die," Nicolai said simply. The king never stood a chance. Her man removed his limbs, one by one. And though the king screamed and screamed and screamed, he didn't once struggle. As if he knew struggling would earn him an even worse fate.

Next to go, his eyes. After that, his groin. At that point, his screams became pleas for mercy. Mercy Nicolai did not have. Oops, there went the king's tongue. No more begging or screaming. Just whimpering.

"Nicolai," Jane finally managed, her voice so weak even she had trouble hearing what she'd said. Fatigue was riding her hard, and she knew she wouldn't be awake much longer.

Nicolai glanced at her, barely able to catch his breath. The need to hurt clung to him like a second skin, visible to all. Never had she seen a more primitive male, wild and uncontrollable, a Pict warrior straight from battle. A sight most people would only ever see in their nightmares.

"Need you," she said.

"Yes." He swung back to the dying king. With a quick flick of his wrist, he removed the man's head, just as he'd done to the others. Then he was poised over Jane, stroking her gently. "I'm so sorry, sweetheart. So sorry."

"Will be…fine. Been…worse. Just need…you."

The words were meant to comfort him. They failed. Absolute anguish cloaked his features. He wiped his arm on a nearby cloth, bit into his own wrist and held the bleeding wound to her mouth. "Drink."

While Nicolai chanted words she did not understand, the warm liquid cascaded down her throat. At first, she experienced the most delicious tingling, starting in her stomach and moving through her veins. To her jaw, her arms, her legs. The tingling soon sharpened, heated, and she felt as if little molten daggers were slicing through her.

What the hell was his blood doing to her?

"Nicolai," she screeched. "Hurts."

"You're healing, sweetheart. I'm sorry. I'm sorry. The hurt is good."

Even as he spoke, her jaw snapped back into place. She screamed, the shrill sound echoing off the cave walls. The lid of her swollen eye split apart, and she groaned. At first, her vision was hazy, as if her corneas had been smeared with Vaseline, but as the heat and the daggers continued to work through her, Windex was sprayed and she could see again. Perfectly.

When the healing process was complete, she lay there, still panting, sweating and trembling, but a woman reborn. She stretched her jaw, and while there was a lingering ache, she could move it unfettered.

"Thank you," she said, tears of relief filling her eyes.

Nicolai sprawled beside her and gathered her in his arms. He held her for a long while before the dam inside her broke and she sobbed against his chest, clutching him tightly to her. All of her book smarts, and she'd been helpless.

"I killed them, sweetheart. I killed them all. They'll never hurt you again. This I swear to you."

The evil of the king stunned her. The complete disregard for her will, the violence he had unleashed... Oh, she'd known there were people capable of such dark deeds, but never before had those deeds been brought to her door. It was frightening and heartbreaking to have seen the evidence firsthand.

"That's the way. Let it out. I've got you," he said soothingly.

"I was so scared."

"Never again. *Never again,*" he vowed. "Unless... were you afraid of me?"

She shook her head.

"Good, that's good. I would never hurt you. Even lost in a temper, I couldn't hurt you."

Soon her tears dried. The physical damage, as well as the pain of the healing, had taken their toll, and she sagged against him, sighing and shuddering. "What were you chanting when you gave me your blood?"

"More of my vampire magic. I cast a healing spell to aid the powers of my blood."

She sniffled, her nose stuffy. "It was better than Vicodin."

"Vicodin?"

"A painkiller from my world."

"A killer of pain. Did you love him?" The words were growled.

A burst of unexpected humor gave her strength. "No. In fact, he was hard to shake. He, uh, stalked me, that kind of thing. I had to pretend he didn't exist."

Nicolai kissed her temple and relaxed against her. "Shall I hunt and destroy him for you, sweetheart? It would be my pleasure, believe me."

"You have enough enemies. Besides, I destroyed him a while back."

Another kiss. "Because you are strong."

Lovely praise, but she was completely undeserving of it and couldn't pretend otherwise. "I wasn't strong enough to save myself today." The tears returned. She brushed them away with a shaky hand. "I took self-defense lessons for a while, but they didn't help. Not really. He would have...he was going to..."

"Never again," Nicolai repeated, tightening his hold. "I will train you further. And when I'm done with you, not even *I* will be able to defeat you."

"Really?"

"Oh, yes. Your safety is a personal mission of mine. A mission I will not fail."

Maybe the turmoil of the day had made her emotional, but she got teary eyed all over again. That was the sweetest thing a guy had ever said to her. Even better than what he'd said to Laila. "Enough about me. I was afraid the giants had killed *you*."

"I doubt even death would have kept me away from you."

Okay. She was wrong. *That* was the sweetest. She kissed the pulse at the base of his neck. "What—what were those things?"

"Ogres."

A yawn snuck up on her, her eyelids dipping heavily. "The king seemed to know you."

He stiffened. "Yes."

And he didn't want to discuss it. She changed the subject, suddenly too tired to reason out why or press for answers. "You found me because you'd marked me, right?"

"Yes," he said again. He traced his fingertips along her spine. "And I have never been gladder for something."

"Have you marked other women?" Oh, God. She shouldn't have asked. She wasn't ready for the answer. Not here, not like this. Not after what had happened. He clearly did not have to be wed or engaged to mark a woman, so there could be a *thousand* out there. She should have….

"Not to my knowledge," he said cautiously.

She sighed with relief. She would be willing to bet "marking" was more than a memory, that marking was an instinct, biology at its finest, a knowledge that went bone deep. After all, dogs did it. Of course, they peed on what they wanted, leaving their scent behind. And they didn't need to remember doing it; they simply needed to smell and catch a hint of the desired aroma.

Nicolai had not honed in on any other woman. As easily as he'd found Jane, he would have found any others, without difficulty. *If* they were out there. So, logically, she had to believe she was the only one.

Yes, logically. He was free.

Maybe you're the one who's as dumb as a box of rocks. A good scientist studies both sides of the coin. Fine. She'd argue in favor of the other side. Nicolai could very well be engaged, as he'd feared, as she'd tried to deny. And maybe he hadn't marked the woman yet, wanting to wait for the actual ceremony to complete the connection.

Or, like the ogres, he could have had a harem of women. Perhaps one woman had not satisfied him for long, so he'd plowed through them like he had a cold and they were tissues. Perhaps there'd been too many to mark. Or perhaps he'd simply never cared enough to do it.

That certainly fit the image of a pampered prince. *Was* he a prince, though? *Had* he been pampered? A man given everything he wanted, never really satisfied?

Sometimes she hated her brain. And coin flipping.

The man she knew was volatile and possessive. He didn't play nice with others, and he didn't know how to share. Yet he was as far from pampered as a man could be. *And he's mine,* she thought, burrowing her head deeper into the hard line of his body. His strong, warm body.

He knew her, and wasn't bothered by her verbal and mental tangents. He'd cared enough about her to come back for her—twice—saving her life. That had to count for something.

"Stop thinking and sleep, Jane," he said.

"All right." Nothing would happen to her while they were together. She knew it. He would guard her with his life. "Hold me and don't let go."

"Always," he vowed.

Oh, yes. He cared. She drifted off to sleep with a smile.

Chapter 12

When Jane awoke, she was still in the cave. She wasn't sure how much time had passed. All she knew was that she'd never felt so rested. She stretched like a contented kitten, warm despite her nakedness, her muscles liquid, and gazed around.

Startled by what she saw, she sat up. Enough time had passed for Nicolai to clean every speck of blood from the floor and walls. He'd also removed the bodies and subsequent body parts. If not for the lingering taint of evil, this could have been some kind of underground resort.

There was no reason for Nicolai to have done such a thing. They weren't going to live here. Weren't even going to spend the day. Unless he'd hoped to spare her any upset. Her eyes widened. That was exactly why he'd done it, she realized. The sweet, darling man.

Hello again, emotional roller coaster. She sniffled, her chin trembling.

"Don't cry, sweetheart. Please don't cry." He was perched beside her, looking away from her, and holding out a bundle of wrinkled material. And God, his profile was gorgeous. Still streaked with blood, though some had been washed away, his cheeks were sharp, his lips lush and his expression relaxed. No ill effects from the fighting. "It kills me inside."

After everything he'd done for her, she would do anything he asked. Besides, despite his relaxed expression, lines of tension branched from his eyes, as if permanently etched there. Something more *was* bothering him, and she wouldn't add to his troubles.

"I won't." She used the hem of the offered fabric to clean her face.

The corners of his mouth twitched, his inner worries momentarily forgotten. What did he find so humorous? "Did you sleep well?" he asked.

"Yes, thank you."

"Good. Now. Will you dress for me?" A question layered with apprehension.

She thought she knew why. Her nakedness aroused him—or at least, she hoped it did—but he didn't want to do anything about it. Not after what had happened here. She was grateful.

She knew the old adage "replace the bad with the good." She also knew there was nothing better than Nicolai's touch. He could play her like a piano, stroking all the right keys and creating a symphony. But she didn't want their first time to spring from any need but the one to be together.

"Jane?" he prompted.

Dress. Right. "With what?" Her robe was ruined beyond repair.

"Your tissue."

"Oh." She chewed on her bottom lip as she studied the "tissue." A faded yellow cotton robe, clean, and free of rips. Perfect. "Where did you get this?"

He motioned behind him with a tilt of his head. "The only other females here were so grateful to be free of their ogre masters, they stayed long enough to help me clean this room and offered you all of their possessions."

"That was thoughtful of them."

"They also offered me the use of their bodies."

"I will wipe the floor with their blood!" She jerked the robe over her head.

When Nicolai came back into view, she saw that he was grinning. That grin…decadent and shameless. Her blood heated. Blood that belonged to him, had once been a part of him.

"I sent them on their way," he said. "*Without* accepting."

"Like I care what you do," she groused. This conversation, on the heels of her harem worries, brought out the fires of *her* temper.

That wiped away his amusement completely. "You had better care."

She sighed. Honesty was needed if they were going to have any kind of relationship. And she wanted a relationship with him, however long they had left together. A day, a week, a month? Or would she remain here forever?

She wouldn't worry about that now.

"Fine," she said on a sigh. "I care." Her stomach growled from hunger, and in the quiet of the cave, the sound echoed loudly. She blushed. "Do you?"

"More than I can say."

"I just…don't want you to be hurt if I leave."

"You won't leave. Now, come." He stood and waved his fingers. "I'll feed you."

He cared! And how could he be so certain she would remain? "What time is it?" she asked, accepting his aid with a tender smile. A smile that quickly fled. Her bones creaked and ached as she straightened.

"Close to midnight."

Back home, she would have been in her bed right now, tossing and turning and dreading the coming morning.

They made their way back to the river. Limping at first, but muscles relaxing with the exercise, she gathered mint leaves and twigs, and they brushed their teeth as they walked. Afterward, Nicolai foraged for fruits and nuts to tide her over. As she nibbled, she kind of expected creatures from childhood storybooks to jump out and grab her, or Laila to scream a curse and appear, but no. The thirty-minute journey was incident free.

Nicolai stepped into the water, dipped all the way in, came up wet and sputtering and motioned for her to do the same. "Bathe, and I'll gather the fish you scare away."

"Ha, ha. Shows what you know. Fish adore me. Don't be surprised if they dance at my feet."

"Are you trying to make me kill the fish in a jealous rage so you can have more to eat?" he teased.

"Maybe." More than gorgeous, he was sexy. Amused, playful, all that wet dark hair plastered to his scalp and dripping down his face, crystalline droplets scorching a path down his mouthwatering pectorals, the ropes of his stomach—and, sweet heaven, there were a lot of ropes—and finally catching in the waist of his loin-cloth.

Without the taint of the cave, there was nothing to dilute her need. Jane hungered for her man more than anything else.

You've gotta clean up if you want to get dirty with him.

"Prepare to be awed," he said, giving her his back.

I already am. She removed her new robe and jumped into the water—such cool, refreshing water—before he could turn and see her beaded nipples. She scrubbed up until her skin tingled. Well, tingled from more than desire.

All the while, she snuck secret glances at Nicolai. He caught several fish and tossed them ashore. As time ticked by, he became more and more apprehensive, his motions clipped. And he was utterly oblivious to her stare. Not once did he glance back at her.

Moonlight spotlighted him, golden and magical. He was so strong, so capable. She chewed her bottom lip as she treaded water. The water might be cool, but the liquid between her legs was warm.

Perhaps she should have been scared or experienced post-traumatic stress symptoms. Flashbacks at the very least. After all, she'd nearly been raped and *had* been beaten. But this was Nicolai. Her protector. Not even bad memories would dare attack her while he was nearby.

"Nicolai," she said, a husky note in her voice. She hadn't meant to call him, but his name had emerged unbidden, unstoppable.

Finally he turned to her. Her breath caught. His eyes were brighter than she'd ever seen them, the gold flecks out to play, mingling seductively with the silver. His cheeks were flushed, his fangs long and sharp.

"Awed yet?" he demanded.

"Yes." Oh, yes. Was that why he was so distressed and distant? She hadn't properly praised his skills? "You're the best fisherman I've ever met. Granted, you're the only one I've ever met, but…"

No hint of a smile. "I'll feed you," he said, adding darkly, "After."

"After?"

"I smell your desire for me, little Jane, and I gave you time to grow used to the idea of being with me. Time is up. Come here." He crooked his finger. "I want you."

After wasn't such a bad word anymore. "About time." She didn't hesitate. She swam the distance, the water caressing her skin. When she was only a whisper away, she let her feet drop to the bottom and stood. The waterline reached just under her breasts.

"I'm going to have you," he said fiercely.

"Yes."

"All of you."

"Yes." Please.

He stepped closer. Every time they inhaled, their chests rubbed together, creating the most dizzying friction.

"Nothing will stop me," he said.

"Not even thoughts of another woman waiting for you?" She hated herself the moment the words left her, but she was still glad they had. Another woman was the reason he had resisted her before.

Shadows couched his features, turning him into the warrior of the night before. "There…is. A woman. Most likely."

Oh, God. "Who?" A plug was lifted, and the desire drained from her, leaving her cold, hollow. "Do you… did you love her?"

"No. My father arranged the marriage. I do not remember my intended's face or her name, or even my proposal. I know only that I promised my father I would wed her."

Don't cry. Don't you dare cry. At least his heart did not belong to someone else. That should help.

That didn't help. She wanted all of him. For herself.

"You're remembering?" she croaked.

"Not everything, only bits and pieces at a time. I tell you this, not to upset you, Jane, but to warn you. No matter what happens, I'm keeping you. You are mine. That will not change."

No matter what happens—as in, if he had to marry another woman. "No."

The possibility of his involvement with another had been so easy to dismiss before. And she could very easily dismiss it now, when it was a reality. *If* he had decided to end the engagement.

She wouldn't be the other woman. She wouldn't! She had too much pride. Didn't she? Oh, God. The fact that she'd even asked meant she already wanted to consider the option.

No. No, no, no. Her parents had loved each other, respected each other, and that's what she wanted for herself. A deep, abiding love that placed her first. She didn't want to spend her nights wondering if her man was in bed with his wife, giving her pleasure and babies. She didn't want to find herself regulated to the fringes of his life. She didn't want to be the one everyone blamed for their troubles.

She deserved better.

When she returned home and thought back on her time here—she knew she couldn't stay now, because somehow, some way, she would find a path home—this was the night that would haunt her. Not those pain filled hours with the ogres. Not even the humiliation of her whipping. *This* hurt the most.

She backed away from him. Not allowing the retreat, he reached out and gripped her shoulders, tugging her back to him. Closer this time, until not even a whisper separated them. They were flush against each other, his erection smashed against her belly.

"I know what you're thinking, Jane."

"What, you're a mind reader as well as an engaged man?" She threw the words like weapons, needing to lash out even in the smallest way.

"No, but I know you. You are not leaving me." The command didn't come from the tender savior who had held her while she'd slept, but from the dangerous predator who had removed a man's limbs just to hear him scream. "I told you these things, not to worry you, but to reassure you. Betrothals can be broken. And mine will be. I will have you, and no other."

"I—I—" Was that a declaration? A proposal? Her emotions ran the gamut, and her mind didn't know whether to release the despair and accept the sudden tide of joy, or wallow in both. "I know you said I wouldn't, but what if I do, in fact, leave your world? You would…" Die. She shouldn't know that, couldn't yet admit that she did, but then, he hadn't asked her to forever mate with him, had he?

If he did, mating could very well tie her to this world

forever. Her eyes widened. Was *that* how he knew she would stay?

"You will not leave," he said. "I will make sure of it, whatever I have to do. Now, we finish this, Jane. Here. Now." He didn't wait for her reply, but swooped down, thrusting his tongue deep inside her mouth.

Joy won.

She couldn't help herself. She welcomed him. He still tasted of mint, warm, wet mint, and she couldn't get enough. And when he tilted her head, taking more, sampling deeper, her nerve endings erupted with sensation. This was what a kiss was meant to be, a possession, a claiming. An awakening of every sense.

Her hands wound around his neck, her fingers sinking into his hair. Later. She'd ask him what he'd meant by "whatever I have to do" later. Right now, she had the most important fact. He wasn't pledging himself to someone else. Here, now, she would enjoy him.

They stood like that, kissing and rubbing against each other forever. And every second of that forever ramped up her desire, until she was trembling, needy, aching with a fever only he could assuage.

"Wrap your legs around me," he commanded harshly.

"Yes." Even the thought left her reeling. She jumped up and did as commanded, expecting him to possess her in the next instant. He didn't enter her, though. No, he carried her to the shore, his hard length sliding against her. She moaned as he laid her down and stretched out on top of her. Still he didn't enter her.

"Don't stop," she breathed.

"I won't." He placed his hands beside her temples, removed his loincloth and anchored his weight.

"So lovely, my female."

"Prove it. Prove that I'm yours."

His lips peeled back from his fangs. "When I'm done, you might regret such a request."

"Promises, promises."

Once again, he defied her expectations. He didn't go in for the kill, didn't deliver instant relief to her raging desires. Instead, he spent the next few minutes kneading her breasts and laving her nipples, his fingers tracing erotic patterns on her stomach, but he never quite reached where she needed him most.

When he began kissing the same white-hot path his fingers had taken, her legs fell open, a silent plea for contact.

He didn't give it to her.

He licked her inner thighs, between her damp lips, even speared her core with his tongue, sinking inside for the briefest of seconds, teasing her with what could be, but he was always careful to bypass her clit.

She needed to come, damn it.

"Nicolai. Stop teasing."

Warm breath trekked over her. "Who do you belong to, Jane?"

Well, well. Now she knew his game. Work her over, tease her with what he could give her, until she gave him what he wanted—what she'd demanded of him. Ownership.

"Look at me," she said.

He rested his chin on her pubic bone. His lashes lifted, and his gaze met hers. Tension strained his features. He wanted to come as badly as she did. "Yes?" he said.

Who would break first? "My turn."

She flattened her feet on his shoulders and pushed.

A second later, he was the one flat on his back and she was looming over him.

"What are you doing, Jane?"

"Having my turn." She laved her tongue over his nipples, loving how they speared her tongue. "If I do anything you don't like, just say stop."

"I'll like." His hands tangled in her hair. His claws must have regrown, because she could feel them biting into her scalp, and she loved it. "Anything you do, I'll like."

"Well, then, let's see what you like most." She licked her way to his navel and dipped inside. His muscles quivered with anticipation. Her breasts cradled his erection, and she rubbed up and down, up and down, fueling his passion. Soon the tip of him grew moist, allowing a smoother glide.

She wanted him out of control. Mindless. Desperate. Exactly as she was when she was with him. She may not have very much experience, but she wouldn't let that stop or intimidate her, she decided. She would learn his body, his every secret desire.

"Jane," he rasped.

"Yes, Nicolai."

"I need… I want…"

"Me to taste you?"

"Oh, gods, Jane." His voice was a croak. "Yes. Please."

She crouched between his legs and peered down at his cock. He was so long, so thick and hard. Down, down she leaned…but she didn't gobble up that delicious length. Not yet. She lavished attention on his testicles, teasing him as he had teased her, until his hips were lifting in supplication.

"Please," he said again.

"Who do you belong to?" she asked as he'd asked her.

He didn't even try to hold out. "You. Jane."

The admission affected her as strongly as a caress, and she shivered. "I'm going to make you so happy you said that." She fit her lips around the head of his penis. His flavor hit her taste buds, and she groaned in eagerness. More, she wanted more. She slid her mouth all the way down, until he reached the back of her throat.

A hoarse cry left him. Up she glided, lightly scraping him with her teeth. Another cry. She hovered there, unmoving, tormenting. Waiting.

"Jane, I like this most."

Down she slid; up she glided, repeating the process over and over, slowly at first, then increasing her speed. Soon he could no longer speak, could only moan and groan as she had. Having him like this, at her mercy, his desire for her consuming him, directing all of his thoughts and actions, was a powerful aphrodisiac to her.

Just as his testicles tightened, signaling the start of his climax, she stilled, clamping her lips on the base of his cock, preventing him from going further. A little trick she'd read about but never tried. His roar of need blasted through the forest.

"Jane," he panted. "Jane, please."

He was trembling, moist with perspiration, but he didn't come. And when the danger passed, she crawled up his body, trembling just as violently. His fangs were so long they'd cut into his lip, leaving trails of blood down his chin.

"Why didn't you…"

"I want you inside me." Her blood was molten in her veins, causing sweat to bead on her brow.

"*Need* to be inside you, but not yet, not yet." His hands returned to her hair, his fingers pulling at the strands. "Must control urge to bite you first."

"Don't control the urge." She leaned down and flicked her tongue against one of his fangs, quickly cutting the soft tissue. "Give in to it. I'm fine."

He groaned as if in pain. "Delicious."

"More?"

The world suddenly spun. He'd tossed her on her back, and was looming over her. "More," he slurred, his gaze locked on her hammering pulse. "No, can't. Not yet, not yet," he repeated. "Baby."

"Yes?" Why *not yet?* Maybe she was greedy. Maybe she was selfish. She wanted now, now, *now.*

He chuckled, a broken sound. "No. Baby. I could give you a baby. Do you want a baby?"

Understanding dawned. Sadness and fear suddenly swamped her, dulling some of her desire. "I can't have children." Would he think less of her? No longer want her?

The woman his father had picked could probably have children.

Oh, ouch.

Jane had thought she'd come to terms with her lack. But now…the thought of starting a family with Nicolai… She wanted that, she realized. Not now, but later. When they were safe. To be with him, to have his child growing inside her… She would never know that joy.

The lack was another reason she'd dumped Spencer when she had. Once, they'd talked about getting married and starting a family, and she'd known how badly he had wanted that. With her, he would never have it. So she'd let him go, knowing he would thank her one day, when he was wed to another woman, his kids running around and laughing in their home.

"After the accident, my body is ruined," she said, pushing the words past the lump in her throat. "So, you don't have to worry about getting me pregnant. Ever. And if you want to stop and never take this thing between us any further, I'll understand."

He peered down at her, a dark warrior whose ire had been pricked. "Jane?"

"Yes?"

"I want you no matter what. *Need* you. Never think otherwise." With that, he gripped her thighs, spread them and surged up, hitting her deep inside with that one powerful thrust.

She forgot her sadness as instant, necessary, all-consuming desire flooded her. He was so big he stretched her; she was so wet, her once-neglected body gave him only minimal resistance.

"Nicolai!" His name, oh, how she loved his name.

"I like this, too," he said. In and out he moved. "Changed my mind. Like this most."

Her mind clouded, her nerve endings razed to the point of pleasure-pain, and she screamed. She'd been so turned on, the slightest stroke would have sent her shooting off to the stars. But this…sweet heaven, this.

Oh, God, it was so good, and she was so lost, she never wanted to be found, wanted this forever… Nicolai, Nicolai, hers, always hers. She was babbling to herself, and she knew it, couldn't control it. Didn't want to control it. Just wanted more. Of him, of this.

"Shouldn't bite, must bite."

"Bite. *Please.* I'm yours, Nicolai. I'm yours."

He growled, and then his fangs were in her neck and she was climaxing, squeezing at him, clutching at him. Taking everything he had to give and demanding more. And he gave it to her.

He rode the waves of her satisfaction, thrusting inside her with a fervor that left her breathless. He was all around her, a part of her, the sole light in her world. Drinking, drinking, oh, yes, drinking. Soon she became dizzy, and little doubts peeked from the shadows of her mind, as if they'd been hiding all along, waiting for her defenses to crumble.

Maybe his words—*want you no matter what, need you*—were preorgasm talk, meant to lure her into bed and keep her from running. Maybe the cloud of desire had been leading him all along. Maybe he would later change his mind about wanting her.

Maybe, when this was over, he would let her go.

No. She fought back. *No.* This wasn't temporary. He wouldn't discard her. Even if he learned the truth about some of the things she'd done to his kind?

Cold, hard reality. Again, she fought back. Nothing would destroy this moment, not even that. Here, pleasure mattered. Only pleasure.

He hooked one of his arms under her knee and lifted, opening her wider, increasing the depths he reached. Instantly her body prepared for yet another climax, needing it just as desperately as the others, as if sex with him was a prerequisite for her survival. She should fear *that.* She needed him too intently, was no longer complete without him.

Hell, if she left, would she be the one to wither? Had

she mated him and just didn't know it? What did she know about the road to mating? Nothing really.

Nicolai took hold of her other leg and lifted, surging impossibly deeper, and she forgot even that. There was no part of her left untouched. She was Nicolai's woman, plain and simple, branded by him, a part of *him*. After this, she would never be the same, didn't want to be the same.

She sank her nails into his scalp and forced his head up. His teeth slid from her vein. "Nicolai…"

"I'm sorry." He eyed her, blood dripping from the corner of his mouth. "I didn't mean…did I take too much?" Agony wafted.

"No." He could have it all, every last drop. "Kiss me," she demanded.

"Yes." He met her halfway. Their lips pressed together, their tongues dueled. His flavor filled her, and this time it was mixed with hers. Together, every part of them together…intoxicating.

"Mine," she said.

"Yours."

Forever, she didn't let herself add, but, oh, did she want to. Later, they would talk. Yes, the dreaded conversation about feeling and intentions. About the future.

The kiss continued, spinning out of control, their teeth scraping together, as he slipped and slid within her. He released one of her legs to move his hand between their bodies, and pressed his thumb against her clitoris. Just like that, she exploded again, spasming around him.

He hissed out a breath, pushed deep once more, and came, every muscle he possessed clenching and unclenching. She'd never made love without a condom, and loved the feel of him jetting inside her.

When he stilled, she wrapped herself around him, holding him as close as possible. He collapsed on top of her, but quickly rolled to relieve the pressure of his muscled weight. They were both sweat soaked and feverish, trembling.

"My Jane," he said, so much satisfaction in his voice she couldn't fear the upcoming discussion.

She kissed his shoulder. "My Nicolai."

Forever.

She hoped.

"Don't leave…need to talk," she breathed, just before drifting off to sleep.

Chapter 13

Panting, sweating, sated in the most perfect way, Nicolai snuggled Jane in to his side. Her blood flowed through his veins like champagne, bubbling and fizzing, claiming every thought and beating back a painful realization he wasn't quite ready to face. He wanted to close his eyes and savor, but he had a few things to work out in his mind first.

She'd wanted to talk. About what? If she thought to push him away after what they'd shared… Well, that wasn't going to happen.

What they'd just done could not be called "sex."

Sex was an urge. Sex was something you could do with anyone. Sex could be consensual or forced, as he well knew. What they'd done was a mating. Primal, wild, necessary, and as essential as a beating heart.

He would have died if he'd been denied access to her body. He'd simply *had* to be inside her. Nothing could have stopped him. Not attack, not death, hell, not even her disappearance. If she had returned to her world, he would have found a way to follow her.

There was no resisting this woman, not for him, and he wasn't going to try anymore. Not in any way. His betrothed might be waiting for him, but so what. Like he'd told Jane, he would have her and no other.

She'd changed him.

When he'd first seen her, scented her, his hunger for her had bloomed. Perhaps he'd become obsessed. Because when he'd watched her being whipped, he'd forgotten his plan to save himself and had gone after her. Then, when he'd heard her scream, had realized the ogres were hurting her, his rage had been unequaled. Seeing her beaten face and body had made a mockery of the rage, however, and he'd become fully beast, his darker nature taking over.

All the times before, he'd only thought he had a temper.

The fighting had ended too early. He'd wanted to torture the king, wanted to keep him at the brink of death and agony for centuries. For Jane's sake, he'd finished the bastard off and gathered his woman close, just like this.

She had slept then, too, but he hadn't calmed. The need to brand her, to let the world know exactly who she belonged to, had been driving him as forcefully as the rage had. But he hadn't wanted to hurt her when he took her—and he'd known he would take her.

So he'd brought her here, intending to swim and pacify himself. He'd meant to feed her the fish, as well, but she'd watched him while he'd captured them, and he'd felt the rise of her desire.

He'd forgotten his good intentions. His hope to be careful.

Now he'd had her, had branded her, just as he'd wanted, needed, but he realized even that wasn't enough. Nothing would ever be enough with her. He would always want her. Always want more.

Were his parents alive, they would understand. He knew this to be true.

He'd loved them, and they had loved him. They would want him to be happy, and he could not be happy without Jane. His father had settled on a neighboring princess only because Nicolai had shown no preference.

Now, he had.

Jane could not have children, and that bothered her, but it did not bother him. He hadn't lied to her. He liked her just as she was. When Nicolai became king in his father's stead—the need lit, caught fire—he would be expected to have an heir. But he had three siblings well capable of seeing to that.

So. His new plan of action: secure Jane to his side, return to Elden, kill the Blood Sorcerer who had slain his parents and claim the throne. He didn't want to wait to discuss this. Urgency rode him. Instinct that drove him to settle things now.

"Jane…"

A moment passed.

"Jane. Sweetheart." Gently he shook her.

"Yes," she muttered groggily.

"We will talk now."

Her slight catch of breath was encouraging. "Really?"

"Yes, really. When you first came to me, you mentioned a book. Where is the book now?"

"Oh. *That's* what you want to talk about." She sounded disappointed. "I left it at the palace in Delfina. I don't think that matters, though. It was the right book, just newer. And blank."

He frowned. "When you read it, the story was about me?"

"Yes. About your enslavement. There was a pink bookmark in the middle, and that's the page that told about your imprisonment. Then, written by the same hand, was a note from you, commanding me to help you, to come to you. The rest of the pages were blank, though."

He'd wondered before if he'd written the thing and forgotten. For all he knew, the witches had cursed him to forget everything but what they did to him. Why had the ink disappeared when Jane had shown up in Delfina, though? Because she'd arrived before he'd actually written the book? But, if he'd commanded her to come here—commanded *her* specifically—he would have met her already. And she would have left him.

He tensed. He did *not* like that notion and he quickly discarded it. He hadn't said "come back to me." He'd said "come to me." So…magic might have shown her to him, and like the book, he'd forgotten.

Still, the fear that he could lose her took root and refused to leave him. "Do you want to stay here with me, Jane?" He geared for battle. A battle he would fight viciously to win. She had a life he knew nothing about, and were the situation reversed, were he stuck in her world, he would have to find a way to leave to avenge his family and home. And he would have stolen away with her, he thought.

Now she was the one to tense. "Okay, I could answer

your question with a question of my own. Do you want me to stay? But I won't. Because I shouldn't have to qualify my opinion. I'm not a coward." She licked her lips, as she did each time she felt desire for him, and he felt the hot slide of her tongue on his chest. "So. Here it is. Yes. I want to stay with you. That's what I wanted to talk to you about."

Thank the gods. He had worried for nothing. "I am glad." Inadequate words. "I want you to stay with me, too."

"Really? You're not just saying that?"

"Jane, when have I ever just said anything?"

"Well, men say stuff they don't mean to get women into bed. All the time."

Some did, yes, but he never had. He'd always been up front, offering a single night of his attention, his body, but nothing else, and no longer. That was it, the end. Although, to get Jane into his bed again, he'd do and say just about anything.

"I will always be honest with you. Always. As long as you desire me. Stop, and I will change my dealings with you."

She laughed, the sexiest purr he'd ever heard. "Thank you for the warning."

Having her near him was arousing. Feeling her lick him, more so. But that laugh…he was hard as a rock in seconds. "I want you with me, Jane. In bed and out."

A tremor drove through her, vibrating into him, relief replacing her humor. "I don't know what I would have done if you'd tried to take away my magic green card. And before you ask, that means get rid of me."

"Get rid of you? Sweetheart, I'm doing everything in my power to keep you."

"Really?" Another soft entreaty.

He would have rolled his eyes if he weren't so happy with her. "Really."

"Thank you. I mean it. Thank you."

"And now you thank me. I should be thanking you. And I do. Humbly. You have become the reason I live, Jane."

He thought he heard her sniffle. She buried her head in the hollow of his neck, rubbing her cheek against him. "So what's next?"

"I need to return to the kingdom of Elden. I think my siblings are there. Trapped, perhaps. I don't know. All I know is that, deep down, I am so hungry to slay the new king, I tremble. Like eating, this is a need. I *must* do it."

She didn't hesitate. "I'll help you."

He did not want her involved in such a violent, dangerous plan, but he did not want her out of his sight, either. "I need to find a way to keep you bound to me and to this land first. Should I write another book for you?" His magic was stronger now.

"If you do, we will be operating under the assumption that I'll return, no matter what we do or try."

"And perhaps such an assumption is what would send you back." Damn this! There had to be a way. "I wonder what spell I used to bring you here. If I knew, I would know if you would leave after a certain time, or after I am truly free. Or if I bound you to the land forever. I remember so many things, but not that, not yet, and I cannot risk another spell. It might interfere with the first."

She eased up, her hair tumbling over her bare shoulder, golden moonlight illuminating her. "When I first read the book and realized it wasn't a joke, I wondered how you could have known me when we'd never met."

"And you figured out the answer." His words were a statement, not a question. He'd known his woman was smart. She was the perfect combination of beauty and intelligence.

"Yes. I dreamed of you before I ever read the book. Saw you chained, but never spoke to you. Now I think they were visions rather than dreams."

"But why have visions of me *before* I used my magic?"

"Maybe part of me crossed into this world long ago. Some things are familiar to me, like the ghost trees and ogres. Maybe you saw me, too, and that's how your magic knew to focus on me."

"That makes sense, but I wonder how you crossed over."

She gulped. "I...I..."

He reached up to cup her cheek. "Don't fear, Jane. We will figure this out. You won't leave. I won't let you."

"There's something I should tell you. About me. My job. You might change your mind about me." She traced the tip of her finger along his sternum. "I said I wasn't a coward and that means full disclosure, even about this. The things I did, horrible things, to learn about your—"

"I told you before, Jane, that your job—" A pang exploded through his head, silencing him, reminding him of what had happened after he'd fought the ogres here in this very spot. The same spot he'd first drunk from Jane. Pain, then opening his eyes in a new location.

He grunted. What was…? Another pang, this one rattling his brain against his skull.

The cage holding his memories and abilities was crumbling, bit by bit.

"What's wrong?" Jane eased to her elbow and smoothed his hair from his brow, her expression soft and luminous with concern. "Are you sick?"

Her emotions were in turmoil, yet she cast aside her own concerns to nurture him. No wonder he'd fallen for her so quickly and so easily. "Drinking your blood empowers me as never before," he confessed, "but as more of my memories and abilities escape, I experience a…wee little pinch of sensation."

Even as he spoke, one of those "wee little pinches" migrated from his head to his chest, and he hissed a breath. That one had been stronger than any of the others.

"Oh, Nicolai. Now I know why you were reluctant to drink from me. I'm so sorry I made you."

"I'm not. And you didn't make me, Jane. I wanted to. Badly. Besides, that isn't why. Want you healthy."

A sound of frustration. "Now you're doing what you said you wouldn't, and weaving pretty words to make me happy."

Another pang, another grunt.

"What can I do? Besides never feed you again?"

"Stay with me. And you *will* feed me again." Every day for eternity. "This will pass."

"I'll stay," she whispered. "Don't worry. And, Nicolai, we've never talked about my job before."

"We haven't? You researched…experimented…" What kind and on who were answered inside his mind, but he was having trouble reaching the information.

The color drained from her face. "That's right. And you still like me?"

"Jane…"

"Yes, of course. We'll discuss it when you're better." A pause. Then a whispered, "Could we have talked in my visions? Could *I* have forgotten conversations? Could whatever magic was used on you bleed into me?" She was talking to herself, trying to reason things out.

"Yes," he replied, anyway. "There's a chance."

"Sorry, sorry. I'll be quiet. You rest."

Trusting her, he closed his eyes, breathed slowly, deeply, and simply let the memories come. The first to hit him was of a pretty maid quietly entering his bedroom. Hinges squeaked as his gaze sought her. He didn't know her name, only that he'd smiled at her earlier that day, and she'd taken that smile for the invitation it was. He was lying on his mattress of plush goose feathers, naked, waiting. She stripped as she approached him.

Just before she reached him, the door opened and closed again. He looked. Another maid. The three of them were going to play. Good. He hadn't looked forward to a night with only one, a single conquest too easy. Too…boring. He needed to try something new.

His mind shied away from that particular memory.

Once, he might have been looking for more than one partner at a time. Once, he might have wanted to try anything and everything. And that one, he still wanted. With Jane. He wanted to do everything with her, but only with her. Everything they did was a new experience. Exciting, and most of all, soul shattering.

That wasn't going to change. She affected him too deeply, too intensely. And she hadn't had much pleasure in her life, he didn't think. Every new touch from him had left her gasping, writhing, her expression one of wonder and need.

He wanted her to wear that expression forever. Would see to it, make it a personal mission of his.

And what she could do with her mouth...*that* was magic.

Darkness suddenly fell over his mind, reality becoming clear. He felt Jane's soft fingers, still smoothing over his brow. Her warm, sweet breath trekked over his cheeks. She had kept her promise. She was staying put.

He couldn't lose her, he thought. There had to be a way to keep her. Forever.

The book, Jane, her dreams of this world. His spell to bring her here. He focused on those things, hoping to spur the memories in that direction. Shifted glamor, the illusion of someone else's face masking her own, he knew that much. Also an incantation in the words he'd written? Yes...yes... He'd murmured a spell as he'd written in the book. He'd wanted Jane to be standing beside him—and then she was.

A memory played.

Don't do this to me. He heard her voice so clearly. *I will find a way to help you.*

She *had* spoken to him before their first meeting. Their first remembered meeting.

I must. I need you. Until your body joins your mind, you are useless to me. His reply. Cold, harsh.

But to take my memory, she'd said.

He had taken her recollection of their conversations?

Their voices faded, and his father's image filled his head. An important memory, but he needed to know about Jane right now. She was the most pressing. The book. Jane. The spell—spells—he'd used.

His father was speaking to him, but Nicolai couldn't hear the words. The book. Jane. The spells he'd used. *Come on. The book. Jane. The spells he'd used.* Gradually, the image shifted. The towering form of his father shrunk. Black hair grew, curling, lightening. Harsh features became soft, delicate. Jane's.

This was his past with Jane, the memory resurfacing. More than a whisper of conversation this time, more than a glimpse.

And there she was, his beautiful Jane, pacing in front of him. They were in his cell. He wore his loincloth and bruises. He lay on his pallet, watching her. From the moment she'd first appeared, untouchable, like a phantom, yet smelling of something wild and primal, he had wanted her.

Honey-colored hair streamed down her back, bouncing with every agitated step she took. She wore a long shirt that bagged on her, and he wished he could present her with silks and velvets.

"How are you tugging me here?" she asked. "Why can't you tug all of me?"

"I told you. Magic. And don't forget, *you* first came to *me* like this."

"As if I could forget. I closed my eyes and just…appeared. As if I'd been teleported, even though I never completed my teleportation research, never tested humans. And the plastic I sent over and back was solid and remained solid. I am not solid!"

"But you wake up at home, and you are always returned to your body."

"Yes." He didn't like that he couldn't touch her or

drink from her, but no matter how many times she appeared—and she had, countless—her condition remained the same. Insubstantial. So, they would talk and she would entertain him.

She'd become something to look forward to, his only enjoyment. And he knew she enjoyed their time together, as well. Knew she liked him. She'd confided in him about her work; he'd told her about his frustration and anger that his memories had been destroyed.

But they couldn't go on like this. He couldn't stay here. He couldn't remain a prisoner forever. There had to be a way to bring her here—all of her. Had to be a way she could aid his escape. A way they could be together physically.

"Tell me the last thing you remember before coming here that first time," he demanded.

"Nothing. I was sleeping! I just woke up, and poof, I was in the Delfina palace and headed straight for you."

"Before that, then. Think. Maybe something was done or said about my world. Years could have passed since it happened, but you would remember."

A heavy pause. "There is something." Though she was spectral, her footsteps seemed to pound into the floor. "Once, I interviewed a vampire at my lab. I asked him question after question, but he refused to answer. I stood to leave. Suddenly he spoke up. He told me to let him go, to let him find his female before it was too late. I couldn't. I didn't have the authority. The next day, I returned."

Urgency filled him. "And?"

"And my boss told me the vampire had screamed all night. I entered his room—he was quiet by then, but this time he spoke up instantly. He said one day I would meet a man, fall in love with him and lose him. Just as my lack of action had caused him to lose his female. Then he broke free of his restraints. I thought he would fly at me, but he merely lifted his hand and used his claw to slash his own throat. He died right in front of me."

Nicolai's stomach dropped. "He cursed you, then. A blood curse." Unbreakable—for the most part.

"That was two years ago, and I thought he was just spouting off. Trying to make me feel guilty for his incarceration!"

"No. He gave his life force to the words, breathing them into existence, lending them his heartbeat. The curse waited for the perfect time to strike."

"So I'm destined to only ever see you while in spirit form? No matter what we do?" She laughed bitterly. "If that's the case, no wonder you end up leaving me. I mean, we can't even touch each other!"

He scrubbed a hand down his face, his chains rattling. He couldn't answer her. Not without condemning them both. "What do you take pleasure in doing at home, Jane?"

"You want to discuss that now? Seriously?"

"Tell me."

She stopped, tossed up her arms. "I exercise and I read. That's all."

"Then I'll write you a book. I'll bespell the words. You will come to me in body, as well as spirit."

"Only to lose you later?"

He pursed his lips.

"I'll take that as a yes. Which means my answer is no. I don't want to come here, be with you, only to lose you forever."

"You can save me."

"And I want to save you, but what I won't do is watch you die." Her gaze narrowed on him. "I know how these things work, Nicolai. You've told me you care about me. And yeah, that could be your incarceration talking, but maybe not. If we take things to the next level and you lose me, you will wither."

He would rather wither than remain enslaved. "That's a chance I'm willing to take."

"I'm not."

"Then I will take your memory, Jane."

Her mouth fell open. "You can do that? You *would* do that?"

"Yes, and yes. I would do that and a whole lot more."

"You know the pain of having memories taken. How could you even think of doing that to me?"

Sound reasoning, which he ignored. "I will only take the memories of me."

"So I'll see you but won't recognize you?" Suddenly she couldn't quite catch her breath. Tears ran down her cheeks, leaving little wet tracks. "Will you recognize me?"

"I don't know. Perhaps."

"Don't do this, Nicolai."

"I must. I need you. Until your body joins your mind, you are useless to me." Useless, but so necessary.

"But to take my memories…"

"You've forced my hand." Flat, no room for compromise.

"And if we hate each other in this new beginning, as we did before?"

At first, she had watched him with those haunted amber eyes, her scent so sweet he could practically taste it. He'd wanted her, craved her, but she had kept her distance.

When at last she deigned to speak to him, he'd been worked into such a frenzy for her that he had lashed out and tried to bite her, only to waft right through her—as well as scare the Abyss out of her. She had vanished. Hadn't returned for days. Frustration and anger had eaten him.

The next time, he forced himself to speak softly to her, to maintain his own distance, gentling her, even though such things went against the very fiber of his nature. After that, she'd come back again, and again, and camaraderie soon morphed into caring.

What he planned to do to her was a betrayal. He knew that.

He did it, anyway. He used his magic to create the book, the pen. Used his magic to write to Jane. Used his magic to send her away, back to her world, to her body. Used his magic to wipe her memories. Used his magic to bring her back to him.

And in the process, his own memories of her *were* taken. Not because of the witches, but because of him. He'd taken them on purpose. He'd known knowledge of his past with her would influence his future. Might even prevent him from using her.

Something was shaking him, dislodging the recollection. He tried to hold on, had to know what happened next, but the shaking continued, and he growled.

"Nicolai. Nicolai, you have to snap out of it." Jane's voice, closer, in the present, frantic and fearful. "Someone's coming. Nicolai, please. Wake up."

Please.

He released the past completely, allowing his mind

to snap back into focus. He'd hurt her enough already. And, as she had feared, he would lose her again. The spell he'd used had not disrupted the very first spell cast on her. The one that would force her to lose her lover. Nothing could disrupt that spell, and none Nicolai had tried had brought her back to him. Until he'd worked *with* the first.

He'd brought Jane here, bound her body to his, on the condition that she leave him when—if—she fell in love with him.

So, he could keep her, as long as he prevented her from loving him.

"Nicolai."

The present. Yes. He heard footsteps. A lot of them. Booted. Spears scraping against the ground. Power saturated the air. Laila, definitely. With her army? Probably.

Different emotions warred for dominance. Fury, elation, anticipation, hatred, anxiety. Nicolai wanted to attack, to kill, but that would place Jane in jeopardy, and that he wouldn't do. Ever.

He jolted upright, a blur of motion. Jane had already pulled on her robe, was ready to go.

"Come." He grabbed her arm, and jerked her away from their camp.

Chapter 14

Nicolai dragged Jane through the forest, branches slapping at him. She was limping again, and he wanted to carry her, but Laila's guards must have caught his scent, because the echo of their footsteps increased, and the sense of magic intensified in the night air.

They were closing in.

He could have moved from one location to another with only a thought. From here, back to the withered, perverted kingdom of Elden. His heart clenched in his chest, and he gritted his teeth. Now was not the time to think of his home. Or the condition of his home. Or his parents and the sorcerer he would soon destroy.

What if he disappeared, but Jane did not go with him? She would be left on her own in an inhospitable environment, the enemy all around.

Damn this. He had to try something. He'd managed to beat the flood of memories back, but they were knocking at his mind, demanding release. If they over-took him again…

He focused on what was most important. He and Jane shared a past he'd barely touched on. One she still couldn't recall. What he knew was that he wouldn't repeat his previous mistakes.

He needed that book, the one in Delfina. Had to write something more inside of it. For when she left him. Oh, gods. Yes, that meant he would be operating under the assumption she would love and leave him, but he *had* to plan for the worst. Maybe, just maybe, a new spell would bring her back.

Elden had not planned for defeat, and look what had happened.

"Nicolai," Jane panted. "I'm used to jogging, but this is like Extreme Jogging, Jungle Edition, and I don't know how much longer I can keep up. Can we rest?"

He heard her. Distantly. Tried to concentrate on her, but the darkness was closing in on him, another memory fighting its way free.

All his life, he had absorbed the powers and magic of others. What they could do, he could then do. That was how he'd formed the air shield inside the palace. The Queen of Hearts had done so; therefore, he had done so, too. And that was why Laila had forbidden anyone from practicing their craft around him.

Some abilities lasted days, weeks. Others lasted a lifetime.

He'd remembered most of this already, so of course his mind tried to shove it aside to make room for some-thing else, something new.

"Nicolai. Please."

He couldn't lock on her. More details unfolded. His

ability to cast illusions, as well as move from one location to another with only a thought, had come from a witch. A lover who had tried to kill him as he lay sleeping. She had wanted to become his bride, but he had wanted only the sex. She'd tried several different identities with him, amusing him.

He'd never told her that he knew who she was, each and every time she approached, because he recognized her scent. He'd let her continue to come to him, and every time he'd made his intentions clear. Still she'd tried, hoping to change his mind. When she realized she could not, in any incarnation, she finally attacked.

One moment Nicolai was leading Jane through the forest, the next he was inside a bedroom. His bedroom, he thought. The one in his memory, with the homicidal witch. He did not realize the switch soon enough and slammed into the wall, propelling backward. He hit the floor with a black curse.

Jane was nowhere to be seen.

Nicolai popped to his feet, his blood flashing hot. He would return to the forest, now, now, damn it, now, and if anyone had touched Jane…

He remained in the bedroom.

Fangs bared, he spun, looking for the way out. Blood stained the walls, crimson splattered in every direction. The floor possessed deep grooves, each in patterns of four, as if multiple swords had been dragged over it and had cut into the wood.

The giant, hairy creatures, their legs—four on each side—sharp and deadly. They had been here. They had come for him.

Nicolai had been pumping into a woman, a servant. His door had flown open, and he'd heard the screams echoing from below, in the great hall. He should have heard them sooner, but his partner had been screaming, too, distracting him.

Nicolai had reached for his blood daggers, the ones he kept on his nightstand, intending to fight the monsters, wondering about his family, but he'd…disappeared, falling straight into a winding black hole.

Had his siblings died alongside his parents? Or fallen into the same hole? He remembered curses around him, echoing.

Now he stopped breathing. He hadn't wanted to remember this, not yet, but… Was he certain his parents were dead? Was there no longer any question in his mind?

He didn't need to think about it. Yes. He was certain. They were dead. The knowledge practically seeped from the mold covered walls around him. He hadn't seen them die, but he'd felt the drain of their life forces. They were gone.

Oh, gods. And his siblings?

No, not dead. Now that he knew what to check for, he could feel their energy swirling inside him still; only, the energy was…different than before. Were they trapped somewhere? Unable to free themselves? Probably. Otherwise, Dayn would have destroyed the Blood Sorcerer and reclaimed the palace.

Dayn and his ability to hunt anyone or thing. Micah, sweet baby-faced Micah, would have been running down the halls and laughing. Breena would have been trying her hand at magic, messing up her spells.

With these thoughts, he wanted to drop to his knees, roar to the heavens, curse, rant and rail, fight everything and everyone. How to find them? How to free them?

Now he also realized he'd heard Dayn's voice in his dreams. Calling to him, telling him to heal himself. They shared a blood connection, something that could never be destroyed. They could speak again.

Where are you, brother?

A moment passed. There was no reply. Very well. He would try again later.

A sense of urgency reignited, and Nicolai checked for his daggers. They were gone, as were his clothing and all his other weapons. The room had been totally cleaned out.

He ground his molars and pictured the rest of the castle, which was surprisingly easy. Towering, more rooms than he could count. Winding hallways and secret passages. He whisked to every bedroom, every cell in the dungeon. He saw people he did not recognize, more bloodstains, more monsters patrolling the gates. Rage consumed him. The need to kill the new king, the sorcerer, intensified. But his family was not here, nor was the sorcerer.

He would have to return. Soon. Always soon. Right now, he had to protect Jane. A full-time job, he was coming to realize. One he cherished and wouldn't trade.

After a last glance at the castle he'd once loved, he closed his eyes and pictured the forest and the last spot he'd seen Jane. He was there a second later—easier every time—but found no sign of his woman. No sign of Laila and her army, either.

He sniffed...sniffed... There. He locked on to Jane's sweet scent, mixed with the disgusting aroma of Laila and her men. They were following her.

He gave chase.

* * *

Jane heard the voices before she spotted the town, and nearly toppled over with relief. She increased her speed, and finally, blessedly, reached civilization. The sun was steadily rising in the sky, casting a violet haze on the people just now starting their day. Warming Jane, and even burning her. Her skin itched, prickling as if little bugs were crawling through her veins.

She did not want to contemplate the possible reasons for such an occurrence.

People—humans?—strode along cobbled streets, some carrying wicker baskets piled high with clothing, some carrying bags of—she sniffed, moaned—bread and meat. Her stomach grumbled as her mouth watered. She was light-headed, her blood supply a little low. She *needed* to replenish.

Jane paused beside a tree, watching, thinking. She had two choices. Keep moving, remaining on her own, and risk being found by Laila. Or enter the town, eat and risk being found by Laila. At least the second option provided a meal plan. So, okay. No contest.

Except, she was still Odette. If these people recognized her, word would spread, and she would be found far more quickly. On the plus side, Laila wouldn't hurt her and Nicolai was no longer with her. He was no longer in danger—she didn't think—and that was a good thing.

He'd disappeared in a heartbeat of time, shocking her. She'd waited in the area for what seemed an eternity, but he'd never reappeared and she'd had to move on. He would find her, wherever she was. She couldn't believe otherwise.

Laila's army had nearly discovered her, marching

right over her hiding place. But they'd lost Nicolai's trail and backtracked in an attempt to find it again. That's when Jane bolted, forcing her protesting body to act before it shut down completely and Laila returned.

If—when—Jane was discovered, she wanted to be well-fed, stronger. So again, no contest. She limped forward, entering the town. The moment the people caught sight of her, they stopped what they were doing, horror consuming their features, and knelt.

Yep. She'd been recognized. What the hell had Odette done to them?

She closed the distance between her and one of the groups with food. "Please. I'm so hungry. May I—"

"Take whatever you wish, princess," the man closest to her said, thrusting the basket in her direction.

"I don't have any money, but I'll find a way to pay you back. I swear." The scent of roasted chicken hit her, transporting her straight to heaven. She stretched out a shaky hand, reached inside the confines of the wicker and claimed a bowl of something creamy. Was she drooling? *You can't dive in like an animal.* "What's your name?"

"Hammond, princess." There was a trace of anger in that husky voice.

"Thank you for the food, Hammond."

"Anything for you, princess." The anger morphed into hatred.

Jane sighed, looked around. "Please stand. All of you. There's no reason to bow."

Several seconds ticked by before they obeyed, as if they feared she would attack them for rising, even though she'd told them to. Other than that, they didn't move. Though she wanted to limp away, find a deserted, shadowed corner and shove her face right into the food, she couldn't. They might suspect she was not who they thought she was.

"I need a room," she announced. "And water. And clean clothing. Please. If one of you could point me in the right direction, I would be grateful."

At first, no one stepped forward. Then, reluctantly, a middle-aged female curtsied and said, "If you'll follow me, princess, I will see to your needs."

"Thank you."

Ten minutes later, an eternity, Jane was inside a bedroom, alone. She devoured the contents of the bowl—some kind of chicken salad—before bathing in the steaming tub the woman had filled with a muttered spell. Not human, after all, but a witch. The water soothed Jane's sensitive skin, relieving the itching. Afterward, she donned a clean, blue robe the witch had laid out for her.

All she lacked was Nicolai, and this day would be perfect.

Where was he?

With a weary sigh, she sprawled out on the bed. Firm, lumpy, but heaven for her still aching muscles and bones. What to do, what to do. Nicolai was, at heart, a protector. Fierce, unwavering. Which meant he hadn't left her voluntarily.

So. Either his abilities—whatever they were—were responsible, or someone had used magic to draw him away from her. The first was more likely. As strong as Nicolai was becoming, she doubted anyone would be able to simply spell him someplace anymore. Because, if that were the case, Laila would have done it days ago.

Laila. The bitch was a problem. A big one. As long as

she was out there, Nicolai would be hunted, in danger. Jane could turn herself in, she supposed, and try to convince the princess to leave "the slave" alone. Would that help, though? Having tasted the man herself, she knew how impossible it would be to forget him.

Laila probably craved him more than the air she breathed. The thought alone caused jealousy to rise up, sharp and biting. Jane ignored the unproductive response. A few problems with turning herself in. One, Laila could wield magic. Jane could not. Two, Jane's secret could be found out. And if the queen whipped her own daughter, what would she do to an enemy impersonating one of her children? Three, what if Nicolai followed her to Delfina? He could be captured again, his memories wiped. His body used.

His body belonged to Jane. No one else.

She rolled to her side, clutching the pillow to her middle, suddenly reminded of the day she had received Nicolai's book. She'd read a few passages and had thought of him for hours afterward. She had been obsessed with him, really. After reading a few more passages, she had fantasized about him, practically making love to her pillow. Then, she had gone to him.

Maybe she could reach him again.

She closed her eyes and imagined him inside her cabin, puttering around, fixing things, then seducing her into bed. There, he touched her, stripped her. Kissed her, tasted her. Consumed her. Goose bumps spread. She could almost feel the warmth of his breath, the slick glide of his skin.

"Nicolai," she breathed.

Jane.

His voice, so deep, so familiar. For a moment, she

experienced a wave of dizziness, felt as if she were floating. Then the mattress was beneath her again, and...cold. Cold? In less than a second, the mattress had gone from warmed to chilled. Impossible. Unless—
Her eyelids popped open, hope unfurling.

Hope dying. She hadn't whisked to Nicolai. She was inside her cabin. On her own bed.

Jane jolted upright, trying to suck air into her lungs. A knot formed in her throat, and nothing could penetrate it. No. She couldn't be here. No, no, no. She popped to her feet, nearly toppling as her knees shook. She rushed around, stumbling a few times, grabbing her knickknacks to see if they were real or imagined.

Please be imagined.

They were solid, dusty, as if they hadn't been cleaned in weeks. They were real. She choked back a sob.

No! Tears blurred her vision. She swiped her arms over her dresser, knocking everything to the floor. A glass vase shattered. A hairbrush clattered. How the hell had she gotten here? She'd wanted to be with Nicolai. She needed to be with him and had to get back. She *would* get back.

She just had to figure out how.

Chapter 15

Jane raged for half an hour. Panicked for an hour after that. Then she did what she did best, reasoned. There was a logical explanation for what had happened. There always was. So, she brushed her teeth, showered and redressed in her robe. No way she'd dress in jeans and a T-shirt. She didn't belong here anymore, and wouldn't dress as if she did.

She belonged there. With Nicolai.

She stretched out on her bed, and her comforter plumped around her. Okay. She could do this. What had she been doing before she'd ended up here? Lying in bed, just like this, thinking about Nicolai. Imagining the two of them making love, actually. Good, that was good. She would just do that again.

She cleared her mind with a little shake of her head, drew in a deep breath, released the air…slowly…and forced her muscles to relax. A picture of Nicolai rose front and center. Dark hair shagging around his head, silver eyes liquid with desire. For her. Lips parted as he breathed shallowly, his own desire raging. His fangs peeked out.

Her stomach quivered, but other than that, nothing happened. No dizziness, no movement whatsoever. *Keep going.* In her mind, she saw him remove his shirt, slowly pulling the material over his head. His skin, his beautifully bronzed skin, glistened exquisitely. His nipples were small and brown, utterly lickable. That scrumptious trail of hair lead from his navel to a cock she'd once loved with her mouth.

Warm moisture pooled between her legs. But again, no floating, no changing locations.

Damn it. She hadn't been this unsuccessful since the age of eight, when she'd read about making synthetic diamonds in the microwave. Diamonds she'd hoped to present to her mother on her birthday. The charcoal bricks and peanut butter necessary for the conversion had survived the lengthy cook time. The dish she'd put them in had not. Neither had the microwave.

A chuckle escaped her as she suddenly recalled her mother's reaction. They'd been standing in the kitchen, her darling mother looking through the thick, dark smoke to Jane, who was holding the book that explained exactly how to do it. Her disbelieving expression was comical.

"Diamonds?" her mother asked.

"I followed every step, didn't miss a single one."

Her mother coughed as she claimed the book. Several minutes passed before she turned her attention to the blackened mess inside the microwave. "You followed every step, did you?"

"Yes!"

"And you used a Pyrex dish?"

Jane blinked. "P-Pyrex?"

Dizziness caused the image to waver, fade, and that dizziness caused a bubble of excitement to burst through her chest. This was it. She was returning....

The moment the dizziness passed, she popped open her eyelids and sat up. For a moment, her unfamiliar surroundings simply couldn't register. She was perched on a linoleum floor in the center of a kitchen. There was a stainless steel stove, a sink, scuffed cabinets. The layout was familiar—she'd just seen it in her mind— but the colors were not.

Once, the walls had been painted yellow. Now they were painted blue. Once the refrigerator had been silver. Now it was black. Still she knew. This had been her kitchen. She'd grown up here. Her mother had stood just in front of that sink, coughing from the smoke wafting from the microwave. A high-pitched scream suddenly echoed, a jumble of words following. "Intruder! Thief! Murderer! What the hell are you doing here?" a woman gasped from behind her. "Who are you? Get out! Get out right now! Billy, call 9-1-1."

Jane whipped around, instinctively holding up her hands in a you-can-trust-me gesture. "I'm not going to hurt you."

Absolute fear coated the woman's features. She grabbed a knife from the counter, waving the sharp tip in Jane's direction. "That's what all the psychos say."

Jane backed away.

"Billy!"

"What?" a sleepy male voice growled from around the corner.

Oh, crap. Reinforcements. Remembering the house's layout, Jane bolted, heading straight for the front door. She raced into the morning sunlight, the length of her robe tangling around her feet. And sure enough, she was in her old neighborhood. Not much had changed. The houses were small, a little run-down and crowded too close together.

Fearing the woman and her Billy would give chase— and grab a shotgun—she sprinted about half a mile along the gravel road, turned sharply and ducked behind Mrs. Rucker's giant oak. She'd hidden here a lot as a kid.

She was panting and sweating as she slid to her ass. And damn. Her feet throbbed. The little rocks had sliced them to ribbons.

Well, that was fun. Not. What the hell had just happened?

She ran the variables through her mind, weighed each of the possible outcomes, compared them and discarded all but one. His blood. She'd had Nicolai's blood; he'd fed it to her to heal her. His abilities must have transferred to her. Like him, she could move from one place to the other, disappearing and reappearing. In essence, teleporting.

She just had to picture where she wanted to go, and boom. She was there in a snap. Amazement filled her. She'd studied the manipulation of macroparticles for years before she'd succeeded in teleporting plastic, basically faxing a small portion from one station to another. Now, to move a living being between planes with only a thought…it was everything she'd worked for, gift-wrapped and handed to her.

So, when she'd imagined her old kitchen, she had

traveled to her old kitchen. Before, in that town, she had imagined Nicolai in her bed, and had therefore traveled back to her bed. So simple, so easy, an answer that made sense. Finally.

She could return to her man.

She was grinning as she closed her eyes and pictured the quaint little bedroom she'd previously occupied. The wooden tub, the feathered bed. Yes, the bed. Where she'd sprawled, hoping Nicolai would find her.

Dizziness rolled through her, and she couldn't contain her gasp of excitement. Next time she opened her eyes, she would be there. Back in Delfina. And if she retained this ability, she would never have to worry about losing Nicolai to magic again. She could stay with him always. If she didn't retain it automatically, she could drink from him every day to ensure that she did.

"Well, well," a female voice said. "There you are, using your magic to become invisible again. Who were you spying on this time, sister dear?"

Dread replaced Jane's excitement as she opened her eyes. She was in the little room, all right, but that room was now overflowing with Laila and her soldiers. Two of them held a teary-eyed woman. The very woman who had brought Jane here, who had fed her, clothed her.

Laila stood at the edge of the bed, peering down at her. There was no sign of Nicolai.

Slowly Jane sat up. *Careful.* "Yes, I was using my invisibility again." As far as lies went, that was a good one. Irrefutable. "How did you find me?"

"Is that any way to greet your loving sister? A sister who has searched and searched for you, desperate to save you from a madman's clutches."

A thought hit her: despite traveling between worlds, the Odette mask was still in place. Sweet! But really, Jane knew if Laila had "searched and searched" for her, it had been to slay her and claim Nicolai for her own. Two could play the deceit game, however.

"Thank you for saving me, darling. All I've done these past few days is miss you."

Emerald eyes narrowed to tiny slits.

"Now," Jane added before Laila could reply. "What are you doing to the woman?"

"Oh." Laila waved a dismissive hand. "I knew you were here, I could sense your magic, but I couldn't find you and feared she had killed you." Was that relish in her tone?

"As you can see, she didn't." As she spoke, she said a prayer that Nicolai did not come for her, yet. She didn't want him walking in on this. Didn't want Laila to see him.

"True." Laila twisted and eyed the guards holding her. "She's no longer of any use to us. Dispose of her."

"Dispose of her" had better not mean... A third guard stepped up behind the woman, who had begun to flail and panic, grabbed her by the jaw and jerked, breaking her neck in seconds. Her body sagged forward, going limp. Lifeless.

Jane could only gape in shock, in horror. "Wh-why did you do that?"

The guards dragged the body away, and Laila shrugged. "She irritated me."

"You..." *Bitch*. The urge to murder the princess flashed white-hot through her veins. And she'd once thought herself unready for such an act.

That she remained in place, seemingly unaffected,

saved her. There was a little voice of reason in the back of her head, reminding her that she was outnumbered and outgunned.

Jane had never been a violent person. Perhaps Nicolai's dark side was rubbing off on her, too, because she *liked* the thought of hurting Laila. Welcomed it. *One day, I will destroy you.*

Laila eased onto the mattress, pressing close. Jane barely stopped herself from scooting away in disgust. "Now, sister dear, we have much to discuss."

Nicolai remained in the shadows, bypassing huts and outdoor vendors pedaling their wares. Jane's scent, so sweet…stronger now…so close…mixed with a hundred others. Some rotten, pungent. Some sweat soaked, some magic ripe.

Laila and her army were here.

The moment realization struck, he stopped caring about stealth. He leaped into action, feet hammering at the ground. The citizens paused when they spotted him, some doing a double take. Murmurs soon arose.

Did they know him?

He caught words like *prince* and *dead,* each a question. They did know him, then. Knew he was a prince of Elden. They'd thought him dead. Did they think the same about his family?

He almost stopped to question them. Almost. Jane was in danger. That preceded *everything*. He quickened his pace. His intense sense of smell took him to a little hut at the edge of the town. Guards spilled from it, filing into the streets. There were even guards posted at the neighboring homes, all watching and waiting for their princess.

Nicolai returned to the shadows. Thankfully no one in this area had noticed him. People were perched in front of their windows, nervously eyeing the guards. Potential allies?

Some were witches, but most were humans. Humans who had crossed into this realm throughout the centuries, for whatever reason. They had congregated here, settled and sprouted roots. That had been a mistake, for this town was part of Delfina and under the rule of the Queen of Hearts. They couldn't help him.

He drew in a heated breath, released it. Well, he didn't need help. He was a prince. A vampire. Powerful beyond imagining. He had led an army of his own, had conquered kingdoms and female hearts. He could absorb the abilities of others, and it was time he used that to his advantage—and not accidentally.

Eyes narrowing, he homed in on the house. Jane was inside. He felt her energy, as sweet as her scent and… now blended with his own. He gave a primitive grunt of approval. *Mine.* He had done more than mark her; he had branded her. *I'm coming for you, sweetheart.*

He switched his focus to Laila. She was rotten to her core, with a scent to match. Magic swirled inside her, dark and potent. Ability after ability, honed over centuries of living with such a slowly ticking clock. He riffled through them.

She could hypnotize others; that could aid him, yes, but she could only entrance one person at a time. She could heal her own wounds. He could already do that. She could *cause* wounds. Another maybe. She could spark false desire. No. A muscle ticked in his jaw, though. How many times had she used that ability on him?

Doesn't matter. He continued his search, discarding…discarding… There! Remote viewing, like what he'd done inside the palace with Jane. Perfect, and now his earlier ability made sense. He wondered how many times Laila had used the ability on him. Watched him without his knowledge.

No matter the answer, she would never be able to do so again.

He grabbed on to the ability and gave a soft mental tug, drawing it closer and closer to him. A little more… just a little more… His chest puffed as his every cell suddenly absorbed the magic necessary to see places he could not physically reach. Still he kept tugging, and tugging, and tugging. Drawing the magic away from her and into him.

Laila wouldn't know what he was doing. His victims never did, until it was too late. Right now, she would be experiencing only mild fatigue. If he attempted to draw *all* of her abilities, all of her power, however, she would know and could try to stop him, erecting mental blocks.

Suddenly his mind opened up. In a blink, he was looking at Jane, as if he were sitting beside her. Only, he saw her through Laila's eyes. And Laila saw the mask. Saw Odette. Odette's dark hair, Odette's green eyes. Her too-long nose and thick jowls.

Knowing Jane rested under that mask was enough to light his body on fire and soothe the sharpest edges of his fear for her safety. She was alive, unharmed. He would have her again.

"What did the slave do to you? Tell me before I perish from worry." Laila ruined the effect of the demand with a yawn.

Jane fluffed her hair, every inch the princess. "Like you said before, he desired me. I desired him, one thing led to another, and we were steaming up the forest, if you know what I mean."

"Did you bespell him to desire you?" Each word was tauter than the last. "You must have. Otherwise, he would be with you now. Yet, I have caught no sign of him. So where is he?"

"No, I didn't bespell him." Jane offered no more.

"Then how did you elicit his desire? He hated you, tried to kill you. You did something, I know you did. Just admit it."

Jane smirked over at her, and it was a glorious sight. "Hold on to your panties, Laila dear, because this might shock you. I—wait for it—treated him with respect. You should try it sometime. You might be delighted with the results."

Hate burned through Laila so relentlessly, Nicolai felt the heat of it inside his own body. "You lie. You've never treated anyone with respect. I doubt you even know what the word means."

"Are we showing our claws now, *darling?* Because I promise you, mine are sharper."

Pride filled him. No one would doubt she was Odette now. Not even the queen herself. She wore confidence as snugly as a cloak.

"I will ask you one more time," Laila gritted out.

"Or what?"

"Where. Is. He?"

"Dead." A casual shrug. "He's dead."

Laila's mouth dropped open, a strangling sound emerging. "You killed him?"

"Yes. Yes, I did." Jane threw her legs over the

mattress, and winced. They must be paining her, he thought, wishing he were there to ease her hurts. She straightened. "Now, let's go home. I'm eager to sleep in my own bed."

Laila remained in place and crossed her arms over her middle. "Where's his body?"

"I fed it to the ogres, of course," she replied blithely. "What's with all the questions, anyway? Nicolai did not belong to you."

She was giving him what he'd told her he wanted, he thought. A chance to destroy Laila, undetected. Time to reach Elden, to kill the new king. And yes, the urgency was still there, simmering inside him, stronger with every minute that passed, but he still couldn't, wouldn't, leave her.

Relief bathed Laila, bleeding into him, but the emotion was as quickly schooled as the hatred. "I found the ogre cave. Nicolai's body was not there. Others' were, which has to mean he killed them and escaped."

Jane didn't miss a beat. "Wrong. *I* massacred the ogres. After they finished with him."

The shock returned. "How?"

A buff of her nails. "A girl never reveals her fighting secrets. She might need them later on."

A heartbeat of silence. A low growl.

"How dare you!" Laila shouted, no longer able to contain her emotions. She jumped to her feet, stomped her foot. "He was mine."

Jane got in her face, putting them nose-to-nose. "Actually, you spoiled brat, he's mine. Was mine."

Tension thickened the air, practically vibrating between them. Long moments passed, the only sound that of their breathing. Finally Laila backed down. She stepped away, widening the distance.

"Of course. You're right." Grudgingly offered. "So tell me. *Why* did you kill him?"

"I no longer desired him."

Even though Nicolai knew why she said what she said, his inner beast did not like hearing those words. Later, he would have to be soothed. Later, he would have to explain his past with her and apologize for what he'd done.

Would her claim then become true?

"Now, then. Let's return to the palace," Jane said. "Guards. Move out."

They hesitated.

"Now!" she screamed, her patience clearly gone.

This time, they scrambled to obey. Jane followed them, forcing Laila to trail after her. Nicolai could feel the princess's desire to stab her sister in the back. But she didn't, and as they marched out of the town, he skulked after them.

Soon…

Chapter 16

Even though, as a princess of Delfina, she was carried on a plush velvet lounge, the sun blocked by a canopy of dark netting, Jane much preferred traveling with Nicolai. Where was he? Close, she thought. She could almost scent him, a hint of magic, a pinch of seductive spice. She prayed he'd opted not to follow her.

Laila thought he was dead. So, in a way, he was finally free of the bitch. He could travel to Elden, and do what needed doing. And Jane could deliver his vengeance—a special care package of lethal—for him.

The princess had killed an innocent woman for no damn reason. No wonder the people in town had been afraid of Odette. The royal family abused their power, and Jane wasn't going to let them do so anymore.

Then she and Nicolai could be together again.

When Laila finally decided to stop for the evening, Jane's legs were stiff from disuse. Not as stiff as they could have been, at least. In fact, not even close to what she was used to dealing with. No throbbing pain, no bone crushing aches. However, a walk would have been nice.

Sadly, a walk wasn't in the forecast for some time to come. She had to continue to lounge as the guards erected her tent. And decorated the inside. And carted in her trunks. Trunks Laila had brought with her, perhaps hoping to bribe her for a night with Nicolai.

When they finished, bowing before her and awaiting dismissal, Laila climbed down from her own raised lounge, stepping on their backs to reach the ground.

"There will be a celebration of your return," the princess announced with a clap of her hands. "We will dine in my tent. My slaves will dance for us, and you may chose whichever you desire to warm your furs."

Gee. Thanks. "Sorry, but I'm tired." Jane climbed down, too, feeling guilty the entire time. Although the guards blinked with surprise at her slighter weight and that sparked a kernel of fear. "I wish only to bathe and sleep. And eat. I haven't been fed properly in days."

"Bathe, yes. Then join me. I will feed you. Since your return from the grave, there has been too much friction between us. I do not like it, and long for the ease of our former relationship."

A lie, Jane knew. Laila hated Odette with the same passion she had craved Nicolai in her bed, but to protest was to, perhaps, act against the real Odette's character. "Very well," she said on a sigh. "I'll join you in an hour." A small reprieve, but a reprieve all the same. She made her way to her own tent.

A long soak in the portable tub did much to appease

her aches and pains. A tub Rhoslyn had filled. The girl was a surprisingly welcome sight.

Jane scrubbed from head to toe, using the floral-scented soap that had rested on the rim. "Did Laila demand that you come on this journey or did you volunteer?"

Frizzy red hair bobbed. "I volunteered, princess." She unfolded a vivid green robe from a trunk. "Just in case we found you, and you had need of me."

I should have been nicer to this girl. "I didn't see you until you entered my tent. Where were you in the procession?"

"Behind the third line of defense, with the rest of the servants and slaves."

"I wished I'd known. You could have ridden in the carriage with me." Jane emerged from the water and grabbed the towel resting on a nearby bench.

"I will help you," Rhoslyn said, rushing over. The robe dangled from her arms.

"No, thanks." There were some things she was now capable of doing herself—things she hadn't been able to do while practically chained to a hospital bed—and she would never again allow anyone to do them for her.

Dried, she pinched one corner of the robe and lifted. Her lips curved down in distaste. Though finely made, the material was too wide for her, and far too thick. She'd melt from the heat. And, where the robe gaped, she'd fry like battered shrimp when in the sun.

"I am sorry if the cloth is not to your liking." Free of her burden, Rhoslyn bowed her head. "You may beat me if you wish."

Jane caught the layer of fear in her voice. "Beat you? Rhoslyn, I'm not going to beat you. Ever."

The girl continued as if she hadn't heard a word Jane had said. "I thought you would prefer something durable, rather than enticing. And your sister was quite eager to reach you, so I did not have much time to pack your things. I am not complaining," she rushed to add. "I simply wished to explain why there are not many robes to choose from, and why I did not bring your very best."

"You did great, I swear. I love the gown. Love it. See?" She dressed and twirled. "I've never felt lovelier."

Rhoslyn offered her a genuine smile. "I am glad, princess. Oh. And I am happy to tell you that I brought your book."

Jane paused, her heart suddenly thumping. "Really? Where is it?"

The girl crossed to the other side of the tent. Slowly, Jane realized, and with care. "Hey. Are you okay? Did you hurt yourself carrying those buckets?" Great. Something else to feel guilty about.

Rhoslyn stiffened, stumbling over her own feet, before continuing on. "I am fine, princess." She hunched over another trunk, dug inside and lifted the leather bound tome.

Jane gasped with horror. As the girl had bent over, her hair had fallen forward and Jane had caught sight of bruising on her neck. Black and blue and clearly spreading farther down. "What happened to your back?" This time, her tone was firm, unyielding, demanding an answer.

Rhoslyn's thin arm shook as she held out the book. "I allowed you to be abducted by the slave. I was punished. As I deserved."

Whipped, then. Laila hadn't given the girl time to

pack properly, but she'd damn sure made time to use the cat-o'-nine-tails. Jane claimed the offered item, hating Laila a little more. "That wasn't your fault. You couldn't have stopped him. Hell, you weren't even there."

No reply was forthcoming.

She sighed. "I'm headed to my sister's tent. While I'm gone, I want you to soak in the tub. If you want. If you don't, don't. Then, I want you to rest. Do not wait up for me. And that's an order."

Eyes wide with surprise, Rhoslyn gave another nod.

Jane stepped outside. Overhead, the sun was setting, muted and a deep purple. And yet, it still managed to burn her newly sensitive skin, making her itch all over again. Now wasn't the time to consider what that meant, either.

Laila's tent was a mere ten steps away. At the entrance, Jane stopped and squared her shoulders. *You can do this.* The sound of laughter and music wafted toward her as she brushed past the flap. She scouted her new surroundings, trying to take everything in at once. To the right, Laila was perched on a hastily constructed dais. Lounging, of course, and eating pastries. There was an empty seat beside her.

Six naked men slow danced in the center. They were tall, leanly muscled and oiled to a glossy shine. Two blondes, two redheads and two with dark hair. Math at its finest. Hands roamed, and bodies bumped and grinded. Each man had an erection, but Jane doubted they liked what they were doing. Their eyes were glazed and lifeless. Were they bespelled?

To the left was a band. Well, the Delfina version of a band. A naked harpist, a naked violinist and a naked vocalist. Jane was sensing a theme. And, well, shit. This had the makings of an orgy. Participation had better not be mandatory. Her body belonged to Nicolai, and no one else.

"Odette," Laila called, catching sight of her. "Thank you for coming."

What ulterior motive do you have? Jane wondered as she closed the distance between them. No way the princess had thrown this little shindig together out of the goodness of her heart. Fact: she didn't have a heart.

Jane eased into her chair and stretched out. "My... pleasure." Something about the princess was off, she immediately realized. No, not off. Different. Yes, that was a better word. She pulsed with power, stronger than before. Had she cast some sort of spell on herself? Could witches even do that?

Wasn't like Jane could ask. She was supposed to be a witch herself.

Laila waved her hand over the tray of pastries. "Have anything you like."

Hmm, sugar. Her stomach twisted with hunger. How many hours had passed since she'd had that delicious chicken salad? The same number of hours that had passed since the princess had killed that innocent woman. Goodbye, appetite. "I'm fine."

"You must drink." Laila clapped. "Fix my sister a goblet of wine."

The servant behind their chairs jumped to obey, and seconds later, Jane was holding a bejeweled, golden goblet. Rather than refuse it, she held on. Drinking the wine was out of the question, though. She needed her wits. All of her wits.

If an opportunity presented itself, she was going to deliver her care package tonight. Poison? A stabbing?

Whatever method she picked, she would have to be careful. She couldn't win against the princess's magical abilities. Especially since she had no idea what the girl could do.

"Now," Laila purred. "Enjoy."

For over an hour, the men danced and Laila watched, eating and drinking. Jane watched *her,* studying her like a lab rat. Soon the princess was giggling and throwing grapes at the men. When the giggles subsided, she became aroused. Unabashedly, she moved her hand underneath her robe and rubbed herself between her legs.

"Touch his chest," the princess called huskily. "Yes, like that. Now lick his nipples. Oh, good boy. That's the way." With her free hands, she cupped one of her breasts.

Jane blushed. She'd nailed the happenings of the night like most of these slaves were probably going to nail Laila. Any minute now, and every single one of them would be orgying.

Oh, gross. She'd just turned the word *orgy* into a verb.

She was just about to excuse herself when the tent flap lifted. A new man, a slave, entered, and he was as naked as the others. He, too, was tall and oiled, though he was lean and lanky. Jane didn't recognize him, and yet, her eyes ate him up. Her heart sped up, her blood heated. Her skin tingled deliciously.

He had hair so pale it was like falling snow. His eyes were as black as a stormy night, and thickly lined with kohl. He was probably five-ten, his shoulders a little narrow, and his belly flat, almost concave. His skin was bronzed to a mochalike shimmer.

There was an almost feminine sense of gentleness

about him. A gentleness that didn't seem to fit the hard gleam of his eyes, as if it were a winter coat that belonged to someone else.

Like Jane had done, he paused in the doorway to take everything in. Anger flared his nostrils. Hate wafted from him, then desire. True desire, overshadowing everything else. He sniffed, gaze panning, then locking on her. He was striding forward a second later. Then he stilled, catching himself.

Breath caught in Jane's throat. She might not recognize that face and body, but she recognized that purposeful, powerful stride. Nicolai. He was projecting someone else's image, she knew it.

He was here. He was alive, healthy and whole, she thought, giddy with the knowledge. She should have been upset. He was ruining her plan, putting himself in danger. And yet, she reacted to his nearness…needed him. His body, his blood.

Her eyes widened as she realized what she'd just contemplated. She wanted to drink…his blood?

Oh, yes, she thought, her gaze zeroing in on his vein. She could see the slight fluttering there and wanted to sink her teeth in. Teeth. Was she…? She ran her tongue along the edge of her teeth. They felt the same, no fangs having sprouted unexpectedly. A wave of disappointment hit her.

She hadn't allowed herself to contemplate such an idea because she hadn't wanted to face that very sense of disappointment.

Vampires were not able to turn humans into blood drinkers. She knew because testing their blood, mixing it with human blood, had been one of her experiments. Nothing had happened, nothing had changed.

Hope did not abandon her completely. Nicolai was a little more…*everything* than any other vampire she'd known, so if anyone could change her, it was him. And she wanted to change. Wanted to live as long as he would.

"Oh, there he is," Laila said. "My special slave. Come here, darling boy. Let me show you off to my sister."

At first, Nicolai did not obey. Jane was glad. She didn't want him anywhere near the princess and her slutty hands. And if the princess *dared* to put those hands on him, Jane couldn't be held responsible for her actions. Actions that would involve the removal of the offending appendages.

Nicolai kicked into gear, and all too soon he stood between the lounges. He bowed his head, subservient.

"So pretty," Laila cooed. "Isn't he pretty, Odette?"

"Yes," she managed to choke out.

Laila sat up and petted his chest.

You are going to die, bitch. Jane fisted her hands on her thighs, her nails cutting, drawing blood.

"I found him days ago, as I was scouring Delfina to save you. He did not wish to travel with me. At first. He had another love, you know, and wished to remain with him. But I quickly changed your mind, didn't I, precious?"

His eyes narrowed, but he offered no reply. Not so subservient, after all.

Petting, petting, the bitch was still petting him. Jane was reaching out before she could stop herself, wrapping her fingers around Laila's wrist and squeezing. "I want him."

Triumph filled those green eyes. "Well, you can't have him. He's mine."

"Laila—"

"No. Do you recall when I wanted *your* slave, and you would not share?"

So. That's what this night was about. Tempting Jane, then denying her. "Let me explain something to you, Laila. I am older than you. Which means I am the future queen. *Your* future queen. What I want, I get. Even if that 'what' belongs to you." She might not know Delfina law, but she knew the construction of a matriarchal culture, as well as social hierarchy.

In the end, top dog always won. Right now, Jane was top dog.

"You—you—"

"Can do anything I want, yes." Jane tossed the girl's hand into her lap. "So don't you dare touch him. I've claimed rights. Do you understand?"

Bright red spots of color bloomed on Laila's cheeks. "Mother will have something to say about this."

"Yes, and I'm sure it will be 'job well done.'" Jane pushed to her feet, standing beside Nicolai. She curbed the urge to link their hands, to bury her head in the hollow of his neck, and simply breathe him in. "Bottom line. She's not here. Is she?"

"No." The color spread to Laila's nape.

"And that means…"

"Your word is law," Laila gritted out. "Very well. I will let you have him without a fight. *If* he wishes to belong to you. Darling," she said, standing and peering deep into his eyes.

Magic crackled between them.

Jane experienced a momentary wave of nervousness.

Could Nicolai be entranced, or whatever Laila was doing to him? "That's enough," she barked.

Laila ignored her. "Tell my sister how much you desire me, precious. Tell her whose body you crave."

His lips compressed into a thin line.

"Tell her! Now."

Even the harp and violin drowned out, overshadowed by the thud of Jane's heartbeat. Then Nicolai shook his head and said, "I desire the princess Odette," and the world outside their circle reentered her awareness.

A shocked gasp. An angry growl. "No. No, you lie."

"Why would he lie?" Jane demanded.

Laila's narrowed gaze swung to her. "What did you do to him? How did you steal his affections from me? *What did you do?*" she screeched.

"She did nothing. I simply want her." There was enough truth in Nicolai's voice to prove his claim.

"I will—" Laila raised her hand, either to hit Nicolai or cast a spell.

Either way, Jane didn't care. She grabbed on to the bitch's wrist a second time. "You haven't yet learned the concept of the phrase *my property.* Touch him, and you'll regret it."

Several seconds passed before Laila schooled her features and dropped her arm to her side. She released a shuddering breath. "You're different, Odette. You never treated me this shabbily before."

Jane shrugged, as if unconcerned, but deep inside she trembled. "Near-death experiences have a way of leaving their mark. Good night, sister dear." Finally she claimed Nicolai's hand and ushered him out of the tent, hurrying to hers.

Rhoslyn had taken her at her word, and had not

remained to see to her needs. Jane and Nicolai were alone.

She whirled to face him. He'd dropped the mask, and she could see his dark, shaggy hair, his bright silver eyes. His towering height, wide shoulders and rock solid strength. Her desire intensified, burning through her.

"We have much to discuss," he said. He cupped her cheeks, his grip strong and sure. "But first, I need you. I missed you more than I can say." And then he wasn't saying anything at all. He was kissing her hungrily, and she was kissing him back.

Chapter 17

Nicolai wrapped Jane in his arms, taking her passion and returning it with equal measure. He'd nearly dropped to his knees the moment he'd spotted her, perched beside his enemy, in danger but alive. Relief, yes, he'd experienced that emotion. Fury, that, too. Laila had been within his reach, his to kill.

Fear had accompanied the fury, however. He'd felt the magical spell protecting the bitch from physical injury, and returning whatever violence was dished to the one doing the attacking.

If he'd gone for her throat…if Jane *had…*

They would have died.

Didn't happen. Jane's safe now.

Laila must know Nicolai was coming for her, or she would not have cast the spell. A spell most witches avoided. No one could hurt her, it was true, but no one could help her, either. If she injured herself accidentally, the spell would turn on *her,* seeing her as the threat. She would not only suffer with her injury, she would suffer a hundredfold with the magic.

"Nicolai," Jane rasped.

He'd feared she would not recognize him, that he would have to steal Laila's ability to hypnotize to force her to leave with him. Something he hadn't known he could succeed in doing, not with Laila's spell waiting to strike. He should have had more faith in his woman. Jane was as aware of him as he was of her. The face he wore didn't matter.

"Yes, sweetheart." The sweetness of her scent infused with his cells. Her decadent taste filled his mouth. His blood heated, and every muscle in his body hardened, anticipating her touch.

"What did you…do with the…real slave?" Her tongue licked at his each time she paused to breathe.

"Set him free." In more ways than one. Laila had scrambled the poor man's brain, until he hadn't known up from down, left from right, making herself the only tangible thing in his world, forcing him to cling to her.

Nicolai could have simply chained the poor man for the night and hidden him, but he'd thought, *That could have been me.* He'd used his own abilities to break through and remind the man of who he was and who he loved, removing Laila from the equation.

"Nice." Jane's hold tightened on him, nearly breaking his ribs. Worth it, he thought. "Shouldn't we…escape, while we…have the chance?"

"No. When the princess sleeps, I can invade her dreams, force her to hurt herself." Another ability he possessed. "Then we'll leave. Return to Elden." Each sentence was punctuated with a deep, wet kiss that rocked him to his soul.

"So we need to do something to pass the time, huh?" Jane returned her full attention to his tongue, sucking and rolling it with her own. Her hands slid through his hair, her nails scraping his scalp and leaving their mark.

He loved that she accepted his need for vengeance so easily. He loved that she clung to him, as desperate for closer contact as he was. But nothing would ever be close enough, not for either of them. He loved that she was smarter than he, and sometimes got lost in her own thoughts.

He just loved…her. Yes, he realized. He did. He loved her. He'd fallen in love with her soon after she first appeared in his world. They'd been strangers, but they'd soon bonded. From the bond, caring had sprung. From the caring, love. But the desire…oh, the desire had always been there.

A glimmer of resentment in his chest. Not directed at her, but to the vampire who had cursed her. Nicolai could never tell her how he felt. She might return the sentiment and vanish.

"I missed you. So much," he said, willing to confess that much but no more. "The separation was like being stabbed." Over and over again, the wound and pain never ending.

"I missed you, too." She kissed and nipped a path along his jaw, his neck, licking and laving. "Where'd you go?"

"Elden."

"Home?"

"Yes."

"Me, too."

"What?" He disengaged from the erotic contact, and peered down at her. "Home *home?*"

She refused to stop. With a little leap, she was back in his arms and sucking on his pulse. "Yes, home home. My world."

Nicolai cupped her chin, forcing her to still, to look at him. Her eyes were glazed with passion, her lids at half-mast. His heart constricted at such a lovely sight. A shake of his head was required to put him back on track. "Let me be clear on this. You left my world and returned to yours."

"Yes."

He'd almost lost her again. And he'd had no idea! "How did you get back?" he croaked.

A secret smile played at the edges of her lips. One that burned through him, deepening his arousal. "Apparently, when you gave me your blood, you gave me your ability to teleport, too."

Dark Abyss. He had never considered that possibility. Maybe because he'd only ever shared his blood with his father, and his father had already possessed some of Nicolai's abilities.

"And you came back to me." He'd never been one to see fate's hand in his life, but now…if Jane hadn't been injured by the ogres, he wouldn't have given her his blood. If he hadn't given her his blood, he wouldn't have found a way to tie her to his side for the rest of their lives.

"I'll always come back to you."

A heavy weight lifted from his shoulders. The curse had somehow lost its power over her. Otherwise, she would have remained in her world.

He traced his thumbs over her cheekbones. "I've told

you this before, but I want you to listen closely. I don't care if I have a thousand betrothed females waiting on me. You are all that matters." He would have only one woman. This woman. Forever.

He swooped back down, plunging his tongue past her teeth and into the sweet recesses of her mouth. She welcomed him with a moan.

He'd been cold and detached with females most of his life. Oh, he'd treated his mother and sister as the treasures they were, but everyone else he had never even given a second thought. He'd been a prince, and they his due. Or so he'd convinced himself.

Fate, he mused again. Had he not been a slave, desperate to escape, he might have treated Jane the same way. And that would have been a shame, to never have known her and the nuances of her personality. Unselfish, brave, stronger than anyone he knew, capable and honorable.

Honorable. Yes. He would never have to wonder where he stood with her. She would always tell him, whether he was a prince or a pauper. She would never be intimidated by him, would always challenge him.

"I want you naked." He tugged at the shoulder straps of her robe, shoving the material to the floor. In seconds, emerald material pooled at her feet. He lifted her out of it, and settled her more firmly against his body. Skin-to-skin. Finally.

Every time she exhaled, their chests rubbed together, and he thrilled at the contact. She was hot and silky against him. Her nipples were beaded, rasping against the fine mat of hair he possessed. His shaft pressed to both their bellies, moisture seeping from the tip. He arched his hips, creating a delicious glide.

She arched to meet him, the friction sparking exquisitely. "I can't ever get enough of you."

"Good." He traced his hands down the ridges of her spine, loving the goose bumps that jumped up to meet him. He cupped her ass. "No panties?"

"None were given to me."

"I'm glad." If he had his way, she'd never wear them again.

"I—I want you. Now."

"You've got me. Nothing will separate us, Jane. Do you understand?"

Her breath hitched. She toyed with the ends of his hair. "I think so, yes."

"Know so. I don't want to lose you. I *can't* lose you. I want to wed you. To be with you always. I choose you, Jane. Over my crown, my people and my vengeance."

Tears welled in her eyes, creating amber pools. Nicolai tensed, waiting, unsure in a way he'd never been before.

"Just as I choose you," she said brokenly.

Thank the gods. He would have dropped to his knees and begged if necessary. "I want to be your family."

"You are."

A soft touch along his check. Jane's expression was so tender, tears filled *his* eyes.

"Jane. I love you." No reason to deny it now. "I want to show you. Let me show you."

Her mouth fell open on a gasp. "You…you love me? I mean, I know you mentioned marriage, but this is the first you've said of love and I…I…"

"I love you. With all my heart."

"Oh, Nicolai." She threw herself at him, laughing and crying at the same time. "I love you, too. So much."

Hearing her declaration was like stepping into a warm ray of the sun after an eternity spent in the cold darkness of winter. Something he hadn't known he needed, but now that he had it, he knew he couldn't live without it.

He drew her down to the floor. Her nipples were flushed and rosy, and he couldn't resist. He circled one with his tongue, flicked it until she moaned, then moved to the other. His fangs extended and ached. Now wasn't the time to indulge in the delight that was her blood, however. He'd fed before coming to her, hoping to dull his hunger for her.

No other blood had ever affected him the way Jane's did. So powerful, so consuming. And while he wanted his memory back in full *now,* he would rather not disappear without warning again and have to track his woman's location, leaving her in danger.

Danger she could handle, as she'd proven over and over again.

He eased up to study her. That honey-colored hair was spread around her shoulders, her eyes glazed and ravenous. She chewed on her bottom lip as she glided her hands along the roped planes of his stomach. She was a wanton sight, a goddess come from the heavens.

He rose to his knees and guided her legs apart. So wet, so pink. He wanted to dive in, both with his mouth and with his cock. Sweat was already sheening his brow, his cells like little knives in his veins, demanding he take her, claim her. His woman. Now, always.

Not yet, not yet.

He had to prepare her. The first time they had sex, he'd hurt her. Not that she'd protested. She'd been too tight, and he'd been too eager. Not this time. This time she would enjoy every second.

He traced a finger up her hot center and she jerked as if struck by lightning.

"Yes!" She fisted her hands on the rug beneath her, and lifted her hips.

With the movement, his finger slid inside her of its own accord. Those inner walls closed around him, squeezing. He could have spilled then and there. *Breathe, damn it.* He worked that finger in and out, in and out, until she was writhing, mindless, gasping his name. Then he worked in a second finger. In and out, in and out.

Soon she was moaning every few seconds, rolling her hips in circles, seeking his thumb on her center. He gave it to her. For a moment. She cried out in relief—and then groaned in distress when he took the pressure away.

A third finger joined the other two, in and out, in and out. Stretching her, spreading that sweet, sweet dew. When her muscles tensed, ready to lock down in climax, he severed all contact.

"Please!" she shouted.

Such a succulent entreaty. He used the hand wet with her juices on his cock, slicking himself up. He closed his eyes in ecstasy, loving the pressure as much as Jane had. Needing it. He stroked up…down.…

"Oh, no, you don't." Her legs wound around his back, her ankles locking just above his ass; she tugged him down. Without anything to balance him, he fell on top of her. She gasped when his weight hit. "Please, Nicolai. Do it."

"Yes," he rasped. He couldn't wait a second more, either.

He guided his tip to her entrance and thrust, deep and sure. They cried out in unison. Then she was coming, clenching around him, driving his need higher...higher. More, he had to have more. Wanted to bite her, wouldn't let himself bite her.

Instead, he sank his fangs into his own wrist. Blood laced his tongue. Blood still flavored with Jane. He wanted to suck, but he forced himself to release his vein and hold the wound over Jane's mouth.

"Drink," he commanded. They would do this every day. Would never risk her losing the ability to move between worlds.

Obeying, she closed her eyes. She looked as if she were...savoring? Oh, gods above, she was. The very idea sent his need soaring. His testicles drew up tight. Any moment now, he would explode. He wanted her with him, though, all the way.

"Harder, Jane," he said, even as he increased the speed of his thrusts. He hit her so damned deep, making her gasp, but she never stopped drinking, and soon her hips were once again rising up to meet him. She was gulping greedily, moaning with every swallow.

My woman. Mine.

Maybe he'd shouted the words. "Yes," Jane responded, inner walls closing tighter and tighter around him as her second orgasm rocked her. "Yours."

This time, there was no holding back. She milked him, and he gave her every drop, shooting it inside her.

They clung together for several minutes, hours, years, shivering and shuddering until finally sagging to the floor. He couldn't quite catch his breath, couldn't quite form a rational thought, but even then he knew he didn't want to hurt her and rolled to his side.

"I thought I was turning into a vampire, then convinced myself I wasn't," she said sleepily. "But I must be. Your blood…it tastes so damn good. I've been craving it, like a drug. And now that I've had more of it—" she shivered "—I feel so *good.*"

He frowned. He hadn't known such a thing was possible. Unlike the nightwalkers, he was a living being, born rather than created. Making others simply wasn't—hadn't been—possible.

Besides, even if he'd wanted to share his blood with others, which he hadn't, his human lovers had not wanted to drink from him. In fact, they had found the very idea disgusting. Same with the witches, and same with the shifters, though their objections had stemmed more from contamination of the species.

"You crave all blood or just mine?" he asked.

"Just yours. Though the thought of drinking from others isn't as abhorrent as it should be."

"Any other symptoms?" He liked the thought of sharing this with her, but the complications scared him to his soul.

"My skin is a little more sensitive than normal. More sensitive than yours, I think. But, if I'm becoming a vampire, a heightened sensitivity would make sense because I haven't yet had time to adjust."

How many other humans would tell him that becoming a vampire "makes sense"? He almost smiled. Almost.

He would have to teach her how to feed, just in case they were parted for any amount of time. He tensed at the thought of her mouth on someone else. *It's the only way*. Cutting through a vein was not a skill you developed naturally, but one you had to learn.

"How do you feel about changing?" he asked.

"A little afraid. A little excited."

"Tell me if you experience any other signs."

"I will."

He kissed her temple. "Rest now, sweetheart. I'll wake you in a few hours."

"And we'll kill Laila?"

See? Jane knew him better than anyone else he'd ever known. "Yes. We'll kill Laila." He wondered if he could draw Jane into the dream, guarding her, preventing Laila from lashing at her while she was defenseless.

"Good." Her warm sigh caressed his skin as she snuggled more firmly against him. "I love you."

"I love you, too."

She fell asleep, and he began to plan their future together, ignoring a sudden and intense sense of foreboding.

Chapter 18

They dressed quickly, quietly, and Jane packed a little bag of necessities. Such as the book—Nicolai had been overjoyed to see it—a few robes, snacks and a canteen of water. Laila had not brought any weapons for Odette to use, a fact that disappointed Jane but didn't surprise her.

"How are you going to invade her dreams?" she asked Nicolai.

"I'll tell you all about it." He moved in front of her and gripped her shoulders. Once again he wore the slave's mask. "When I'm done."

She knew what that meant—he would be in danger—and her answer was hell, no. "I'm going with you."

He sighed as if he'd expected such a response and had already resigned himself to it. "I do want to take you into the dream with me, and I will try to do so. Having never done something like that before, I don't know if it will work. Meanwhile, I want you to stay here."

"Why?"

He flicked his tongue over an incisor. "If I can't force her to harm herself, I'll have to absorb her powers. All of her powers and all the spells she has cast upon herself."

Jane's eyes widened. "You can do that?"

A stiff nod. "Most likely I will have to go that route. I tried to invade her dreams while you were sleeping and encountered an unexpected resistance. If the resistance is still there, while I'm in close proximity to her, I'll have to do something to lower her guard to steal her magic. Something…nonviolent."

She began to understand, and wanted to throw up. Or maybe throw a punch. "Like…kissing her?" Or more?

Another nod, this one barely discernable.

"You can't just stab her?" she asked hopefully.

"Not without dying myself. She's cast a spell that causes any injury I attempt to inflict on her to be directed at myself."

"Okay, so that's out." Jane nibbled on her bottom lip, felt the cuts already there and realized she had been doing a lot of nervous chewing lately. "That explains the power I felt wafting from her, I guess."

"You felt that?"

"Yep." She squared her shoulders. "And okay, fine. If you have to kiss her, you have to kiss her. And believe me, I do not envy you. That's taking one for the team a little far. I mean, I think I'd rather endure the stabbing myself instead of having to kiss her."

He nearly choked on a laugh. "This is not funny, Jane."

"I know." But she'd much rather he laugh than worry over her reaction. "As long as you survive, I'm good with the plan. Please tell me you'll be able to hurt her once you absorb her powers."

"Yes." Absolute determination radiated from him. "I will."

"Then I guess sticking your tongue down the devil's throat has a nice enough payoff." She punched him in the arm. "Good luck, tiger."

He laughed again, this time far less strained. "Thank you. Now. Will you please stay here?"

"Nope, sorry. I may not possess any magic of my own, but Laila still assumes I'm Odette. You might need me. Therefore, I'm sticking to your side as if I've been glued there."

A moment passed in silence, then another. Finally he pinched the bridge of his nose. "All right. You may come with me. If things do not progress as I hope, you are to run to Elden, and search out the prince Dayn. Trust no one else. Tell him you belong to me. Tell him you are my betrothed."

How sad he suddenly sounded. At the thought of losing her? "And he'll believe me?" Not that she would leave. She wouldn't, not for any reason. They *would* be together.

"I've marked you, so yes. Yes, he will. He is a blood drinker, like me."

When he turned away, she grabbed his arm. A puny move but one that worked all the same. "You found your brother?"

"Not yet. I have a feeling you will succeed where I have failed."

Again, he went to leave. Again, she held on to him. "So you *are* a prince?"

"Yes," he repeated. "The crown prince, destined to rule all of Elden."

This time, he remained in place, awaiting her response. She released him and shrugged. "That explains *a lot.*"

He blinked down at her. "That's all you have to say on the subject?"

"Yeah." He was royalty. So what? Everyone had a flaw.

She bent down, grabbed the strap of her pack and hefted the heavy thing onto her shoulder. The cord dug into her muscle, but she didn't allow herself to wince. Nicolai would take the burden upon himself, and he needed his hands free.

"Just don't expect me to be all humble and obey your every whim. That's not going to happen. So are we doing this or what?"

His lashes fused, hiding his irises, as he leaned down, wrapped her in his arms and kissed her, softly, sweetly, a tender lover expressing his gratitude. For what? she wondered, then she forgot the question. Her lips tingled. Their tongues met briefly, and she tasted him. Wanted more. Always, she wanted more.

He straightened and sighed. "I do not want her magic affecting you, Jane. If I fail and she turns on you—"

"Sticks and stones may break my bones, but I might be a vampire so I don't give a shit. I'll heal."

His brow knitted with confusion and anger. "No one will be breaking your bones."

She patted his cheek. "I believe I've already told you

that I'm going with you and that's final. Stop trying to talk me out of it."

Maybe he could feel her determination. Maybe he hated the thought of being apart as much as she did. Either way, his hands left her and he nodded. "Stubborn baggage."

"I'll take that to mean *delightful female*."

"You'd be right." He twined their fingers and ushered her outside, into the night. The moon was hidden behind thick, dark clouds, the air cool and moist. A storm must be brewing.

There was a campfire crackling a few feet away, casting golden rays and heat, but no guards around it. Actually, there was no sign of life anywhere. Not even in front of Laila's tent. Jane knew men patrolled the perimeter, however. She could hear their hearts beating. *Thump-thump. Thump-thump.*

"Something's off," Jane said.

"I know," Nicolai replied, his voice flat.

"She should have guards in front of her tent. Why did she send them away?"

"She must be expecting me."

Could they never catch a break? "We should leave. Come back another day. If she knows who you are, she'll attack."

"Oh, yes, she will." His voice was still flat, but resolve gave it a dangerous edge. "We may be giving her too much credit. She may not know, may only suspect. Either way, she dies tonight."

He spoke like a man who knew he didn't have a lot of time. Jane recalled his need to return to Elden. A physical need that was slowly killing him, he'd said. Perhaps that was the case here.

So, when he strode the short distance and swept inside the tent without pause, Jane made no protests. Lanterns were still lit, and her eyes adjusted instantly. Unlike earlier, no slaves danced in the center.

To her consternation, Laila was not asleep on her bed. She still lounged on her chaise, sipping from a goblet. Waiting.

"Finally," she said casually. She stroked the timepiece hanging around her neck. A timepiece that had not been there earlier. "And now I have my answers."

"About?" Nicolai shoved Jane behind him.

She placed her hands on his back, felt the muscles knot.

Fury colored Laila's expression for a split second before she smoothed her features. "You'll stay where you are, slave. And believe me, you won't be able to move from one location to another with only a thought, so don't even try."

Had she used her magic to root him in place? Jane moved beside him—and yes, that was exactly what Laila'd done, she realized as her own feet became as heavy as boulders. Laila hadn't moved, hadn't even blinked, yet somehow she'd used her magic.

Dread blasted through her, little bombs that spread their poison quickly. "Mother will be very disappointed in you," she said.

"Will she?" Laila smiled, shifting her attention to Jane. "Or will she be proud of me for destroying an imposter?"

Breathe, just breathe.

"Earlier, when I had that human female killed, I felt your upset and disgust. I wondered why. That is not something my sister ever felt. Then, I felt someone

digging through my powers. I wondered who, but I
didn't cast a spell to stop—or hurt—the person, because I also wondered what they wanted. Imagine my
surprise when they—he—chose my magic mirror."

She wouldn't ask. Couldn't. Not yet.

"Then, imagine my further surprise when my very
loyal slave ceased to desire me. The same way another
slave of mine ceased to desire me."

"Nicolai never desired you," Jane spat.

Laila shrugged, unconcerned. "He never desired you,
either. In fact, I think he was relieved when I took over
his care. Then, suddenly, you return from the grave, and
he can't tear his eyes away from you. He yearns for you,
abducts you. Not to use you as a shield, but because he
can't bear to be away from you. Something was wrong,
and I knew it. Now, I know what that something is."

"And just what do you know?" Nicolai asked as
calmly as if they were having Sunday brunch and dis-
cussing the next day's forecast.

Jane looked up at him. He'd dropped the mask. There
was his dark hair, his silver eyes. His wide shoulders,
his muscles stretching the fabric of his dark blue robe.
A beautiful man she would protect with her own life.

"The woman beside you is not my sister," Laila said.
"Her name is Jane, correct?"

Breathe. "I am Odette. You can't prove otherwise."

"Really? Well, perhaps you are right." Anger laced
the princess's tone, the words as sharp as daggers.
"Once, I could look through the eyes of others. Now
that ability has been taken from me. No matter, though.
I remembered how Nicolai used to talk to someone
inside his cell. A woman. Jane. No one else could see
her. We assumed him insane." She laughed smugly, and

even her humor sliced. "But your name is Jane, I would bet, and you are human."

Jane could feel the fury pulsing off of Nicolai. "Perhaps you're the insane one."

Laila unfolded from the chair and stood. Her gaze swung to Nicolai. "Oh, no, you don't, slave. As you can tell, I've cast a spell to prevent you from stealing any more of my powers. While the two of you…frolicked, I fortified my magic." Had he tried?

"Except," he said with a smile of his own, all white and lethal, "any powers you use are mine to use, as well. That, you cannot prevent from happening."

"No, you can't…" Laila screeched. She'd tried to step toward them, but her foot had stopped midair.

"Yes, I can. Holding you in place doesn't harm you physically, and, in fact, saves you from my claws. So you should be happy. Your protective spell is working."

"Release me, or I will scream for the guards."

He arched a brow, taunting her. "And you think they'll believe you concerning Odette? They won't, and we both know it. Your only chance is to release her. Do it, and we'll talk. You and I. Alone."

"Right. Because I'm a fool."

"Well…" Jane said.

Laila scowled at her, but continued. "Vow that you won't try to kill me or use the powers that I use, and I'll consider it."

Nicolai opened his mouth to reply, probably to agree, but Jane stopped him. "I'm not going anywhere. I don't care what the two of you decide." And as soon as she was able, she was taking a crash course in Magic 101. She wanted to know the rules. What a witch could and couldn't do. She wanted to know how to stop them. How to defeat them.

"How about this, Nicolai," Laila said, smiling again. "We'll find out what kind of damage I can do to your Jane without ever taking a step."

A moment later, Jane felt as if her head was about to explode. She cried out, clutched her ears, felt warm drops of blood spill onto her palms. Her entire world focused on her throbbing brain, and she lost sight of everything around her.

Her knees buckled, but her feet were still locked into the rug covered floor. She could only crouch, screaming and crying and praying for death. An eternity seemed to pass. But then, the pain stopped just as suddenly as it had hit her.

Gradually she became aware of her surroundings and realized *Laila* was now screaming.

Nicolai, Jane thought distantly. Nicolai must have stolen her ability to squeeze minds—or whatever she'd done—and was using it against the princess. But he was grunting, too, as if the pain was exploding through him.

Laila's screams ceased abruptly. Nicolai quieted a second later.

The only sound to be heard were panting, labored breaths. Jane tried to stand, but didn't have the strength. She saw that her bag had fallen and rested a few inches away. She was soaked with sweat, her robe seemingly a hundred pounds heavier.

She managed to turn her head and glance up at Nicolai. He wasn't looking at her, but at Laila, his eyes narrowed, hatred radiating from him.

"You saw what I saw," Laila gritted out. "Your precious human studied your kind. Cut them up, hurt them. Tell me, were they your friends?"

Oh, no, Jane thought. No, no, no. Somehow he'd known she had researched and done experiments on his kind, but he hadn't known the identities of her victims. *Had* she hurt one of his friends?

"Do you still wish to protect her?" Laila demanded. "Do you still wish to be her lover?"

Silence.

Such heavy silence.

Please don't tell me you knew any of them. If he had, he would hate her.

"What do you want, princess?" Nicolai said, his voice devoid of all emotion.

A knot grew in Jane's throat, practically cutting off her air. He did. He hated her. She needed to apologize, to explain, but couldn't do so here, now.

He can't hate you. He loves you. He'll forgive you. Eventually. She hoped.

Laila's chin lifted, triumph flashing through her eyes. Such cruel green eyes. "I want you to bind yourself to me. Forever."

He snorted. "No. What do I gain in return? Nothing."

"I'll allow you to kill the girl." She motioned to Jane with a wave of her hand.

Acid burned a hole in her stomach.

"I'll kill her," he said, matter-of-fact, "but I don't need to enslave myself to do it."

Oh, God. Jane had become one of his enemies, his hated, must-be-destroyed-at-any-cost enemies. "Nicolai. Please. I'm so, so sorry."

He didn't deign to look at her. Just held up his hand

to silence her. "I took your memories. *Me*. I wanted you
to save me. So, as you can see, I never truly wanted you.
Only what you could do for me. Save your apologies."

He'd…what? Why would he…?

Everything rushed back, as if a glass cage had been
shattered inside her mind. They had talked, they had
shared. Discovered that she was cursed. He'd known
that forcing her to cross over, to save him, would en-
danger him. For that very reason, she had refused. He'd
taken her memory and forced her to do it.

At the time, she'd thought she would resent him. Instead, she was glad he'd done it. Glad she'd helped him,
freed him, made love with him. She even understood
his reasoning. When she had been bed bound, she had
tried to bargain with God for freedom. In that state of
mind, you did things. Things you weren't always proud
of.

Why hadn't she returned home permanently, though,
as the curse dictated? She loved him. She should have
lost him already.

Or was his hatred the thing that would keep them
apart, not her absence? Her stomach somersaulted.

"*I'll* kill her, then," Laila said.

"With magic?" Nicolai laughed. "Please do. Then
I'll have the power to kill *you*."

"Not if I kill you, *then* the girl."

"You don't want me dead, princess. You want me
pliant." His head tilted to the side. "Why did you bury
my memories? Not of the girl, but of everything else.
I know why you blocked my powers, but the memories…"

A smug gleam entered her eyes. "You want to know,

fine. I'll tell you. I'm not the beast you think me, you know."

He crossed his arms over his chest.

"You appeared at the slave market in Delfina, and everyone assumed you were a Prince Nicolai look-alike. Everyone wanted to buy you. Me, Odette. The wealthy, the poor. Only Odette and I knew you truly were Prince Nicolai of Elden, crown prince, vampire, powerful beyond imagining." Again, she stroked the timepiece. "You fought wildly and managed to slay several people who simply approached you to study you closer. Then, you escaped."

His eyes widened ever so slightly, an involuntary reaction Jane was sure. She figured he hadn't recalled that part of his life yet. She wanted to reach out to him, but feared he would reject her.

"Odette had set you free, after blocking your powers. She wanted you away from the market, away from the prying eyes of others. News had just come from Elden that the king and queen had been slain."

A sharp intake of breath was Nicolai's only response. How Jane ached for him.

"As you can guess, Odette wouldn't have freed you if she had no way of capturing you. Yet still you proved elusive. She nearly succeeded a dozen times, because you kept trying to return to Elden, yet you always found a way to abandon her. When she at last caught you, she scoured the depths of your mind. You might not have witnessed the event, but you knew. You had heard the news, as we had, and magic had filled in the rest."

"Tell me," he rasped.

"In a bid to gain control of the lands, the Blood Sorcerer attacked. Your mother and father lay dying, and each cast a spell. Your mother, to send you away to safety. Your father, to fill you with a need for vengeance."

Jane could feel Nicolai's fury growing...sharpening....

"Odette couldn't allow you to keep trying to return," Laila went on. "Nor could she allow you to search for your brothers and sister. Had they known you still lived, they would have come for you. So, they had to think you were dead, slain with your parents. That way, no one would ever come to your rescue."

His hands fisted.

"And now," Laila went on, "now it's too late."

"What do you mean?" he gritted out.

"Twenty years have passed since the Blood Sorcerer attacked the palace."

"No." He shook his head, once, twice. "No."

"Oh, yes." A fleeting smile. "You were as unaware of the passage of time as you were of your past. Odette made sure of it." Laila lifted her chin. "So. How about this for a bargain? I will help you defeat the Blood Sorcerer, *if* you kill the human. Right here, right now."

"And forget the crimes *you* have committed against me?" he seethed.

At least he hadn't accepted right away, Jane thought darkly, dryly. That he would turn on her so savagely... she could not forgive. Unless, this was a trick. Unless, he meant to gain Laila's trust.

Hope eternal.

"It's either that, or I let the healer wipe your memory once again. We've had to do so several times, you know."

Tighter and tighter those hands curled. "You would trust me not to hurt you?"

"No. You will take a blood oath not to. *Before* I release you, and after you kill the girl."

Jane gulped, her mouth going dry.

This time, Nicolai didn't hesitate. "Very well. Release us from your magical hold, and I vow never to kill or hurt you. Help me slay my enemy, and I…I will kill the girl."

Chapter 19

Suddenly Jane's feet were freed. Nicolai snaked out an arm, catching her before she could bolt. Not that she would have. Or, yeah. She would have. Actually, even with his grip, she still could. All she had to do was disappear. To disappear, all she had to do was think of her home.

As the man she loved tugged her closer...closer... panic took over, her thoughts too chaotic to tame. Then, an unexpected calm took hold of her. This *was* the man she loved. The man who claimed to love her. The man who *did* love her. He might be angry with her—furious, even—but he wouldn't kill her.

This *was* a trick to trap Laila.

He wouldn't ever hurt her. She knew that on a bone-deep level. He was beautiful and wanton, wicked and yet principled. She'd given herself to him body and soul. Now and forever, just as he'd given himself to her. Nothing would change that, not even her past. She trusted him.

Blind trust had never come easily to her. She'd always believed in proof. Testing theories, changing variables and watching reactions, but blind trust was what she was giving her man. He'd come through for her time after time, and he would again.

Yes, she knew there was a dark side to his nature. Hell, she'd seen him in action on multiple occasions. No matter what, however, he would never turn that dark side on her. So, he had a plan. Pretending to want to kill her was part of it.

"Release me, too, princess," Nicolai said.

"No. Just the girl."

He growled, but that was the only indication he gave that he'd heard her.

Jane couldn't let another moment go by without telling him how she felt. "I'm so sorry, Nicolai. I didn't mean to—"

"Silence." A lash, and yet he gave her the subtlest of nods, as if he wanted her to continue.

Still he dragged her closer, until her body was flush with his. His heat enveloped her, so familiar she relaxed.

"I worked for the government, and yes, I studied your kind, but I never tortured and I never killed. I didn't know you at the time, and I didn't know what I did would hurt you or someone you loved. I just tried to help my people understand what—"

"Be. Quiet." His fangs flashed down at her, but again, he gave her the barest hint of a nod.

"I love you. No matter what happens or what you have to do, I will always love you."

"What are you waiting for?" Laila snapped. "Do it."

Jane could hear the rush of Nicolai's blood. While his expression was calm, stern, his heart beat erratically. He was not as unaffected as he seemed.

He didn't look away from her when he said, "I'm going to drink from her neck, princess. I'm also going to cover her mouth to prevent her from screaming."

"Let her scream," Laila said, anger soothed. "I'll like it."

"I will not have anyone rushing into this tent and watching. Nor do I want you nearing us until she's... dead."

Pretend. This is pretend, she reminded herself. Otherwise, he would have simply swooped down, savagely bit and sucked the life right out of her. Yet, here he stood, arguing with his tormentor, demanding certain concessions.

"Do not tell me what to do, slave. I—"

"Will accept my terms or we are back to where we started."

A pause. Jane drew in a deep breath and tilted her head to the side as she exhaled, giving him easier access to her vein. His eyes widened, his pupils flaring. His fangs lengthened and sharpened a little more.

"I want her on the floor," he croaked. "Release my feet, Laila. You can stop me again if I lunge for you."

Another pause.

"Very well," Laila said on a sigh.

A second later, Nicolai was urging Jane the rest of the way to the ground.

He loomed over her as he had countless other times. Her hair splayed around her shoulders, and her robe sagged.

"Nicolai," she breathed.

"Not another word, Jane." The gold flecks in his eyes seemed to swirl. Down, down he leaned. Breath emerged from her lungs and mouth shallowly. Just as his teeth sank home, he flattened his hand over her mouth.

Her eyes flared. Her body bowed. Warm, electric pleasure entered with his teeth, shooting through every inch of her. He was sucking slowly, so slowly, taking little sips. And his hand…his hand was cut, his blood dripping into her mouth, down her throat and swirling in her belly.

He was feeding her even as he drank from her. His fingers tapped at her cheek, a bid for…something.

She had only to reason this out.

He'd told Laila he would kill her. Therefore, he was pretending to kill her. And any time Jane had spoken up to soften him, he'd told her to shut the hell up but had really wanted her to keep talking. So…he must want her acting panicked and disbelieving while acting un-caring himself.

She tested her theory, struggling against him, giving Laila a show. When Nicolai grunted his approval, she knew beyond any doubt. She pounded her fists into his shoulders, as if trying to shove him away. She bucked, as if trying to dislodge him.

When the wound in his hand closed up, he ground his palm against her teeth to reopen the flesh. Once again, his blood trickled down her throat.

Then, he groaned, sucking a little harder at her vein, drawing a little more blood.

Enough, she thought she heard him say, but that was impossible. His lips were still on her vein. *Enough. You have to stop.* He lifted his head, panting, licked his lips, then dove back down, biting her in a new place. This, too, pumped pleasure straight into her veins.

Careful, careful, careful. Don't take too much. Slow down.

Jane frowned. Nicolai was speaking, but he was doing so straight into her head.

Have to time this just right. Again, his voice drifted through her head. The pressure against her vein eased.

Nicolai?

His body jerked against hers. *Jane?*

Yes. I can hear you, and now I'm guessing you can hear me. How is that possible?

He licked her neck, careful not to let Laila see. *Some blood drinkers share a mental connection.*

"Hurry," the princess snapped.

I need you to kill the princess for me.

Though he wanted the pleasure of doing so, he couldn't. He'd vowed not to. Which meant, someone had to do it for him. So, that was his plan. To have Jane strike the lethal blow.

Consider it done.

Thank you. A pause. *I'm sorry for what I did to you. Before. And now.*

I'm sorry, too. Her heart skipped a beat.

The princess has lowered her defenses, just as we hoped, and I've absorbed some of her power. The spell that stopped anyone from hurting her is now mine. She'll still be strong, however, just not as *strong.*

Nicolai didn't drink much more. He even dribbled several mouthfuls of blood down Jane's neck and onto the ground. He was creating a mess, she knew. The illusion of death. She forced her struggles to slow...

slow…until sagging limply, arms falling uselessly to her sides. She lay there, breathing as shallowly as possible. So much so she knew not even Nicolai could see the rise and fall of her chest.

Through tiny slits in her eyelids she watched him lift his head. Blood continued to drip from his chin, splashing on her collar and absorbing into her robe. He pressed two fingers into her nape, searching for a pulse. She knew what he felt: a wild, strong beat.

"It's done." Nicolai severed all contact as he stood. "I've done my part. Now you do yours."

"Step away from her," Laila said. "I will check for myself."

He didn't hesitate. He moved to the other side of the tent, away from Jane, away from the princess.

But…just how was she supposed to kill the woman? She had no weapons, and Laila wasn't devoid of all her powers. She could cast a spell in the blink of an eye.

Come on, Parker. Think. Footsteps pattered. Body heat wafted. *Think faster.* Then the creak of bones echoed as Laila crouched. The body heat drew closer… closer…as the princess reached out.

The flicker of an idea presented itself. Dangerous, untested, but the only way. *Nicolai, can she travel with only a thought, like you?* Jane rushed out.

No.

Perfect. Laila's fingers pressed into Jane's neck. Jane opened her eyes, reached up and latched on to her wrist. A gasp of shock sounded. At the same time, Nicolai swooped in and grabbed the timepiece from around Laila's neck.

"Mine," he snapped "Jane. Now."

"What are you—?" Laila began.

Before the princess could begin casting, Jane closed her eyes and pictured her home—with Laila in it. Now that her mind was calm, her focus cold, it wasn't difficult. She saw her kitchen, experienced a wave of dizziness. Laila struggled against her, but as the dizziness intensified, the struggles slowed. For a moment, Jane felt as if she were floating, and tightened her grip on the princess.

"What are you...what...?" Laila's voice was weak, and Jane could hear an underlay of pain.

"Jane," Nicolai shouted. "Jane! What are you doing?"

When the dizziness left her, when she felt something hard and chilled pressing into her back, she looked around. She and Laila were inside her kitchen. Sunlight streamed in through the window, burning her so badly she actually sizzled. She rolled away with a hiss of pain, seeking the shade.

Nicolai hadn't teleported with Jane that night in the forest, but then, he hadn't been operating at full tilt. Most of his abilities had still been locked away. Tonight, he'd been like a powder keg—and so was Jane.

She stopped, flat on her back, Laila still in a crouch. The princess was pallid, sweating and...falling. She hit the floor, face-first.

Jane meant to leap away, grab a knife. That's the reason she'd brought the witch here. Suddenly she could scent Laila's blood. It wasn't an altogether pleasant smell, and yet hunger twisted her stomach. Such raw, consuming hunger.

Before she realized she'd even moved, she was angled toward the princess, her teeth sinking into her vein. Only a trickle of blood met her tongue. Frustration clawed at her. She angled her head, bit again. Again, only a trickle. She lifted, found the princess's pulse with her gaze, then swooped back down. This time, the blood flowed like a newly awakened river.

She should have had to chew to get what she wanted, a thought that grossed her out, but her gums were aching terribly, and her teeth—fangs?—had slid right in.

Warm, rushing life continued to fill her mouth. She moaned, dug her teeth in deeper, sucked harder, replenishing what she'd lost.

She must have hit a nerve because Laila came out of her faint with a jolt, and tried to push Jane away. She tightened her hold, gulping and gulping and gulping. Soon, Laila ceased struggling. Went as limp as a rag. Jane continued to drink, physically unable to pull herself from the drug that was this woman's blood. Drug, yes. Because, with the blood, something else, something warmer, almost…fizzy, rushed through her.

Her cells practically exploded with energy.

Stop, you have to stop. If she took any more, she would kill the princess. She could hear the distant *thump-thump* of a heartbeat, and knew it was slowing, almost beyond repair. The flow of blood was trickling off, thinning.

I don't want to stop. I brought her here to kill her. Stopping defeats the purpose.

But in the back of her mind, she knew—somehow, as if the memory were not her own—that to kill this way was to live this way. One death would not be enough. She would drain everyone she drank from. Always. No one would be safe from her. Not even Nicolai.

Nicolai.

Panting, she jerked her teeth out of Laila. She flicked her tongue and, sure enough, she had fangs.

Nicolai had made her a vampire.

With a shaky hand, she brushed the hair from her face. When she caught sight of that hand in the light, she gasped.

She…glowed. Bright, golden, white lightning exploded from her skin. And the crackling in her veins… she felt like she could do *anything*. Until she moved her hand into a ray of that sunlight and started sizzling. She groaned with pain, her arm falling to her side.

Note to self: avoid the sun.

Another thing of note: *You're here for a reason. Don't forget.*

As if she could.

She leaped up and, knowing exactly where her knives were, grabbed one, careful to remain in the shadows. As she peered down at the woman who had enslaved Nicolai, taken away his rights, abused him physically and sexually—for over twenty years!—she found that she couldn't stab her. Couldn't kill the bitch that way, either.

Death would be too easy for Laila. *You have to do* something. *When she wakes up, she'll use her magic against you.*

Could she, though? This world was different from Laila's, with different metaphysical laws, different atmospheres. Would her magic work here? Nicolai's ability to cross from one world to the other worked in both places, but while Nicolai could withstand his own sun, he would not be able to withstand Jane's. Proof: she could tolerate his, but not hers. And she'd dealt with this sun all her life.

She wished she had interviewed or dissected a witch—and she didn't care what kind of monster people would think her for such a desire. But one had never been brought to her lab. Could that be because no one had known they were here? Could they not use any of their powers in this world, and were rendered human?

There was one way to find out.

Jane dragged the princess to her bedroom, which was hard to do with her windows and drapes all open, found rope and tied the bitch to the bedposts. Not once did Laila awaken. Jane showered quickly, cleaning off the blood, then dressed in familiar jeans and a T-shirt. Felt odd, wearing her "normal" clothes. Felt…wrong.

Trembling, she threw the robe in the washer. *Nicolai?* she cast out mentally, hoping for a reply. *Are you out there? Are you okay?* Soon as she took care of Laila, she would go back to him.

They hadn't yet bonded fully. Otherwise, neither of them would have been able to drink from others. She wanted to bond fully.

Jane returned to her bedroom, pushed a chair in front of the princess and waited. She wouldn't let herself think about Nicolai yet.

Hours passed, ticking by slowly. Finally, though, Laila cracked open her eyes. She moaned, tugged at her bonds, frowned. Realization jolted her upright—or rather, as much as possible.

"Relax," Jane told her. "I haven't done anything to you that you haven't done to someone else."

"You'll pay for this," Laila snarled.

"And you're stuck here."

A moment passed, then another. Then, suddenly, Jane could hear the woman's voice in her head, as clearly as she'd heard Nicolai's. *What did she do to me? Why can't I use my magic?*

Jane smiled. Well, well. One blessing at least. "You can't use your magic because you're in my world now."

Laila gasped. "How did you know that?" *Oh, great goddess. She has my powers. She has my powers!*

"No, I don't. I am a vampire, though."

"Stop that!" *She's reading my mind, the bitch. I hate her! Now clear your mind. How did she become like Nicolai?*

"I drank his blood."

"Stop doing that, I said."

Jane chewed on her bottom lip. If she could read minds, she could go deeper than surface thoughts. Right?

She focused more intently on Laila's thoughts.... *Have to escape... How do I escape without my powers? I have to steal my powers back.*

She probed a little deeper. Suddenly she was reliving the episode on her kitchen floor. Except, she saw and felt and heard through Laila's senses. Waking up to untutored fangs in her neck, weakened, unable to use her powers. Powers she'd relied on her entire life.

She *had* taken the princess's powers, Jane realized. That was what fizzed inside her veins.

Nicolai could absorb other people's powers, and when Jane had consumed his blood, she must have developed that ability just like the teleportation.

She probed even deeper. There seemed to be a thousand different voices, a thousand flashes from the girl's life. She listened and watched for the things concerning Nicolai... There!

She watched, listened. Hated the princess all over again.

"*You* wiped Nicolai's mind," she growled as she came back to the present. She was shaking. "You told him—and he thought—a healer had done it."

Laila paled. "I'm not saying anything to you."

"You don't have to." Laila had wiped his mind and bound his powers, then planted a new memory, one of the healer doing so. She hadn't wanted him to blame her. She'd also tried to plant suggestions of love and adoration, but while she had manipulated his thoughts, she hadn't been able to manipulate his emotions.

And now I can do so, Jane thought. She wasn't exactly sure how to use the ability, so she latched on to every memory she could, pictured a black box and stuffed them inside, hiding them away.

"What are you doing?" Laila demanded. "Stop… What…why…?"

Jane remained silent. She worked for hours, grabbing and stuffing, grabbing and stuffing. When she finished, the cabin was dark and musty, and her body so weak she had already slid out of her chair.

She met Laila's gaze. A blank gaze. "Who—who are you?" Panic sprouted. "Who am I?"

"Tit for tat," Jane said with a forced smile. When the sun set, she loaded Laila into her car, drove her into the nearest town and dropped her off. She was without powers, memory and money. She would have to place herself at someone else's mercy.

Mercy she might not find.

Jane returned home, pulled on her robe and threw herself on her bed. She pictured the tent where she'd last seen Nicolai, but…nothing happened. She tried again…with the same result.

She tried for hours, the entire night. By morning she was a sobbing mess, weak, sick to her stomach. She couldn't do it. She couldn't return.

The curse had finally kicked in.

Chapter 20

Three days. Within three days, Nicolai's full memory was returned.

And now, holding his timepiece, he knew exactly what had happened to his parents. The Blood Sorcerer had launched a sneak attack, going for the king and queen first, allowing his monsters to ravage them. The hideous monsters from Nicolai's nightmares, the ones he'd seen on the castle walkway and inside his bedroom.

Laila had it right. As the pair lay dying, they had cast separate spells. The queen, to send her children away. The king, to spark a need for vengeance. Both spells had bonded with him—and his timepiece. A gift from his parents. All their children had one. Even Micah, the youngest.

Micah, just a baby.

Now, twenty years had passed. Micah was a man.

Unless he'd been trapped in a time standstill like Nicolai. And if he still lived.

Nicolai knew Dayn lived. Now that his memory and abilities were restored, so was his mind connection to the other blood drinker in the family. He could hear the turmoil of his brother's thoughts. Could feel the man's desperation.

Breena was out there, too. Rumor was, she was living with Berserkers. An impossibility. Berserkers had been wiped out long ago. So…where was she really?

And Jane…his Jane. Sometimes he could hear her as he heard Dayn. Distantly, the words and emotions muted. *Don't think about her right now. You'll collapse.*

He'd never gotten to tell his beloved siblings goodbye. Nor had he gotten to tell his parents. His father had wanted so badly to see him wed. Betrothed at the very least, and Nicolai had agreed to bind himself to someone. Only, he never had. Not really. He'd finally settled on the princess of Brokk, but he had never made a formal offer. And, oh, how his father had despaired.

While he could not give his father a bride—if he couldn't have Jane, he would have no one—he could at last give his father the vengeance he'd used his last breath ensuring.

Nicolai knew he was not too late, for the timepiece continued to tick. When the hands stopped, then and only then would it be too late. But the hands were moving more quickly than they should have, meaning time was running out.

He would return to Elden, kill the sorcerer and claim his rightful place on the throne. Nothing would stop him. Tomorrow, he added. Nothing would stop him *tomorrow*. He could not bring himself to leave

Laila's tent. Not yet. This was the last place he'd seen and held Jane.

Jane.

You aren't supposed to think about her.

Beyond the tent, he could hear the rest of the camp rousing. Footsteps pounded closer and closer and he knew it was only a matter of minutes before someone ventured inside again. He pictured the Princess Laila, as he had done before, cloaking himself in her image.

Sure enough, the tent flap rose and two guards stepped inside, awaiting orders.

"Leave this place," he found himself saying. "Gather everything and everyone else and return home."

"What of you, princess?"

"I'm staying. Now go."

They bowed and exited, used to her abruptness. He'd been casting illusions for years, and had once teased his brothers and sisters, pretending to be them—in front of them. They had laughed, and begged for more.

The memory had his chest constricting. He would have liked to tease Jane that way.

Jane, he thought again. Her blood flowed through his veins, heating him up, making him ache and tingle. How was he supposed to live without her?

He didn't care what she'd done in the past. How could he? She had already confessed her past to him, when he'd been imprisoned, and she'd appeared to him in phantom form.

He knew she thought he blamed her and perhaps even hated her. Was that why she stayed away? Had he failed to convince her otherwise when they'd spoken in their minds?

There'd been no other way. He'd had to convince

Laila he would kill her. So even though he'd wanted to hug and kiss her and tell her how much he loved her, how there was nothing she could ever do to earn his hatred, he had glared at her, snapped at her.

She'd returned to her own time. To save him. And now, enough time had passed that he feared she no longer possessed the ability to travel here. Or was the curse keeping her there? The curse he'd thought he'd overcome. Oh, yes, he realized. There was his answer.

He stalked to Jane's bag and dug inside, withdrawing the book. He'd flipped through the blank pages a thousand times already. Each of those thousand times he'd imagined casting another spell, one to bring her back to him.

Yet, how could he make such a spell work? How could he circumvent the curse that separated them? So far he had not…thought of…

A way.

Heart galloping, Nicolai found a pen, sat on Laila's lounge and started writing.…

Two weeks later, Jane returned from her midnight jog and found a box on her porch. The same box she'd found before. She knew what rested inside it and gulped.

Not a day had passed that she hadn't thought about Nicolai, cried for him, prayed to see him again. She found herself racing up the porch steps, grabbing the box and shoving her way inside the cabin.

Every day she'd changed a little more. She still ate food, still needed it, but she also needed blood. Her midnight jogs, which she no longer needed to work the stiffness out of her muscles because her muscles didn't get stiff anymore, had become snack time. The deer ran from her, but like a lion with a gazelle, she always caught one.

The biggest change of all? She was pregnant. She'd realized the truth only a few hours ago, and had been in a shocked daze ever since. She should have figured it out before now, having spent the past several mornings vomiting. More than that, Nicolai's blood had healed her spine and legs, so why not her reproductive system, too?

She wanted to see Nicolai, needed to tell him. Had to make love with him, laugh with him, hold on to him and never let go.

The bookbinding creaked as she opened the front flap. There was a tattered pink ribbon—from one of her robes, she realized, her eyes filling with tears. Heart pounding against her ribs, she mentally read, her voice too wobbly to speak.

"My name is Nicolai, and I am the crown prince of Elden. I will become king the day I kill the Blood Sorcerer. And I will kill him. After I tell my female that I love her."

She swiped at her burning eyes.

"I will always love my Jane, and I am miserable without her. She thinks I despise her, but for the first time in her life, my too-intelligent woman is wrong. I did and said what I had to only to save her life."

"I know," she managed to work past the knot.

"Her life is far more important to me than my own."

The words swam. Again, she swiped at her eyes.

"But she is cursed. Cursed to lose the man she loves. And she has. She's lost him. Absolutely. But now…

now she can find him again. If not through magic or
abilities, than with her mind."

Jane wiped her eyes with the back of her wrist, trembling, hopeful, joyous, excited and scared. Scared, because Nicolai was offering her the world, but she had
no way to tell him.

"Come back to me, Jane. Please. Come back to me.
I await you. I will await you forever."

The rest of the pages were blank.

Oh, Nicolai. I want to. I want to so badly. She stood
on her shaky legs and walked, trancelike, into her
shower. She sat and let the water pour over her, clothes
and all. Nicolai wanted to see her, but she couldn't
return. Every time she tried, she destroyed a little piece
of her soul.

And yet, she gave it another try.

She closed her eyes and pictured the tent. Just like
before, nothing happened. Just as she'd feared. She tried
again. And again. And again. Only when the water was
cold as ice did she emerge from the stall. *Don't give up
hope. There's another way.*

Yes. *Yes.* With her mind, he'd said.

Her mind.

The next evening, she gathered all the necessary
tools for transfer. Crudely, quickly constructed, but
hopefully adequate. She donned her robe and placed
the sensors of the machine along her bedposts. Trembling, she stretched out on her mattress, flipped the
switch and closed her eyes. If she died because of this,
okay. If she hurt herself, whatever. She refused to allow
fear or anything else to stop her from doing whatever
was necessary to reach her man. Refused to deny her
baby the chance to know a father's love.

A slight buzzing in her ears. Sickness in her stomach. Her machine could work, she reminded herself, and *had* worked with plastic.

I'm not plastic. Oh, God. Jane pictured her destination, trying to use Nicolai's ability alongside the man-made appliance. Several seconds ticked by. Seconds that felt like separate eternities. Finally she felt her body begin to heat…heard the buzzing increase in volume… felt the bed disappear from beneath her… Heat…more heat…

Buzzing, gone. Nothing. She was nothing.

"Jane. Sweetheart."

Nicolai. There was his voice, so close. Panting, she pried her eyelids open, and she saw that she was lying on the floor of the tent, Nicolai looming over her, his hands wrapped around her arms as he shook her.

She'd done it. She'd crossed over. Traveled to him, her mind the guide.

"Jane," he said on a sigh of relief. There was no need for more words. Not yet.

An instant later they were kissing and pulling at each other's clothes. In seconds, they were naked and falling to the floor. No preliminaries. Nicolai shoved open her legs and thrust deep. Thrust home.

Jane cried out, already wet for him, needing him like she needed air to breathe. He pounded in and out, pushing her to heights she'd only dreamed about these past two weeks.

Her nipples rasped his chest, sparking a fire. An inferno. Spreading through her, consuming her, and she erupted, screaming, screaming, clutching at him, scratching his back. And then his fangs were in her neck, and he was drinking, and she was climaxing again, angling her head and biting into *his* neck.

He roared as she drank him down, bucking against her, going even deeper, and soon shooting inside her. Glorious, necessary, life affirming.

When he collapsed against her, she held on tight. She didn't think she'd ever been happier. She was with her man, her love, the future bright.

"You got the book," he said, planting little kisses along her jaw.

"Oh, yes. Thank you for sending it. I couldn't get here. I wanted so badly to come back to you, but I couldn't move from one location to another in a blink anymore."

He propped his weight on his elbows and peered down at her. "Thank you. Thank you for coming back."

"My pleasure." She cupped his cheeks. "You'll be happy to know Laila is now in the same position she placed you in." She'd watched the news. Laila had been found, her image flashed, calling for anyone who might know her. And until someone claimed her, she'd been locked in a mental institution for the violently insane.

"I don't care about her. How are *you?*"

"Good." Now. "I have something to tell you."

He lost a little of his good humor. "You look worried. Jane, you can tell me anything. I will never hate you. Never turn away from you."

"I… Do you remember when I told you I couldn't have children?"

He nodded, his brow furrowed.

"Well, I can." A smile grew. "And I'm going to. I found out a few days ago. We're going to be parents."

His mouth fell open, snapped closed. Fell open again.

"Jane…I… Jane!" With a whoop, he leaned down and kissed her again. "You are sure?"

"Yes."

Another kiss. "Are you happy?"

"Yes."

"Me, too." His smile was radiant. "Oh, Jane." He kissed her again and again, his hand constantly rubbing over her still-flat belly. "I love you, and want you with me. Tell me you'll stay. Tell me you'll live with me. Marry me."

"Yes, yes, yes!" She laughed, hugging him tight. "In case you don't understand, yes means yes."

He chuckled against her lips. "I must still return to Elden."

"And so you will. With me. I adore you, Prince or King or whatever you are!"

"As I adore you, Jane. My heart and my queen."

"Good." She cupped his cheeks, loving him more with every minute that passed. "Now let's go to Elden and kick some ass."

* * * * *

A sneaky peek at next month...

NOCTURNE™

BEYOND DARKNESS...BEYOND DESIRE

My wish list for next month's titles...

In stores from 21st October 2011:

☐ Lone Wolf – Karen Whiddon

☐ The Vampire Who Loved Me
  – Theresa Meyers

In stores from 4th November 2011:

☐ Lord of Rage – Jill Monroe

Available at WHSmith, Tesco, Asda, Eason, Amazon and Apple

Just can't wait?

Visit us Online

You can buy our books online a month before
they hit the shops! **www.millsandboon.co.uk**

1011/89

Have Your Say

You've just finished your book.
So what did you think?

We'd love to hear your thoughts on our
'Have your say' online panel
www.millsandboon.co.uk/haveyoursay

- Easy to use
- Short questionnaire
- Chance to win Mills & Boon®
  goodies